THE END GAME

by

Bill Rogers

CATON

ALSO BY BILL ROGERS

DCI TOM CATON
MANCHESTER MURDER MYSTERIES

The Cleansing
The Head Case
The Tiger's Cave
A Fatal Intervention
Bluebell Hollow
A Trace of Blood
The Frozen Contract
Backwash
A Venetian Moon
Angel Meadow
The Girl and the Shadowman
The Opportunist

JOANNE STUART
NATIONAL CRIME AGENCY SERIES

The Pick, The Spade and the Crow
The Falcon Tattoo
The Tangled Lock
The Blow Out

INDIVIDUAL WORKS

Teenage and Young Adult Fiction
The Cave
Short Crime Stories
Breakfast at Katsouris
Eight walks based on the Manchester Murder Mysteries
Caton's Manchester

The author asserts the moral right under the Copyright, Designs and Patents Act 1988 to be identified as the author of this work. All rights reserved. No part of this publication may be reproduced, stored in a retrieval system or transmitted, in any form or by any means, without the prior consent of the copyright owner, nor be otherwise circulated in any form of binding or cover other than that with which it is published and without a similar condition being imposed on the subsequent purchaser.

While this book is based on factual research, and actual police operations are referred to as background context, all of the characters in this book are fictitious, and any resemblance, if any, to actual persons, living or dead, is purely coincidental. Any references to businesses, organisations, places, or localities are intended only to give the fiction a sense of authenticity. All of the events and behaviours described as taking place in those settings are fictional. The End Game was written in real-time, and changes will inevitably have taken place post publication, including the rebranding of the Brecon Beacons as Bannau Brycheiniog.

A CIP record for this book is available from the British Library.

Published by Caton Books

Paperback ISBN: 978-1-909856-31-8

Cover Design by Bill Rogers
Cover Image ©@gettysignature via Canva.com
Design and Layout: Commercial Campaigns
Editor: Monica Byles

First published May 2023
Copyright © Bill Rogers
First Edition

"He that dies pays all debts."

Stephano, Act 3 Scene 2 , The Tempest,
William Shakespeare

Prologue

So near and yet so far. Crouched on a ledge, behind a wall on the crest of the hill, he had a clear line of sight. Or would have done, were it not for the sun setting behind the blue-grey mountains.

He counted eleven buildings in all. Seven single-storey mud-walled houses with flat roofs and holes for eyes, scattered around a central compound behind whose high walls stood a large concrete two-storey house and three small outbuildings with corrugated iron roofs.

According to intel, this was where the hostages were being held. Three women aid workers from the US, France and the UK. Five hundred thousand dollars by midnight tonight or they would all be executed. He looked at his watch. It was 18.39 local time. Less than six hours left.

He checked on the other seven members of his patrol. All eyes were on the compound, through the scopes of sniper rifles or glued to their M22 binoculars. His colleagues' body language told him that they shared his apprehension.

Between them and the village lay stony open ground, across which snaked low broken walls, half a dozen irrigation ditches and scattered yellowed stalks of crops long harvested. Poor cover and multiple traps for the unwary. No time and too exposed to check for improvised explosive devices. In short, a tactical nightmare.

Worse still was the eerie silence and the absence of any sign of life. It was as though the scene had been frozen in time. Or that they were expected. He slid from the ledge and sat with his feet against the wall. Nothing to be done but wait for the sun to go down.

A blood-red sky. The shadows of buildings, cast in sharp relief, were spectral fingers probing towards him. In the afterglow, seconds before darkness descended, he glimpsed a solitary eagle as it spiralled upwards.

He checked the safety on his compact carbine and pulled his night-vision goggles down. Turning his head from left to right and back again, he cursed their limitations as he scanned the scene below.

The fields glowed pale green, the stone walls, and the buildings, a darker forest green. The hairs on the back of his neck prickled at the absence of any lights in the compound. This was all wrong. Even worse, one of the two helicopters had been diverted on an evac' mission. They were waiting for news of the remaining Apache before commencing their assault. The chopper's role was to provide covering fire for the attack and then evacuate the hostages and the troop. Timing was everything – too early, and the hostiles would be alerted; too late, and Taliban reinforcements could arrive.

Three clicks in his headset. He turned to see the sergeant raise his right arm, point to the eastern sky, and signal, *Helicopter incoming*. They crouched on the ledge, waiting. The sergeant's hand was still aloft. He counted down from three with his fingers and then waved his men forward.

Over the wall and down the slope, heels sliding on the rocky scree. Eyes focused on the open ground ahead. He sensed his colleagues a metre or so behind. His lead leg slipped. He slid on his back the final stretch to level ground. Vaulting the first of the walls, he jogged across the field beyond, leapt the ditch and hunkered down behind a second wall to take stock. Less than sixty metres to the gates of the compound. His heart was pounding. In spite of the cold night air, sweat trickled down his forehead, stinging his eyes. He peered over the wall, scanning from left to right. Still nothing.

Up again, and into the next field. One wall to go, and then a short sprint across open ground to the compound. Believing that they had the crucial element of surprise, he felt a surge of adrenaline.

The End Game

Behind the compound walls, a blinding flash launched an emerald ball of light into the sky. Seconds later, it briefly flared to the east, then slowly drifted to the desert floor.

'Grey Eagle down!'

Lasers probed the killing ground where he now stood frozen to the spot. As he threw himself to the ground, automatic fire erupted from every roof and window. He saw three of his troop fall like puppets. And then he watched in disbelief as multiple bullets tore his body apart.

***

Harry cursed, tore off his headset, and threw it on the desk. On the screen, he could see the enemy doing their victory dance on the roof of the compound. In disgust, he ended the game, and scooted his chair away from the desk.

If only he'd been able to purchase a set of thermal and infrared overlay googles, he'd have seen it coming, been able to take evasive action and warn the patrol. And then they might win the day, affording him a chance to open the treasure box that contained an MK14 enhanced battle rifle and a clutch of grenades.

'Harry!' he heard his mother shout. 'Your dinner's on the table!'

He sighed, sent his laptop to sleep, and left the room.

Chapter 1
Wednesday 31st August 2022

Naval Street, Ancoats, 9 a.m.

'Come on, guys!' Jake said. 'Get a shift on! This is important.'

He sat on the edge of the sofa, left heel pumping up and down, exuding more than his usual macho enthusiasm. Louie added milk to his lungo intenso and came over to join him.

'Do I detect an excess of excitement, boss?'

'Wholly justified,' Jake said, 'as you're about to find out.'

Louie sipped his coffee and put his cup down on the wooden table. 'Go on then,' he said.

'Not till Nuan's joined us.'

Louie looked over his shoulder. She was sitting at her desk, wearing headphones, eyes on the screen of her high-resolution monitor.

'Nuan!' Jake shouted.

She placed her hands over her earphones, shook her head as though mildly irritated, and began to type at the keyboard.

'For God's sake!' Jake said. 'Sometimes she's impossible. Go and get her, Louie.'

'Not just sometimes,' Louie grumbled as he heaved himself up. He walked over to Nuan and tapped her on the shoulder. She looked up, bemused.

'We're waiting to start the meeting,' he told her.

'Meeting?'

Louie leaned in and lowered his voice to a whisper. 'Jake's reveal for this new game that's going to take the world by storm? We agreed last night. Eight o'clock this morning, on the dot?'

Nuan frowned. 'He was late,' she said.

The End Game

'Well, he's here now.'

'Okay.'

She stood, picked up her metal vacuum flask, and followed Louie. She sat facing her colleagues, unscrewed the top of her flask, took a leisurely drink, screwed the top back on, and placed the flask on the table.

'Ready now?' asked an exasperated Jake.

'Yes, thank you,' she replied.

'Right,' Jake began, 'here's the premise. Multiple threats face humankind. Chief among them, global warming and climate change.' He began to use his hands, punching the air to make his point. 'Forest fires, killer heatwaves, floods, famine, loss of habitat on land and on sea. Pandemics, mass migrations and political instability. Each player has the chance to become one of the...' He waggled his fingers to indicate speech marks. '... "Global Heroes" who save the planet.'

'How exactly?' Louie asked.

'By assuming multiple roles.'

'Such as?'

'Scientists, environmentalists, wildlife specialists and zoologists, campaigners, political leaders . . .'

Nuan raised a hand, seeking permission to speak.

Jake frowned. 'Go on,' he said.

'It'll require a truly extensive scientific information resource.'

'Not a problem,' he told her. 'We can start with basic and intermediate levels that require less sophisticated info banks and build them up after the initial development phase.'

It was Nuan's turn to frown.

Louie jumped in before she had time to formulate her next question. 'Sounds brilliant, mate,' he gushed. 'Have you come up with a name yet? What about *Global Hero*, or *Become a Hero*? Better still, *Save The Planet*?'

Jake shook his head. 'All taken. Along with all the other obvious ones. I was thinking something with a strong Manc connection. Like, *Bee a Hero*? *Bee Heroes*? *Beecome a Hero*?'

'I like,' Louie responded.

'Nah,' Jake said, 'work in progress.'

'I don't see the win/ lose motivation,' Nuan observed.

Jake raised his eyebrows. 'Thought it was obvious. The survival of humankind is at stake. You're either a hero or a failure.'

'Are you thinking single role and linear progression?' she asked.

'Both. Each player can choose linear progression or jump from role to role – hero to hero.'

She cut him off mid-flow. 'There are loads of eco games out there already. What do you see as its USP?'

Jake's expression flagged annoyance, both with the interruption and her need to spell it out. As ever, it was lost on Nuan. She was a stranger to emotional intelligence. Her colleagues made allowances because it was more than compensated for by her logical, mathematical and spatial intelligence that was way off the chart.

'There are multiple USPs,' Jake told her. 'Obviously, it's highly relevant, educational and ethical like all the other games out there. But ours will highlight the moral dilemmas in making different choices about how to save the planet. Parents and teachers are gonna love it.'

'Brilliant!' said Louie. 'Where's the bonus income stream?'

Jake grinned. 'Initially, the hacks and fixes will be free. Once the players are hooked, they'll be happy to purchase special hacks and fixes in-game without even thinking about it.'

Harriet, their new temp, appeared from behind a potted palm, and stepped nervously towards them.

'Not now!' Jake told her. 'Can't you see we're in a meeting?'

'I'm sorry, Mr Gorlay,' she said, 'but I thought you might need to see this.'

She held out a large brown envelope. There was no postage stamp. He beckoned her towards him and took the package. It was addressed to *The Directors, MancVG*. And printed in bold red letters, the words URGENT & PERSONAL.

With a wave of his hand, Jake dismissed the temp, tore the self-seal strip across the back of the package, and shook the contents onto the coffee table.

Chapter 2

Out slid a single folded A4 sheet of paper and a mobile phone. Jake unfolded the sheet. There were three lines of text. His face registered confusion, followed by annoyance.

'What does it say, boss?' Louie asked.

> You are about to play The END GAME.
>
> Failure to engage will have consequences.
>
> Read your text messages.

'Some punter trying to flog us a game he's designed?' Louie suggested.

'Or *she's* designed?' Nuan said.

'Or *it's* designed,' Louie added, not to be outdone. 'Whatever, they've got a bloody nerve. What are you going to do, Jake – bin it?'

Jake dropped the paper on the table and picked up the phone. 'It's a novel way to grab our attention. Intriguing even. Since they've gone to the expense of buying a phone, we may as well see what they have to say.'

'Some expense,' Nuan observed. 'That phone is out of the ark.'

It was small, plain and black, like something from the mid-1990s. Jake pressed and held the start button. After a few seconds, the screen lit up.

'That's odd,' he said. 'There's no number and no message. There's nothing on here except for this one app – BlackOp. Anyone know what that is?'

Louie shrugged. 'Sounds familiar. Is it a game, maybe?'

Nuan began to search on her phone. Jake opened the app.

'There's no email,' he told them, 'and it says all calls are disabled. The only application seems to be for text messages, but there aren't any.'

'Stone Age,' Louie observed. 'Some game this is going to be.'

'BlackOp is a Dark Web app,' Nuan reported. 'Maximum privacy. VoIP number. All texts, messages and calls military-grade encrypted. Messages self-destruct when read.' She looked up from her phone. 'Less Stone Age, more state of the black arts.'

'You don't want to be messing with something on the Dark Web,' Louie said. 'Seriously, mate . . . bin it.'

Jake thought about it for a moment, then placed the phone on the table and proceeded to rip up the note. As he did so, the phone pinged.

The three of them stared down at the screen. Jake picked it up and examined it.

'It's a long text. What do I do?'

'Open it,' Nuan said, 'but no links. It's only words. Words cannot kill you...'

'Not true,' said Louie. 'Honestly, mate, I think...'

Jake touched his screen to access the message.

'Read it out,' Nuan said.

> Welcome to the END GAME, Jake. I am The Boss. You and your fellow directors are the players. This is a reality game... A game of challenge and survival. Played in real time. The gameplay is as follows.
>
> WARNING: There are 5 levels. On each level you must complete one task. If you complete the task, you will proceed to the next level.

The End Game

> Failure to complete a task will result in a sanction. Following each sanction, you will be required to proceed to the next level, where you will face another task.
>
> Tasks will become progressively more challenging. No barter allowed.
>
> Sanctions will increase in severity. Once a sanction has been applied, it is irreversible.
>
> WARNING: Bad manners will not be tolerated and will result in sanctions. Failure to engage with the END GAME will result in total wipe-out.
>
> You will shortly receive instructions for Level One.

'Is this your idea of a joke, Louie?' Jake demanded. 'Because I am not amused.'

'Not me, boss,' Louie protested. 'On my life.'

'Give me the phone,' said Nuan. 'Quick!'

'Why?' said Jake.

'Because I want to copy it before it disappears.'

He held it up so she could take a screenshot. As she did so, the image dissolved.

'What are you doing that for?' Jake demanded.

She checked the image. 'Because it's evidence.'

'Evidence of what?'

'I don't know, but it feels threatening.'

'Everything seems threatening to you, Nu,' Louie said. 'You're not supposed to take it literally – it's a game.'

'A *reality* game,' she reminded him, 'with *sanctions*.'

'I'm with Louie,' Jake said. 'Someone's trying to mess with our heads. That's all.'

'I don't like people messing with my head,' Nuan responded, 'especially anyone on the Dark Web. Better to be prepared.'

The End Game

Jake put the phone down. 'Enough of this. We need to make a decision about my game.'

'*Our* game,' Louie pointed out.

'Only if you two buy into it.'

'This'll be extremely time-consuming, especially for Louie and me,' Nuan said, 'and if you want to keep it authentic and engaging, we'll have to pay for some of that expert advice you talked about.'

'That'd be true whatever game we go for,' Jake replied. 'The only question is, are you in or out?'

Louie grinned. 'I'm in, on condition you come up with a strong storyboard.'

Jake turned to Nuan. 'What about you, Nu?'

She was in a world of her own, staring down at the coffee table.

'Nuan?'

She looked up. 'Er... yeah... I'm in.'

'Great,' said Louie. 'In the meantime, why don't we go with *BeeHeroes?* We can use the Manchester Bee logo.'

'Isn't that a bit close to home for a game we want to go global?' Nuan wondered.

'Nah, bees are fundamental to people's survival all over the world, and they're a threatened species.'

'Let's stick with that for the prototype,' Jake said, 'and see if it grows on us. We can do some market research on the name when we've got a product to trial.' He looked at his watch. 'It's nearly lunchtime – let's have a bite to eat and a drink to celebrate.'

As the three of them got to their feet, the mobile phone gave out an ominous ping.

Nobody moved.

Chapter 3

'You going to answer that?' Louie said.

'You can't answer it,' Nuan reminded him, 'it's read only.'

Jake picked it up. 'Shit!' he said.

'What's it say?' Louie asked.

Nuan held her phone out. 'Show me, quickly,' she said. She took a shot of the screen.

Louie peered over her shoulder and read the message out loud.

> END GAME Level One
>
> You must donate £200,000 to the End In-Game Purchases charity within 24hrs of receiving this text.
>
> WARNING: Failure to complete this task in its entirety will result in a Level One sanction: denial of service.

'Bloody hell!' Louie exclaimed. 'That's what he means by a real-life game. This is blackmail.'

Nuan shook her head. 'Extortion.'

'This is not the time for political correctness,' Jake said. 'This is serious.'

I agree,' she said. 'We have to tell the police.'

Louie began scratching his neck. 'What can they do?' he said. 'This guy's on the Dark Web. They'll never track him down. And even if they do, it'll be too late to stop whatever sanction he's got planned.'

'They can try and trace where this phone was purchased,' Nuan suggested.

'On the Dark Web. So good luck with that. And as we've all handled the damn thing, you can forget about forensics.'

'Stop arguing!' Jake shouted. 'I need to think.'

The phone pinged again. Nuan seized it. She copied the text, and read it out from the photo on her own screen.

> WARNING: Do not involve the police. To do so will constitute bad manners and result in further sanctions.

Jake snorted. 'What is he, a mind reader?'

Louie's scratching intensified. 'Or maybe there's a recording device in the phone?'

Nuan turned and strode over to to her work desk. 'I'll find out.'

'How are we going to deal with this, Jake?' Louie demanded. 'We can't do as he says or he'll just keep upping the game till we're bankrupt.'

'Not necessarily. *If* this is just about the in-game stuff, and he starts demanding that we stop all of our add-ons, it wouldn't force us to liquidate, though our annual revenue would take a sizeable hit.'

'How much?'

'Twenty per cent from our two free-to-play games that rely completely on micro-monetisation, and another twenty-five per cent from power-ups, skins and loot boxes in the rest of the products.'

'Forty-five per cent!' Louie exclaimed. 'That's not just sizeable – that's massive.'

'That's gross revenue, remember,' Jake pointed out. 'Our costs would go down a bit, and we'd be paying less tax, so it would mean a reduction of around thirty-six per cent of net income.'

'It's still over a third,' Louie said. 'On the plus side, if we did donate that money, we'd come out of this smelling of roses, looking like the good guys holding the moral high ground.' He warmed to the idea. 'We'd get brilliant publicity. Might even pick up a bigger market share on the back of it.'

'Not if people find out we were forced into it,' Jake said.

'How would they know?'

'This maniac will probably tell them, if the police don't.'

'But if we don't go to the police . . .'

'Then he'll keep ramping up his demands. Don't you see? If we pay two hundred thousand now, he's going to be demanding two million by Level Five!'

Nuan returned and handed the phone back to Jake. 'It doesn't record,' she said, 'just like it doesn't give us the right of reply.'

'Louie wants to pay up,' Jake told her, 'and he wants to issue that statement too. I said that's not a good idea. The demands will escalate.'

'What about that sanction?' Louie said. 'Denial of service?'

Jake shook his head. 'How's he going to manage that? There's no supply chain. We distribute everything ourselves.'

'If he's a hacker,' Nuan said, 'or has access to hackers, a DOS attack on our servers could disrupt our streaming service and our comms. But we have state-of-the-art firewalls, and even if they do get through, I am sure that I can rectify the situation within twenty-four hours.'

'Bad for publicity then, but not fatal,' Jake observed. 'I vote we call his bluff.'

'Or hers,' Nuan said.

Chapter 4
Day 1
Friday 2nd September 2022

Millgate Lane, Didsbury, 7.30 a.m.

Caton wiped the traces of egg and crispy bacon from his lips with the back of his hand and pushed his plate to one side.

'That was a treat,' he said. 'What did I do to deserve it?'

'Nothing that I recall,' Kate replied, with a mischievous smile. 'I thought you might need it. Especially after your early morning training session. Besides, you never know what might be waiting for you.'

Caton's mobile rang, as though on cue.

'There you go,' she said.

'It's not work,' he told her, 'it's Helen – she's probably checking on Harry.'

'You'd better take it,' she said. 'I'll make you a coffee and some toast.'

Caton took the phone through to the hall. 'Helen,' he said. 'How are you?'

'I'm fine, Tom,' she said, 'and you?'

'Fine. Except it's back to work today.'

'Welcome to my world. How did Harry's sleepover go?'

'Has he not told you?'

She paused. 'He did, but you know what teenagers are like. I need to hear it from you.'

There was something in her tone that told him this was not a routine call. It was also the first time that Helen had given the slightest indication of not trusting their son.

The End Game

'It went exceptionally well,' he told her. 'In spite of the age difference, he and Emily got on well. In fact, on the day out we had in Morecombe, Harry took her under his wing. Even went out of his way to keep her amused. He was very protective of her. I was impressed. You'd have been proud of him, Helen.'

'I'm glad to hear it,' she said. She didn't sound it.

'What's the problem, Helen?' he asked, 'I can tell there's something troubling you.'

He heard an intake of breath. When she spoke, it came out in a rush, as though she'd been waiting for the opportunity to let it all out.

'It's Harry, Tom. I'm worried about him. All he wants to do is stay in his room and play his video games. I'm dreading it on Monday when the Autumn term starts. As soon as he gets home from school, he's straight up to his room. When I ask if he's done all his homework, he either says they didn't get much because it's nearly the end of term, or that he did most of it on the bus coming home . . .'

It didn't sound that much of a problem to Caton. It might even be true. Not difficult to check. Helen was still on a roll.

'...I'm worried about the amount of time he's spending on those games, especially with the holidays looming. I mean, what's he going to do while I'm out at work? Stay closeted in his room, glued to the screen, not even bothering to have lunch...'

Caton thought she was catastrophising, which wasn't like her at all.

'...I want to sign him up for the Latics Premier League Kicks school holidays sessions. He'll get top coaching, and the opportunity to play in local and regional tournaments. He'll even get to play against clubs from across the country. There'll be talent scouts. The club even organises free giveaways, and he'll have the chance to sign up as a volunteer for all sorts of activities.'

She paused to take breath.

'I'm guessing he doesn't want to?' Caton interjected.

'No, he doesn't. And it's all because he's obsessed with these damn video games! I want you to talk to him, Tom.'

The End Game

Caton felt ambushed, and he certainly wasn't going to rush into anything without thinking it through first. Helen had other ideas. He heard her call Harry's name, and the sound of her knocking on his bedroom door.

'Helen,' he said. But she wasn't listening to him. He could just about hear their conversation.

'Harry! Harry! Take those earphones off. It's your father. He wants a word with you.'

'Can I just finish this, Mum? Please?'

'No, you can't. It'll only be a couple of minutes. Your father has to be off to work. Why don't you just press pause or something?'

Caton grimaced. He imagined Helen's hand in Harry's back propelling him into the room, and his bewildered expression.

'Dad? It's me, Harry. What d'you want, Dad?'

He sounded anxious. Anticipating a telling off for something he wasn't even aware that he'd done, and barely managing to disguise his irritation. Not the best basis for a friendly father and son chat.

'Dad?'

'Harry!' Tom began. 'Sorry about this. Sounds like you were in the middle of something?'

'Nah, I was just trying out a couple of new games.'

'Two? Sounds exciting. What are they called?'

'One's called *A League Of Your Own*. It's a Football League game where you build your own team and compete against other players.'

'Sounds good.'

'It is. And the other one's even better. Everyone's playing it.'

'Everyone?'

'Everyone at school.'

'What's it called, Harry?'

'SEEL.'

'Seal? What's that, a nature programme?'

Harry's laugh made Caton feel ancient.

'No, Dad! It stands for *Seek, Evade, Eliminate, Liberate*. It's based on real US Special Forces operations in Afghanistan. You have to parachute behind enemy lines to

The End Game

rescue hostages, evade hostiles along the way and eliminate any that stand between you and your objective.

'Ah, I see,' Caton said. 'It's a play on words... *Navy Seals*.'

'Get with, Dad!' Harry responded. 'It's got nothing to do with the Navy, we're talking Afghanistan. Afghanistan is landlocked – everyone knows that.'

Not just old, but ignorant too. Caton decided to let it go. There was more to worry about here than exploring semantics with a fourteen-year-old. Fourteen? Where had all those years gone, the last seven of which he'd spent playing catch-up. He decided to change the subject.

'Speaking of football,' he said. 'What do you reckon about Wigan Athletics' new right back?'

'Promising,' Harry replied. 'He's got great pace, and his crosses are belting. And he can be a bit of a beast if he needs to be. On the other hand, he's getting on a bit.'

'Remind me,' Caton said, 'how old is he?'

'Thirty.'

And here's me approaching a half-century, Caton reflected.

'While we're on the subject of the Latics,' he said, 'your mum's been telling me about these Premier League Kicks sessions...'

***

'Tom, you're a genius!' Helen said. 'How did you manage to persuade him?'

'Like you said, I'm a genius.'

'I wasn't serious,' she told him. 'What did you do, Tom, bribe him?'

'Not exactly.'

'What does that mean?'

'I simply pointed out that he needed a healthy balance between relaxation and exercise, and that it wasn't healthy for him to stay cooped up in his room in the middle of summer.'

'And?'

The End Game

'And, if he signs up for at least a couple of sessions a week during the holidays, as a *reward*, I'll treat him and me to this season's home cup matches at the DW Stadium.'

Her tone hardened. 'What happens if you have to work?'

'Come on, Helen. You know I'm free at weekends, ditto night matches, unless there's a time-critical investigation.'

'And then I'd have to take him.'

He was tempted to remind her that Harry was her son too and she was big in PR at the stadium and had a free pass to all of the games. He resisted.

'Tom?' she said. 'Are you still there?'

'I'm here, Helen.'

'I thought we'd agreed we would never use bribery to persuade him to cooperate.'

'It wasn't really a bribe, more a reward for giving up some of the time he spends on his beloved video games.'

'I'm not sure I get that,' she said.

Caton wasn't entirely convinced himself. 'Try not to worry, Helen,' he said. 'Just be a little firmer. Why don't you follow up on my breakthrough by persuading him to draw up a timetable that fits the video games around all the other stuff and gives him more balance in his day?'

Caton heard her slowly exhale. He imagined her shoulders relaxing, and the stress leaching away. He felt sorry for her. It couldn't be easy being a single mum with a teenage boy. But he refused to feel guilty. She'd kept Harry's existence from him, and as soon as he'd discovered he had a son, he had stepped up. So had Kate, come to that, thank God.

'I'll give it a go,' Helen said, 'and thank you, Tom.'

'No need. And give yourself a break, Helen. You're a great mum.'

'I'm not sure about that,' she said.

'I am,' he told her. 'Harry will be fine.'

Chapter 5

'Sorry, he said, 'that took longer than I expected.'

Kate placed his mug and slice of damp toast on the table. 'I had to put your coffee in the microwave, but even that was four minutes ago, and your toast's cold. I couldn't heat it up because I'd already buttered it.' She put her hands on her hips. 'What did Helen want?'

Caton told her.

'She's right to be concerned,' she responded. 'One of my PhD students is writing his dissertation on the potentially addictive consequences of video gaming. It's opened my eyes. But you were right to caution her about coming down too heavy on Harry. At his age, that could just push him further into himself, and really get him hooked on those games. How's the toast?'

'Perfect,' he said. 'The butter's seeped right through, just how I like it.'

She raised her eyebrows. 'First I've heard of it.'

'Only joking.'

'Well, I wouldn't if I were you. Just in case I take you at your word.'

Caton blew on his coffee. 'What are your plans today while I'm hard at work?' he asked.

'For your information,' Kate said, 'I'm still at work, just working from home. I'm in court tomorrow giving evidence in that case I told you about. I need to prepare.'

He nodded. 'The woman who killed her husband with a bread knife because he'd been abusing her for years.'

'That's for the jury to decide, but my expert testimony, along with forensics evidence, will be crucial in helping them to decide between murder and manslaughter.'

The End Game

'They're the tricky ones,' he acknowledged, 'where nobody knows what really happened apart from the victim and the accused. Then it all depends on how the jury sees it. I've a similar one the CPS wants us to wrap up, even though with a little more time we could probably nail it down. There's a lot riding on it.'

She sat down facing him. 'How so?'

Caton sipped his coffee. He was surprised how quickly it had cooled off – like some of the investigations he had worked on over the years. He took a sip, then pushed his mug away.

'We've got a fourteen-year-old boy who stabbed another youth. His version is that it was self-defence. He says he was bullied and threatened by this other lad over and over again until he was out of his wits. He began carrying a knife for self-protection. He claims that on the day of the stabbing, the other youth produced a clasp knife. The defendant pulled his knife from his pocket to put the other boy off. He alleges that someone behind him pushed him towards the other youth, and he stumbled and fell. He put his hands out to break his fall, and his knife entered the thigh of the other youth, slicing his femoral artery. But for the swift action of a teacher, the victim would have bled to death.'

'Poor kid,' Kate said. 'What's he likely to get?'

Caton frowned. 'The problem is that the clasp knife went missing, and the witnesses are either too scared to corroborate the accused's account or are suggesting that it was deliberate. Given time, we may be able to get some of the waverers to help us.'

'If not?'

'He's got no previous, and plenty of good character references. It's going to depend on how the jury sees it, and who the judge is.' He shook his head. 'He's a nice lad – too nice. He'll be easy meat in Young Offenders. There's every chance he'll come out broken or criminalised.' He pushed the bench back and stood up.

'Are you going to finish your coffee?' Kate asked.

Caton recognised the subtle warning signs: the hurt behind the eyes, the hint of accusation in her voice. He lifted his mug and downed the contents. It was stone cold. He grimaced.

'Serves you right,' Kate said, as he walked off towards the hall. 'Shouldn't have been so long on the phone.'

Caton consider an appropriate riposte. He decided there wasn't one – there rarely was.

'Have a lovely day!' he said.

Chapter 6

8 a.m.

The map on the satnav indicated long tailbacks on the anticlockwise section of the M60 north of Stockport. Caton decided to cut across the city and then pick up Ashton Old Road. Halfway up Wilmslow Road, he recalled that shortly before the first lockdown he'd been intending to visit the restoration of the Marcus Rashford mural. He slowed and turned left into Copson Street.

It was some years since he'd driven down here but the street was still recognisable from when he'd grown up back in the early days. At less than one hundred and eighty metres long, he was surprised at how lively and diverse it had become. He passed a smart cafe, two dentists – one boasting twenty-four-hour emergency care, a pharmacy, an opticians, a solicitors, a range of shops, and five restaurants and fast-food outlets offering Lebanese to South Indian cuisine. And that was in the first fifty metres alone. There were precious few towns in the area with a high street as vibrant as this. Caton swung into Moorfield Street and parked up outside Age Concern.

On the opposite side of the road, Akse's mural, five metres high and over fifteen metres across, covered the entire gable end of the Coffee House Café. None of the spray-painted graffiti remained. The young footballer stared down at him – strong, proud, defiant, challenging. A riposte to the sad individual who had thought that missing a penalty for England was more important than the twenty million pounds plus the footballer had raised towards the FareShare food charity of which he was its most famous ambassador.

The End Game

An elderly woman, laden with two carrier bags of groceries, stepped off the pavement and came to stand by his open window. 'Scum!' she declared.

'I beg your pardon?' Caton said.

She nodded towards the mural. 'Saw you looking. Scum! The ones that defaced that with their dirty words and filthy drawings. Not fit to lick the dirt off his boots. Or Sancho's, come to that.'

'I'm sure you're right,' he said.

''Course I'm right!'

She put her bags down, then leaned with one hand on the roof of the car, settling in for a chat. Caton retreated into the cabin, wishing he'd been wearing one of the facemasks sitting in the glovebox, and wondering if they'd ever see the light of day.

'They should've knighted him by now, and that's from a dyed-in-the-wool, true-blue City fan,' she said.

'Me too,' he responded.

She leaned in closer, her blue-rinse perm brushing the window frame. Blue-rinse perm. He hadn't seen one of those in years.

'D'you know how much we locals raised to get this mural restored?'

'No.'

'Just under forty thousand pounds in less than two hours on Julie's *JustGiving* page.'

'That's impressive,' Caton said.

'Too bloody right! And before you ask, it only cost a fraction to put it right. All the rest went to the charity.'

'Well, it's been lovely talking,' he said, 'but . . .'

'You've things to do, places to be. Of course you have.'

She retrieved her bags, straightened up with a grunt, and set off down the street, muttering as she went. 'Scum!'

Caton returned his attention to the mural. Across the full width ran a quote from Rashford's mother, Melanie, that had inspired him:

'Take pride in knowing that your struggle will play the biggest role in your purpose.'

'Isn't that the truth,' Caton murmured.

As he pulled away from the kerb, a call came through.

It was DI Carter.

'Where are you, Boss?'

'On my way in, why?'

'Where exactly?'

'I'm about to join Wilmslow Road, just north of the old White Lion pub.'

'Good,' Carter said. 'We're needed in Ancoats. There's been a suspicious fire at a business on Naval Street. Everything points to an arson attack.'

Caton slowed at the junction.

'See you in ten,' he said.

Chapter 7

Caton had a fondness for Ancoats. Just over half a square mile bounded by Ashton Old Road, Ancoats Green and the Rochdale Canal. As a sixth-form student at Manchester Grammar, it had been one of his favourite local history projects. The world's first industrial suburb, it was packed with cotton mills and silk mills, glass factories, warehouses, churches, chapels and schools, together with rows and rows of back-to-back houses and squalid courts.

In the mid-1880s, it had also housed gangs of Manchester's most notorious Scuttlers, the city's own version of Birmingham's Peaky Blinders. Naming themselves after the streets in which they lived, the Bengal Tigers, Poland Street Lads, and Pollard Street Scuttlers, waged turf wars and vendettas against each other, as well as gangs from the neighbouring Bradford and Miles Platting districts. But their real venom was reserved for the gangs of Salford. In that respect, it was much the same as today, Caton reflected, except that the axis of power had shifted to South Manchester, and pointed, brass-tipped clogs and leather belts with large brass buckles had been replaced by knives and guns.

By the outbreak of World War One, several thousand Italian émigrés fleeing civil war had joined a substantial Irish community, and the area of Ancoats around St Peter's Church swiftly became known as Little Italy. Utilising the surplus ice from a massive fruit and fish warehouse on Blossom Street, around seventy Italian ice cream vendors had fanned out from here on horse and cart and tricycle across the city. Caton smiled as he turned onto Great

Ancoats Street. If he remembered rightly, it was on this street that Antonio Valvona, biscuit-maker, had created the world's first ice cream cornet, replacing the shared 'penny lick' glass bowls that were thought to be spreading typhoid and cholera across the city. In doing so, he had saved the ice cream industry.

By the time that Caton joined GMP, Ancoats had become a shadow of its glory days. The mills and warehouse were either derelict, in ruins, or had been demolished, the canals lost or stagnant. The population had dwindled to just over a thousand souls.

His musing ended abruptly. A white van had stopped suddenly in front of him, one brake light missing, the other smeared with dirt. Caton stamped on the brake and cursed as his seat belt dug into his chest. His car skidded the final few feet and came to a stop with a discreet thump, bumper to bumper. The door of the van slid back, and the driver got out. Bald, red-faced, short and stocky, his chest swelled with righteous indignation. He thumped his beefy hands on the roof of Caton's car, and leaned in.

'What the fuck were you doing?' he demanded.

Caton lowered the window a fraction, held up his warrant card in his right hand and, with his left, pointed to the dashcam mounted below the rear-view mirror.

'Are you aware,' he said, 'that it's illegal to drive with only one brake light? Even more so when it happens to be obscured. You're looking at a sixty-pound fine, three points on your licence, and a vehicle rectification notice.'

He paused to allow the man time to process the information. Waited for the aggression to wilt, his shoulders to sag, for him to remove his hands and step away.

Caton lowered the window. 'Or I could issue you a verbal warning?' He raised his eyebrows. 'What's it to be?'

'I'll take the warning,' the man muttered.

'I didn't catch that?' Caton told him.

'I said, I'll take the warning.'

'Good,' Caton replied. 'You have ten days to get your lights fixed.' He leaned out of the window and called after the retreating van driver. 'And don't forget to clean that light before you set off!'

The End Game

The man checked his stride, swore beneath his breath, leaned sideways, spat on his left hand, and rubbed the offending light, exposing the red plastic but leaving a thin smear of dirt. Caton decided to let it go. He had already ridden his luck. In theory, because he was on official business, he should make out a report. In theory. He rubbed his chest, hoping that his ribs were only bruised, started the engine, and set off in the wake of the van.

He turned into Redhill Street, entering Ancoats proper, and drove between the canal and the redbrick and sandstone buildings. Former palaces of industry, these mills and warehouse had been transformed into elegant apartments. In the spaces between, and on the pedestrian-friendly streets and squares, had sprung up dozens of restaurants, bars and shops, and several craft breweries. What less than twenty years earlier had been a scene of utter neglect and desolation had become a desirable destination to live, work and play. It seemed an unlikely place for arson. Caton turned left into Bengal Street, sharp right into Naval Street, and stopped. The way ahead was blocked by a police van slewed across the street. Parked outside a Victorian redbrick warehouse, he spotted a fire service incident unit, a patrol car, and several unmarked cars. Caton locked the car and set off on foot.

Chapter 8

Nick Carter was on the other side of a tape marking off the inner cordon. He was talking to a man, a head and shoulders taller, wearing a blue T-shirt, and white forensic trousers tucked into a pair of wellington boots. Caton gave his details to the female PC holding the log, and ducked under the tape.

'This is DCI Caton,' Carter said. 'Boss, this is Jadyn Brown, group manager of the Greater Manchester Fire Scene Investigation team.'

The two men shook hands.

'Why don't you tell Mr Caton what you just told me?' Carter said.

All of six foot five tall, and seventeen stone in weight, Brown was built like a second row forward. Caton could see him rescuing people from a first-floor window without the aid of a ladder, given which his voice came as a surprise. He was softly spoken yet authoritative, with just a hint of Caribbean heritage.

'Preliminary findings,' he began. 'We received a call in the early hours of this morning reporting a fire at these premises. The appliance arrived less than three minutes later, and quickly extinguished what was left of the fire. It was immediately evident that this was not your average petrol through the letterbox.'

'In what way?' Caton asked.

'It *was* an explosive incendiary device,' Brown said, 'but the perpetrator wasn't out to burn the building down. Far from it.'

'And you know because...?'

The End Game

'Firstly, it was placed next to one of these ventilation inlets where it would do specific but limited damage.'

Caton stared at the two large steel panels with louvred slats, set into the wall close to its base. One was bowed and twisted beyond recognition.

'What's behind there?' Caton asked.

'A bank of computer servers. Part of a dedicated server farm for a small digital company. Looks like someone was out to damage this business without actually gutting the building.'

'Because of the placement of the device?'

'And because the 999 call was received immediately *before* the device exploded. There are two reasons we know that to be the case. Firstly, because the call was made at 2.28 a.m., and yet a resident in one of those apartments behind you stated that she heard the sound of a small explosion just *after* 2.30 a.m. She'd just come in from work at a bar in the Northern Quarter and had not yet gone to bed.' He paused. 'Furthermore, the company's own equipment shows that the servers affected by the explosion stopped working at precisely 2.30 a.m.'

'They wanted you to get here before the fire had a chance to spread?'

'If so, it worked. Manchester Central is only a quarter of a mile away. Like I said, our appliance arrived in just under three minutes.'

'Where did the call originate?' Caton said.

Brown pointed. 'The far end of the street. And before you ask, the number was untraceable.'

Caton stared at the blackened metal. 'How bad is the damage?'

'The two servers immediately behind there have been ruined.'

'There are others?'

'Follow me,' Brown said.

He led Caton around the corner of the building and pointed to four identical ventilation panels on the south wall, intact and untouched.

'There are eight more servers in there,' he said. 'The room was equipped with an inert-gas suppression system that all but put out the fire before we arrived. There's also a powerful heat extraction and ventilation system to keep the servers at optimum temperature. The smoke was sucked out, leaving the rest of the building unaffected. As I said, the server units next to where the explosive device was located are out of action, but all the others are still functioning.'

'So, either the perpetrator wasn't aware of their existence, or this is some kind of warning? Extortion, maybe?'

Brown nodded. 'Or an insurance scam. That's for you to find out.'

'How long before you have something concrete for us to work on?' Caton asked.

'There's not a lot to the scene. Your best chance is with whatever CCTV is out here, and with the device itself. I'm liaising closely with your crime scene manager, so there shouldn't be any delay in getting you a report.'

'Where are the owners?' Caton asked.

'Follow me,' Carter said.

Chapter 9

It was an enormous room, occupying the top floor of the old warehouse.

Cast-iron pillars one foot in diameter supported the vaulted ceiling. The stains on the bare wooden floorboards had been retained as witness to their history. What might have seemed stark and cavernous had been softened by pale blue paint on the ironwork, including the bars on the arched windows. Modern works of art hung on the bare brick walls. Large potted plants, quiet uplighting and black industrial-style hanging lamps contrived to minimise the sense of space and define the purpose of different areas.

Caton was unconvinced. Neither reflective of its historical weight, nor comfortable in its modernity, it left him feeling disappointed.

He and his DI were led past a drinks station, a breakout space with flip charts and whiteboards, a meeting space with a table and chairs for ten persons, and six workstations, each equipped with a bank of computer monitors, keyboards, laptops and tablets, and an ergonomic chair.

At the far end of the room, hidden behind a screen of tall plants, they found the directors seated in a conspiratorial huddle – an impression reinforced by the expression on the faces of the two men. It was as though they had been caught smoking behind the school bike shed.

Following a brief introduction, the young woman went over to join her colleagues, freeing the sofa on which she had been sitting for the two detectives. Caton sat down and sized up the three of them, judging them all to be in their early to mid-thirties.

Jake Gorlay, who had been introduced as the CEO and creative director, was tall, athletic and in his early thirties.

He kept his blond hair short and his designer beard was artfully modelled on that of an A-list movie star. He wore a grey sports jacket over skinny-fit washed-out jeans and sported highly polished light tan brogues.

Beside him on the sofa, Louie Ellish, senior artist and animator, looked more like Caton's idea of the archetypal graphic designer. Of medium height and build, he had black curly hair, designer glasses, and wore a cardigan over a white T-shirt and jeans. On his feet were a pair of white trainers. Of the three, he looked the most nervous.

Nuan Lau, senior programmer and head of production and distribution, returned Caton's gaze with an intensity that was almost unnerving. She was short and slim, with coal-black eyes. Her auburn hair, shot through with crimson highlights, hung halfway to her waist. In her left hand she held a mobile phone. Her right hand clutched a stainless steel and BPA-free plastic vacuum flask, one of those claiming to have been designed to help save the planet, or, at the very least, the oceans.

'Perhaps we could start with you telling me what it is you do here?' Caton said. The three directors looked at each other. Through some unspoken agreement, it was Jake Gorlay who responded.

'We're an independent video game producer and publisher,' he said. 'Medium-sized, not in the same league as Google or Sony, but we do alright. I come up with ideas, we knock them around, then I come up with a storyboard. Louie works on the graphics and oversees a team of designers we contract work out to. Nuan here does the programming. When a game is ready, Nuan produces a pilot. We tweak it, then install it on one of our servers, and market and stream it direct to people's devices. They get the full video and audio. When gamers start to play the game, all of their inputs come through the controller on the server and they play in real time, independently or with others.'

'If the server's damaged, none of them can play the game?'

'Exactly.'

'And that's what's happened here?'

'Two of our high-clock CPU servers have been destroyed.

The End Game

That means that two of our most lucrative games are offline.'

'It's costing us five grand in lost revenue every day,' Louie Ellish said. 'Not to mention the stream of complaints from our customers.'

Gorlay glared at him.

Nuan Lau raised the hand in which she held her flask. 'But I've already uploaded our most popular game onto one of our other servers which had spare capacity.'

'And,' Gorlay added, 'I'm exploring the possibility of having our games hosting outsourced to a specialist provider instead of maintaining a server farm of our own.'

'I told you we should have done that two years ago,' muttered Ellish.

'Not helpful!' Gorlay responded.

'Do any of you have any idea who might be responsible for this?' Caton asked.

A glance passed between the two men. Lau stared at them, as though curious to see how they were going to respond.

Jake Gorlay replied for all of them.

'No,' he said.

Caton could tell Gorlay was lying, and it was clear from the look on Carter's face that he wasn't alone in thinking all three of them were hiding something.

'So,' Caton began, 'someone, who just happens to know how important your servers are to your company, and where they are located, causes a fire that destroys two of them, and you have no idea what that person's motive might be, or his or her identity?'

'It's a mystery,' said Gorlay.

'Like one of your games?'

Gorlay shrugged.

'Okay,' Caton said. 'Let's see if we can help. Is there anyone who might wish to harm your company?'

'I can't think who,' Gorlay said. He turned to his senior artist. 'What about you, Louie?'

Ellish shrugged unconvincingly. 'Me neither.'

'What about CDC?' Nuan suggested.

That prompted a sharp intake of breath from her CEO.

Caton stared at him. 'CDC?' he said.

The End Game

Gorlay's response was reluctant. 'Castlefield Digital Creations. They're just another gaming company like ours. One of over twenty in Manchester alone.'

'And how might they benefit from damaging your server units?'

'They've been trying to buy us out,' Nuan Lau responded. 'They've been very persistent.'

'Really?' Caton said. 'Why might that be?'

'Because we have six high-profile and very profitable games.' Gorlay said 'If they were able to add them to their portfolio, it would make them a major player. Then the big boys might come sniffing and make them an offer they can't refuse.'

'Or big girls,' Lau said.

'What are they offering you?' Caton asked.

The two men looked at each other.

'That's confidential company information,' Gorlay said. 'It might give someone a competitive advantage.'

Caton smiled. 'I wasn't aware that Greater Manchester Police are into video game production,' he said. 'Nor are we known for industrial espionage.'

Gorlay remained tight-lipped.

'We could always check with Companies House,' Caton said.

Gorlay shook his head. 'That won't give you the answer you're looking for,' he said.

Caton leaned forward. 'Which is?'

Gorlay surrendered. 'Two and a half times our annual sales revenue.'

'Which comes to?'

There was a long pause.

'Fifteen point three million pounds.'

Carter couldn't help himself. 'For video games?'

'Believe me, that's small fry compared with what the big companies are making,' Gorlay told him.

'And the industry multiple for takeovers is actually three times sales and revenue,' Louie Ellish chipped in.

'And we have above average market traction and growth, a highly sustainable competitive advantage, and the market is growing exponentially,' Nuan Lau added.

The End Game

'Couldn't you just take the money and then start up under a new name with some new games?' Carter said.

Gorlay groaned.

'Any such agreement,' Nuan Lau said, 'would include a binding agreement to cease operating in the same market in a competitive manner for at least two years. Standard practice.'

'Besides, this is our baby,' Gorlay pointed out. 'There is no way we're giving up now.'

'Apart from this rival firm, CDC, does anyone else come to mind?' Caton asked.

None of them responded. Nuan Lau was looking at the floor, and Louie Ellish had given his CEO a brief sideways glance before staring at a spot on the ceiling.

Caton lost patience with them. 'You're behaving like children,' he said. 'I shouldn't need to remind you of the gravity of this attack on your business. Never mind the damage – someone could have died. Who's to say that next time they won't?'

Nuan Lau raised her head and stared at each of her colleagues in turn. 'We should tell them,' she said.

Caton sat back. 'Tell me what?'

'She's right, Jake,' Ellish said, 'If this is a Level One sanction, God knows what's coming next.'

'Sanction?' Caton said. 'Are you saying this is about extortion?'

'Yeah,' Gorlay finally admitted. 'We're being blackmailed.'

'Extortion.' Caton told him. 'Not blackmail, extortion.'

Gorlay bristled. 'Same difference, surely?'

'Not in a legal sense,' Caton replied. 'Although both involve threats or require a specific course of action in order to obtain money, only extortion involves threats of physical violence against a person or persons, or destruction of their property. Blackmail uses the threat to expose secrets or knowledge that might harm the intended victim or someone close to them.'

Gorlay raised both hands, less in surrender than in irritation. 'Okay,' he said. 'We're being *extorted*.'

Here was someone, Caton decided, whose inflated ego was such that he was quick to take offence, and even quicker to give offence to others. He could see a line of potential suspects reaching around the block.

'Finally, we're getting somewhere,' he said. 'It's time you told us what the hell is going on.'

Chapter 10

The two detectives put on their forensic gloves as the envelope, sheet of paper, mobile phone, and the images from Nuan Lau's phone were set out on the coffee table in front of them.

'How many of you have handled the package and its contents?' Caton asked.

'All of us,' Nuan Lau replied.

'Then we'll need your fingerprints and DNA swabs,' he told them.

'Is that really necessary?' Gorlay asked.

'Only if you want us to catch whoever is doing this,' Caton replied.

He and Carter took their time examining the evidence before them, ending with the screenshots of the text messages.

'The terminology used strikes me as unusual,' Caton said. '"Boss", "bad manners", "levels" and "sanctions"?'

'They're common terms used within the gaming community,' Lau told him.

'So this could be a gamer, or a designer of games?'

Gorlay scowled. 'Obviously,' he muttered.

'Or someone who knows how to Google?' Carter said.

'What else does it tell you about the person who sent these?' Caton asked.

'That he's out to hurt our business, obviously,' Gorlay said.

'Or she, or they,' Nuan Lau added.

'That he . . . or she . . . has a thing about in-game purchases?' Louie Ellish suggested.

'Unless that's just a cover?' Lau said.

Gorlay snorted.

'Well, there's nothing else in it for he, she, they, it or *them*, is there?' he said. 'Not if the money is going to this charity.'

'Have you heard of a charity called . . . ' Caton checked his notes. '. . . End In-Game Purchases?'

'Oh yeah,' Gorlay replied, 'this one is a bloody pain. It only started campaigning to put a stop to in-game gambling and purchases a couple of years ago, but they're gaining ground.'

'There's no mention of gambling in these messages,' Caton pointed out.

Louie Ellish sat forward. 'The thing is,' he said. 'we don't have any gambling within our games, and we actively discourage people from doing so.'

'We agreed when we started the company, no gambling,' Nuan Lau added. 'It's against our ethics.'

'So why do you think you're being targeted?'

'Million-dollar question,' Gorlay said.

'Or two hundred thousand quid in our case,' Ellish pointed out, 'and that's only for for starters.'

'I assume that the three of you have discussed how you intend to respond to these demands?' Caton said.

'We're not paying, if that's what you mean!' Gorlay responded. 'And we won't be issuing any statements or stopping any in-game purchases. Besides, there's no point now your lot are involved.'

'Good,' Caton told him. 'Our advice is to never give in to ransom demands. Even if you do, there's no guarantee that the perpetrators won't come back for more, or still carry out their threats. And, taking a wider perspective, giving in may embolden them to target other companies.'

Gorlay stood up. 'I don't give a shit about other companies. I want to know what we're supposed to do now, and how you're going to protect us, and our business?'

Caton refused to be provoked. 'Keep us informed of every communication,' he said. 'Record any calls on your mobiles. I'll see if we can arrange twenty-four-hour surveillance on this building. Ring 999 immediately if you have any reason to fear for your personal safety. I'm going

The End Game

to arrange for one of my colleagues to take each of you through a risk assessment that will include your personal routines and the security of your homes: their accessibility, locks, alarm systems, CCTV coverage, and so on. In the meantime, DCI Carter will need to speak with each of you separately.'

Gorlay bristled. 'Are you suggesting that one of us could be involved?'

'Not at all,' Caton said. 'This is routine procedure in a case of extortion. The more we know about each of you and your company, the sooner we'll be able to find out who's behind those messages, and the attack on your servers.

'Now, if you'll excuse me, I'm going to check with the Fire Service Investigation team and our crime scene manager.' He stood up. 'Try not to worry. We'll deal with this.'

'Easy for you to say!' Gorlay responded.

Caton gestured for Nick to join him. The two of them moved out of earshot.

'I suggest you start with Lau,' he said. 'Of the three of them, she's been the most forthcoming.'

'That was my instinct,' Carter agreed. 'Let's hope she's even more enlightening when she's not got Gorlay watching her every move.'

Chapter 11

'Ms Lau. Why don't you start by telling me a little about yourself,' Carter began, 'and how you came to be working here?'

Ignoring the carafe of water and the glasses on the table, she took a sip from her flask.

'I came to Manchester to study at the university. It has a highly esteemed computer science department. Did you know that it's also the birthplace of computer science?'

Carter did.

'Alan Turing,' he said.

'Alan *Mathison* Turing,' she corrected.

'And where did you come from?' he asked, instantly regretting the ambiguity of the question. 'I mean . . .'

He needn't have bothered.

'Swindon,' she replied, without a flicker. 'My parents adopted me when I was two years old.'

'Right,' he said. 'And when did you meet Mr Gorlay and Mr Ellish?'

'They were also studying computer science here in Manchester. Jake was in my year, Louie a year behind. We all developed an interest in the development of computer-generated video games.'

'And whose idea was it to work together?'

'Jake and Louie decided to start up the company. They approached me because they were aware of my programming expertise.'

It was said as a matter of fact, without affectation or modesty.

'That must have taken some investment?' Carter said.

The End Game

'We were fortunate. Jake's father lent him twenty thousand pounds; mine lent me five thousand pounds. It was enough to get us started. Within two years, we had repaid them with interest.'

'And Mr Ellish? Did he contribute anything?'

There was a hint of surprise in her eyes.

'His expertise – that was priceless.'

She began to unscrew the top of her flask again. Carter used the time to gather his thoughts. He waited until he had her full attention.

'Are you happy here?' he asked.

She seemed surprised by the question.

'Happy? This is where I do my work. It provides me with challenge and intellectual stimulation. I'm thankful when my endeavours are deemed successful. I don't come here to be happy.'

Carter wondered if anything ever made her happy. And what on earth she could do with the considerable sums of money she was making that might bring a smile to her face.

'But you're not unhappy here?'

'I am neither happy nor unhappy,' she replied. 'I do my work to the best of my ability, and then I go home.'

'And where is home exactly?'

'I live in an apartment overlooking New Islington Marina. I've been there for over six years.'

Carter looked up from his notes. 'Really? Detective Chief Inspector Caton used to live there. You must have been neighbours.'

'I don't recall having ever seen him,' she said.

'And do you live alone?'

'Yes, and no.'

'Yes, and no?'

'I have a partner. She lives with her son on a converted coal barge on the marina. Sometimes she comes to stay in my apartment when her son is visiting his father.'

'What's their marital status, your partner and her son's father?'

Carter was prepared for her to be affronted. She was not.

'They were divorced two years ago, before she and I met.'

'And what are the names of your partner and her son?'

'Thelma Dundas and Langston Dundas. Langston is ten years old, and profoundly deaf. It's the result of an acquired congenital recessive gene inherited from his father.'

'I'm sorry to hear that,' Carter said.

'There's no need to be sorry, detective inspector,' she responded. 'Langston is a very bright and happy boy. His abilities are many and more than compensate for his deafness.'

Carter was about to say he was glad to hear it, but he'd already had two put-downs and wasn't eager for another. 'What does Ms Dundas do for a living?' he asked.

'She works for the Manchester University Library Service. We met when I was searching for a scholarly article on fifth-generation advanced game design. Thelma showed me where I could refill my flask with filtered water. We got talking.'

Carter wondered who had initiated the conversation, and how exactly that had gone. Lau didn't strike him as a social animal.

'When we discovered,' she continued, 'that we both lived at the marina, she invited me to visit her barge, and to meet Langston. He was named after Langston Hughes, the poet, social activist, and playwright who was a central figure in the Harlem Renaissance...' She checked to see if Carter knew what she was talking about and realised that he did not. '... A flowering of black intellectual, literary and artistic life that took place in the nineteen-twenties.'

She made it sound like a quote from Wikipedia. Carter decided it was time to wrap this up.

'Ms Lau,' he said, 'do you have any suspicion about who might be behind this attack on your company?'

For the first time, her gaze faltered. She looked down at her flask as though surprised to see it there and began to unscrew the lid. As she took a series of small sips, Carter's interest grew. She was playing for time.

The End Game

'Ms Lau,' he said, 'Nuan, if there's something we should know, you must tell us. Forget about any loyalty you may feel you owe to others. This is already an extremely worrying situation. If we don't quickly get on top of it, your colleagues, their families, even your partner and her son, could find themselves in grave danger.'

The mention of her partner and her son did the trick. She stopped what she was doing and looked directly at him.

'There's something I think I should tell you. It's to do with Jake.'

'Go on,' he said.

'I think he may be cheating on his partner.'

'And what makes you think that?'

'He has a history with women. Jake is wealthy and personable. I'm told he can be very charming. He also enjoys the good life, not that there's anything wrong with that. It is understandable that many women find him attractive.'

She paused. Carter held his breath and waited.

'However,' she said, 'he's had many relationships, some very short, some long, and it's not unusual for him to have more than one at the same time. He's also very tactile. I don't think he can help himself when it comes to women.'

'And how do you know all this?' Carter asked.

'I overhear them talking, him and Louie. He confides in Louie. It's a male thing, I think.'

Carter nodded. 'Bragging.'

'Sharing conquests,' she qualified. 'When they become aware that I'm in the vicinity, they quickly change the conversation. Also, we get calls here at the office. Sometimes when everyone else is out and I'm working alone, I answer the phone. These women give their names. Leave messages asking for Mr Gorlay to call them back. Even confirm that they'll be at such and such a place, at such and such a time. When I tell Jake, I get the impression that he's annoyed that I took the call.'

'And you believe that his partner . . .?'

'Becky. Becky Kerson.'

'Becky . . . is aware of these liaisons?'

She nodded. 'I think so. She's been calling the office

more frequently, asking for Jake. It's clear that she has no idea where he is, and that upsets her. She's even started dropping into the office when she's in Manchester, which she never did before. She smiled a lot at the start of their relationship, but not now.'

At best it was circumstantial, though thought-provoking.

'Do they live together? Mr Gorlay and Ms Kerson?'

She nodded solemnly. 'In a big house in Cheshire.'

Before Carter had time to ask anything more, she added something that further sparked his interest.

'Jake also has an apartment here in Manchester. In the Northern Quarter.'

'Really?'

'Yes. He says it's so he can carry on working if he needs to, and get into the office early in the morning. Or if he and Becky have had a late night in Manchester, they can sleep there rather than have to drive home.'

'But you think he may be taking other women there?'

She lowered her eyes. 'Yes.'

'Because?'

'Sometimes, when I'm in town with Thelma, in a bar or a restaurant or just wandering around, I see Jake with another woman. Often this is when I happen to know that he has planned to stay the night at his apartment.'

'I see,' Carter said. 'And is this a recent thing, or would you say it's been going on for some time?'

'A long time.'

'And has it always been the same woman, or have there been other women?'

Nuan raised her head and looked him in the eyes. 'Yes,' she said, 'other women too. But this one for a longer time.'

'How long?'

She shrugged. 'Five months, maybe six?'

'I see,' Carter said. 'One last question, Ms Lau. Where were you between midnight and four o'clock this morning?'

She was surprised by the question but not affronted. 'Last night? I was at home. In my apartment.'

'Alone?'

'No, Thelma was with me. Langston is staying with his father.'

The End Game

Carter made a note. 'And is there anything else you think might help us with our investigation?'

She shook her head. 'No.'

'In that case, thank you, Ms Lau,' he said. 'Please ask Mr Ellish to join me.'

Chapter 12

'Perhaps you could begin by telling me how you first met Mr Gorlay and Ms Nuan?'

Ellish visibly relaxed.

'It was at a computer animation and visual effects fair at Manchester Met. I met Jake and Nuan at PLAY Expo at the Bowlers Exhibition Centre in Trafford Park.'

'PLAY Expo?'

'It's an annual hands-on exhibition of modern gaming – or it was before Covid struck. You'll find everything there to do with computer animation and visual effects: retro, indie, arcade, VR, LAN, tabletop, tournaments – the works. I was running a workshop on animation rigging.'

'Animation rigging?'

'It's the way in which we get our characters to interact with the environment we create around them. There are three main components to animation rigging: the base object of the character; the mesh that gives the character form; and the rig, or character skeleton . . .'

Carter was sorry he'd asked. But at least it had got Ellish talking. He held up his hand.

'That sounds fascinating, Mr Ellish, but I've got the gist. Can I assume that Jake and Nuan were impressed by your work and invited you to join them in the enterprise they were planning?'

'Yes.'

'Good. And the idea was for the three of you to set up a limited company in which you would all invest, and all of you have shares as directors. Is that correct?'

The End Game

Ellish was slow in responding. Carter had the impression he was trying to work out where this heading.

'Ye . . . s.'

'And what form did your investment take?'

Ellish expressed surprise. 'Well . . . me.'

'Your expertise?'

'That's right.'

'So they brought their own unique skills, plus hard cash, and you just brought yourself?'

'They couldn't have created any games without someone like me!' Ellish protested.

'I get that, Louie,' Carter said, 'but surely, the same is equally true of your fellow directors. So if you weren't bringing cash to the party, did that affect the number of shares you received compared to them?'

Carter already knew the answer. A cursory search on Companies House before he started the interviews had, if little else, at least furnished that information. He could tell that for Ellish the penny had finally dropped.

'Well, yes. But that doesn't . . .'

'How many exactly?'

'Nineteen per cent.'

'And your fellow directors?'

'Nuan has thirty per cent and Jake fifty-one per cent.'

'Giving Mr Gorlay the majority stake.'

'Well, yes.'

'And you having such a small stake in the company when, as I understand it, your work is clearly of equal worth... how does that make you feel, Louie?'

Ellish folded his arms, and adopted a more forceful and defensive tone.

'I know what you're implying,' he said. 'And you're wrong. I'm fine with it. The only dividends that have been drawn down to date were to pay back our investors – Jake's father and Nuan's father. The rest has been ploughed back into developing the company. In lieu of dividends, we've been paying ourselves a handsome annual salary that is the same for each of us.' He paused. 'Besides, the initial agreement was only intended to be temporary, until such time as the investors had been repaid with interest, and the company was on a sound footing.'

'And what's supposed to happen then?'

'At that point the articles will be revised to give each of us one third of the shares, to reflect the fact that we founded the company together and have an equal share of the copyright to every game we've produced.'

'And Mr Gorlay's happy with that?'

Ellish's eyes narrowed a fraction. 'Why wouldn't he be?'

'Because it was his idea? Because without his father's investment none of this would have happened? Because he's the CEO?'

'Look,' Ellish said, stabbing a finger in Carter's direction, 'Jake's a stand-up guy. As part of the agreement, he'll receive an enhanced salary to reflect his role as CEO. Besides, I told you, it's already been agreed.' He sat back and folded his arms.

'And this agreement,' Carter said, 'was it in writing?'

By the time Ellish replied, his actual words were redundant. The way his face had clouded over was answer enough.

'Well, no,' he said. 'It was a gentleman's agreement, but...'

Carter didn't let him finish. 'And when is this gentlemen's agreement due to take effect?'

'At the end of our current financial year.'

'Which is when?'

'The thirty-first of January.'

Carter tried to work out the implications and if they had any relevance to the case. He failed.

'Moving on,' he said, 'tell me about yourself. Where do you live. Do you have a partner?'

Ellish sat up a little. He tugged nervously at the seam of his cardigan. 'I live with my parents in Barlow Moor. And I don't have a partner. And before you start jumping to conclusions, I'm a *voluntary* incel.'

Carter looked up from his notes. 'Come again?'

'The fact that I am currently single is a life choice,' Ellish told him. 'If I did want female companionship, I can assure you there would be no shortage of offers.'

The End Game

Carter hadn't begun to speculate about the reason that Ellish was single, let alone his likely gender preference for a partner. It all seemed unnecessarily defensive.

'I don't doubt it, Mr Ellish,' he said. 'You said *currently*. I take from that there have previous relationships?'

'I don't see the relevance of that,' Ellish snapped.

'It's just routine,' Carter replied. 'Often the relevance or otherwise of information we request only becomes clear later on. So, humour me, Mr Ellish. Answer the question, please?'

Ellish reached forward and poured some water into one of the glasses. He drank slowly, and then put the glass down. His tone was matter of fact.

'There've been a few since I left university, but none of them serious. And none within the past year or so.'

Carter waited until he had eye contact. 'None in the last year or so,' he repeated. ' Could you be a little more precise, Mr Ellish?'

Louie had to think about it. 'Well, it was shortly before Christmas the year before last. So, eighteen months?'

'And you parted amicably?'

'Yes.'

'And what about Mr Gorlay?'

At first it seemed that Ellish had misheard. Then he replayed it in his head and appeared to be astonished.

'Jake? What about him? What are you implying?'

'I'm not implying anything,' Carter said. 'I was just wondering what you know about the current state of Mr Gorlay's relationships . . . marital . . . or otherwise?'

Ellish rubbed his left eye, then stroked his chin. 'I've no idea what you're talking about,' he said. 'Why would I?'

Carter smiled. That was two physical tells, and one verbal when he asked that question. He was lying.

'So you wouldn't know about Mr Gorlay's current mistress then?'

'No, I wouldn't! Mainly because I can't believe that he would ever cheat on Becky.'

Now he was rubbing his neck, just above the collarbone.

'Really?' Carter said. 'I'm surprised. I'd have thought you'd have been the first person in whom Jake would confide something like that. You know, man to man?'

The End Game

'No, because I'm sure there was nothing to confide.' He said this with an exaggerated frown, while avoiding eye contact and feverishly massaging the back of his neck.

Carter was sorry this wasn't being videoed. Louie Ellish was a living encyclopaedia of tells. It would have gone down a bomb at the training centre at Sedgley Park. Of course, Carter had a few tricks of his own. He faked surprise and slowly shook his head.

'I must be mistaken then,' he said. 'I'm sorry to have troubled you, Mr Ellish. Especially after you've been so helpful.'

He stood up. Ellish scrambled to his feet.

'Is that it then?' he asked.

'For now,' Carter replied, 'except that I'll check the names and details of those *few* women with whom you say you have had relationships since you left university.'

Ellish's face blanched. He began to stutter. 'B... b... but it's so long since I've seen most of them. I... I... I don't know where they are now, what they're doing e... e... exactly.'

Carter had the feeling that this was about embarrassment rather than anything more sinister. He felt genuinely sorry for the guy.

'That's alright, Louie,' he said, 'just do your best and leave the rest to us. And don't worry, we'll handle it sensitively. Oh, and before you go, can you tell me where you were earlier this morning, between the hours of midnight and 4 a.m.?'

'At home,' Ellish told him. 'In bed. All night. Mother brought a cup of tea at 7 a.m.'

'Thank you,' Carter said.

Ellish stood up. 'Would you like me to ask Jake to come and join you?' he said.

'That's very kind of you,' Carter responded, 'but I think I'll ask him myself.' He smiled. 'I could do with stretching my legs.'

Chapter 13

Jake Gorlay's body language had been defensive from the moment Carter told him he was ready to see him.

Carter guessed that the worried expression on Louie Ellish's face as the two of them passed each other had unsettled Gorlay. He knew something was wrong, but he had no idea what it was. Which was precisely what Carter wanted. He waited for Gorlay to settle into a slouch in his chair and began.

'Now you've had time to think, Mr Gorlay,' he said, 'I wondered if you'd had any more ideas about who might be behind this attack on your company?'

'Such time as I had,' Gorlay replied, 'has been taken up by one of your minions asking me a load of questions that didn't seem to have any bearing on your catching the bastard. So, no, I haven't.'

Carter rested his tablet on his knees and stared hard at Gorlay. 'Firstly,' he said, 'I don't have any minions, I only have colleagues. Secondly, if the questions to which you refer were to do with where you live, who you live with, the security arrangements at your properties, what vehicles you use, your working and social habits, and so on, then they were all designed to assist our investigation and try to keep you safe. I would have thought that after what happened here earlier this morning, you'd have been okay with that?'

Gorlay looked uncomfortable. He shifted in his seat. 'I suppose,' he growled.

'Good,' Carter said. 'And I think you'll be pleased that the questions I have for you are all designed to help us catch the perpetrator, or perpetrators, as quickly as possible. So, just to clarify, apart from this business seeking to acquire your company . . .' He consulted his notes.

'CDC. Castlefield Digital Creations,' Gorlay supplied.

'Thank you,' Carter said. 'So, other than CDC, you can't think of anyone who might attempt to extort money from your business?'

'No.'

'All of the communications you've received – the letter and the text messages – were addressed to you, Mr Gorlay. Have you considered that it might be a personal attack on you, rather than on the business?'

Gorlay pushed himself upright. His hands gripped the arms of the chair. 'Absolutely not!' he said. 'I'm the CEO of this company. Of course, they're addressed to me.'

'It doesn't necessarily follow,' Carter said, 'but I take your point. However, you must have considered the possibility that this might be someone out to get back at you?'

'Back at me? What the hell for?'

Carter shrugged. 'I've no idea, but I had to ask – it's just procedure.' He paused. 'So, not personal?'

'No!'

'There's no one you might have upset?'

Gorlay looked askance. 'Upset? Some bastard has just set fire to my business and is trying to blackmail us by threatening worse. Because I've upset them? Are you serious?'

'Mr Gorlay,' Carter said, 'you would be surprised what lengths some people will go to because they feel they've been slighted. It would be in your interest if you let us know of anyone who's unhappy with you because of something you've done recently, or in the past.'

Gorlay sat back in his chair. 'Well, there isn't.'

'In that case,' Carter said, 'let's move on.'

'Let's,' Gorlay muttered.

'The details you shared with my colleague about the properties you own,' Carter said. 'Did they include the apartment in the Northern Quarter?'

Gorlay reddened. 'No.'

'And why was that?'

The End Game

'Because she asked me where I live, not what else I owned.'

Carter made a mental note to check. 'In that case,' he said, 'when we've finished here, you'd better give me the details of the apartment, including your security arrangements there, so we have the full picture.'

He made a quick note so he wouldn't forget, and pressed on.

'How often do you stay at the apartment, Mr Gorlay?' he asked.

Jake Gorlay shrugged. 'Hard to say. Once or twice a week, maybe. It depends.'

'On what?'

'On whether I've got a late finish or an early start. Or if me and Becky are out on the two that night.'

'And then you both stay over?'

Gorlay's eyes narrowed. 'Obviously.'

Carter nodded his understanding 'Does anyone else ever *stay over* with you?' he said.

Gorlay's eyes widened a fraction. Enough to tell Carter that this line of questioning was something he had feared.

'Like who?' Gorlay said.

The classic defensive ploy. Buy time with a question of your own while you work out how the hell you can get out of this.

'Like another woman, for example?'

Gorlay's eyes flared, his fists clenched. Carter could tell he was really angry. At being exposed, or because one of his colleagues had ratted on him, most likely both. He raised a hand.

'Please, Mr Gorlay,' Carter said, 'let's be clear – I'm not here to judge the way you conduct your private life, but we do need to know about everyone who's part of it. And I mean, everyone. There is no reason why any of it should become public knowledge unless it turns out to have a direct bearing on our investigation. But if you're not straight with me, we'll have to start asking around. So, let me put my question another way. Are there any women other than Becky with whom you have, or have had, a relationship?'

As Gorlay sat processing the implications of everything

the detective had said, the anger leached from his body like a balloon deflating. He reached forward and poured himself a glass of water.

Carter sat back and gave him all the time he needed.

Gorlay put the glass on the table. 'Okay,' he said, 'I've always brought girlfriends back to the apartment, of course I have. All completely innocent and above board, short-term, no complications, till this last one.'

He paused while he worked out how best to spin the narrative, nodded to himself, and then continued.

'Two years into my relationship with my partner, Becky, we went through a rocky patch. About the same time one of the accountants at the firm we use started coming to my gym in town.' He grinned. 'Mylene Terry, good-looking girl, bright, keeps herself fit – I'd always fancied her. There she is on the joggers and the bikes, on the mat beside me. She started flirting.' He shrugged, as if to say what is man supposed to do? 'We met for coffee after one of the sessions. It went from there.'

'When was this exactly?' Carter asked.

'Becky and me have been together just over five years, so it would've been around Easter 2019.'

'Carry on,' Carter said.

'Ironically,' Gorlay said, 'not long after that, Becky and I patched things up. I'd been working all hours to launch a new game, and she'd been peckin' my head like mad. But now the work had eased up, and I was with Mylene a couple of nights a week, I was a lot more relaxed, and to be honest, bending over backwards to keep Becky happy. It was working for both of us. Mind you, Covid nearly put a spanner in the works. But in June, when the lockdown restrictions eased, me and Mylene were able to meet up every now and again in the afternoons at the apartment.' He grinned. 'After being cooped up working from home for over three months, Becky was glad to see the back of me.'

'And what is the situation currently?' Carter asked.

'Well, me and Becky are solid, and Mylene is history. We're no longer an item.'

Carter looked up. 'Since when?'

'A month ago.'

The End Game

'And why is that?'

Gorlay grimaced. The wounded party. 'Because she wanted more. She was planning to leave her husband, and she wanted me to leave Becky. Better still, throw Becky out so she could move in with me. She'd gradually been getting more and more intense. Texting and calling to see where I was. When I realised what was happening, I tried to cool it. But then she started ringing the office. She even called in a couple of times on the pretext of checking something to do with the accounts. I could see where it was heading, so I broke it off.'

'How did she react?'

Gorlay took another sip of water, sat back and crossed his arms. 'Not good. She all but trashed the apartment. It cost me four grand to replace the stuff she broke, but it was worth it to get rid.' He shook his head. 'What makes a woman turn from a lovely, thoughtful, romantic being into a raging beast?'

It wasn't rocket science, Carter reflected, but it was clearly beyond a narcissist like Gorlay. 'Has she been in touch since you split up?' he asked.

'No.'

'She hasn't contacted your partner, Ms . . .?'

'Kerson. Becky Kerson. No, she hasn't, thank God.' Gorlay uncrossed his arms and leaned forward. 'But if you think she's behind this business, the arson and the blackmail, you're wrong.'

'What makes you so sure?' Carter responded. 'After all, if she has access to the accounts, and some basic understanding of your business, surely she'd be capable of cobbling together that letter and those texts?'

That gave Gorlay pause for thought. 'But not the arson,' he said. 'It's not like it was a petrol bomb. She wouldn't have the know-how?'

'How do you know it wasn't a petrol bomb?' Carter asked.

'I overheard a couple of the firemen talking. Saying something about an explosive device. Besides, even I could see there wasn't any glass.'

'Right,' said Carter. 'Well, I'll need contact details for

The End Game

Mrs Terry.'

Gorlay sat forward. 'You will tread carefully, won't you?' he said. 'Her husband doesn't know anything about us. If he was to find out now, it would finish their marriage and likely set Mylene off again. Not to mention the damage he might do . . .' He paused. '. . . He's one of your lot.'

Carter looked up. 'Our lot? You saying he's a police officer?'

'That's what she says, not that I've ever met him.'

Carter checked his notes. 'One last question,' he said. 'Where were you between midnight and 4 a.m. this morning?'

'At home with Becks,' Gorlay said. 'I told you, we're mint.'

Chapter 14

Nexus House, 1.30 p.m.

'Thank you, DI Carter,' Caton said. 'Does anyone have any questions?'

The major incident room was packed for the syndicate briefing, with some people seated at their desks, others perched on them. It was lunchtime, and over a third were eating sandwiches or snacks. Detective Constable Powell was the first to raise a hand.

'From what you've said, DI Carter, do we take it you're ruling out an inside job?'

'We don't rule anything out,' Carter responded. 'You know that. Not until everything they told me has been checked. But if you're asking if I think any of the directors has anything to gain by attacking their own business, then I have to say I doubt it. Gorlay's ex-mistress and his partner, however, is another matter.'

'I know we've not got the forensics back,' DC Nair said, the young detective who had transferred from the Met eighteen months ago, 'but given what we do know about the cause of the fire, is it likely either of them would have known how to put that together?'

'Point taken,' Carter responded, 'but they may know someone who does.'

'What about the husband of Gorlay's ex?' DC Franklin asked. 'The one he said was in the police. What do we know about him?'

Amit Patel, a civilian analyst on Duggie Wallace's team, stood up. 'I can answer that,' he said. 'Derek Terry was in the same office as me at Central Park. He's not a police

The End Game

officer, he's an IT performance data manager. When I left, he was working on the backlog of GMP unrecorded crimes.'

'That'll keep him busy,' someone quipped.

'What's he like?' Carter asked when the laughter had died down.

'I didn't really know him well,' Patel replied. 'I got the impression he has a chip on his shoulder and a bit of a short fuse. I do remember someone telling me he was in the Army Reserve – what used to be the Territorials. In the office, they called him "Saturday Night Soldier Boy".'

'He'd have the know-how then,' Carter observed. 'Thank you, Amit. Anyone else? No? All yours then, Boss.' He sat down.

'Right,' Caton said, 'that's everything we have so far. Scene of crime analysis by the fire investigation team, and that of our own SOCOs, suggests that the device was carefully placed to produce minimal but precise damage. Enough to disable two of the servers, but allow the rest to carry on running. That, together with the anonymous 999 call in advance of the explosion, supports the theory that the perpetrator, or perpetrators, wanted to send a message rather than destroy the business. The question is, why? Anyone?'

The suggestions came thick and fast. Almost as quickly, they appeared on the whiteboard.

To ensure the company is recoverable if bought out?

To make sure they can still generate the income so they can meet the ransom demand.

To prove intent?

To avoid accidentally killing someone?

Competitor trying to force them to sell, without destroying the business?

'It all seems a bit drastic?' ventured Detective Sergeant Jimmy Hulme.

'Their revenue is five million pounds a year and growing,' Carter responded. 'It's not exactly chicken feed.'

'Always thought I was in the wrong job!' Franklin joked.

'You're not wrong there,' someone told him.

'If Castlefield Digital Creations have offered MancVG fifteen million,' Caton said, pulling them back on track,

The End Game

'they must want it badly, and they may not be the only ones.'

'But extortion, Boss,' Nair said, 'not just with menaces but with real consequences? I'm inclined to agree with DS Hulme. It doesn't sound like the kind of risk a creative company would take.'

'In my experience ...' DC Franklin began.

'That's an oxymoron, for a start,' someone at the back observed.

'...the thing about creative types is that they don't have a firm grasp on reality,' Franklin continued unabashed.

'Something you have in common then,' the same person muttered.

Several newer members of the team snorted.

'Enough of the banter!' Caton told them. 'Those of you who are new to the team need to know that while I appreciate occasional genuine humour, I will not tolerate anything that crosses the line and threatens the harmony of this syndicate. You have been warned.'

He waited for the message to sink in before continuing.

'I know some of you regard anything less than a murder investigation as a waste of time, but I shouldn't need to remind you that this has been declared a local critical incident. And we have no way of knowing how it might escalate.'

He turned to his senior intelligence analyst.

'Duggie, I want all the intel you can get on CDC and their directors and give their details to DS Whittle and DC Powell. Carly, Henry, I'd like you two to then arrange interviews with those directors.'

He looked at the whiteboard.

'Now, before we move on, does anyone have any suggestions as to other potential business-based motives?'

He was met with a deafening silence. Then DC Nair tentatively raised a hand. Caton was glad to see that he'd recovered from the nasty bout of Covid he'd caught from his grandfather, who had sadly died.

'Go on, Josh,' he said.

'What about industrial terrorism, Boss?'

'It's hardly an attack on the nation's economy or infrastructure,' Carter said.

The End Game

'True,' Caton conceded, 'but Josh is right. I doubt it's the case, but we can't rule it out. What the messages strongly suggest, however, is that this is less about business motives than a political or personal campaign against video game in-app purchases and gambling.'

DS Powell's hand went up. 'Unless it's a personal vendetta against the company or one of the directors?'

Carter turned to look at him. 'Then why link their demands to a charity? Why not keep the money for themselves?'

'To avoid suspicion falling on them,' Powell replied. 'If it's all about revenge, then where the money ends up is not going to be important.'

'Fair point,' Carter acknowledged.

'Right, I think we've covered all the options,' he continued. 'Let's move on to tasks. Calls to MancVG are already being monitored to track the source. Although if they keep using burner phones, that'll only give us brief geolocations. Unless we can find the phone or the store where it and/or the SIM card was bought, there's no chance of tracking it. The likelihood is our unsub bought a bunch of phones from dodgy brick and mortar stores without CCTV, and he's going to use a different one for each message, and ditch said phone and SIM card straight afterwards. But I'll request our Computer Branch to look for similar activity on the Dark Web and see if they can hack into this BlackOp and identify the purchasers.'

'That'll be like hunting for a needle in a haystack, Boss,' Duggie Wallace said. 'Especially after that joint Aussie, FBI, ANOM-app sting.'

'I get that,' Caton said, 'but we have to try. And I'd like you and Amit to search for any mentions in social media related to video game in-app purchases or gambling.'

He turned to DI Carter.

'Given that Mr Wallace's team will be busy with all of that, I'd like you to task members of the team to gather as much information as possible about all of the remaining names on that board.'

The door opened. Benson, the crime scene manager, entered.

'Great timing, Jack,' Caton said. 'Please tell me you have the initial forensic results.'

'Yes, Boss.'

'Then the floor is yours.'

Chapter 15

'Preliminary findings are that the fire was caused by an explosive device,' the SOCO began. 'Further analysis is being carried out at the military Explosive Ordnance Disposal unit labs, and they've already confirmed that the device came within the definition of an explosive substance in the Explosive Substances Act 1883. To be precise, it was an RCIED.'

'Remote controlled improvised explosive device,' Henry Powell explained.

'Thank you, DC Powell,' Carter said. 'We're all aware of your previous career in the military. But let's hear what Mr Benson has to say.'

Henry Powell didn't look the slightest bit abashed. One thing he'd grown after seven years in the Queen's Dragoon Guards, and six years in the police force, was a thick skin.

'Sorry, Boss,' he said.

'That's okay,' Caton told him. 'Carry on, Jack.'

'DC Powell is quite correct,' Benson said. 'For the uninitiated, these devices are improvised explosive devices armed by radio control and detonated using either passive infrared switches, or wirelessly using a phone, personal radio, Wifi, or even Bluetooth. They're made up of four main components: a switch, a power source, an initiator – also known as a detonator when used to set off high explosives – and a container.'

He consulted his notes.

'In this instance, there were two rocker switches connected to a circuit board, and the power source consisted of eight C-cell batteries and one PP3 nine-volt battery

The End Game

connected to a mobile phone. The detonator consisted of mercury fulminate and a small flashbulb. All of this sat in the first half of a square container, three sides of which were made of fibreglass resin. This half had been filled with expanding foam to keep the components in place and stable. In the second half was a thin plastic bottle containing paint thinner, surrounded by dozens of six-millimetre diameter carbon steel ball bearings. The end wall adjacent to the plastic bottle consisted of what they believe to have been a thin perforated sheet of acetate.'

He looked up from his notes.

'The container was hooked onto the ventilation grille. The EOD guys' narrative is that when the phone signal triggered the detonator, the explosion ignited the paint thinner and propelled it, together with the ball bearings, through the apertures of the ventilation grille. The ball bearings penetrated the outer casing of the servers creating access for the flaming paint thinner.'

'Ingenious,' someone said.

'But improvised,' Benson reminded them, 'in the sense that it was not an off-the-shelf military-style device.'

'Home-made then?' DS Carly Whittle asked.

'Yes, and in that sense, amateur,' the SOCO replied. 'But it was clearly made by someone who knew exactly what they were doing.'

'Have the unit seen anything like this before?' Carter wondered.

'Not exactly the same, but close,' Benson said. 'All of the components have been found in RCIEDs at home and abroad. Used by domestic terrorists and hostile actors all over the globe. However, there were two things that they found particularly interesting. Firstly, the use of mercury fulminate, not because it's unique, but because there are many more readily available and less tricky alternatives out there, such as nitrate-based fertilisers, stump remover and blocked drain remover, and because it would not usually be employed as a squib in what is essentially an incendiary device. The second thing is the use of ball bearings as precursor projectiles, rather than as a weapon to kill or maim. This suggests quite a sophisticated perpetrator.

Someone who is confident, and possibly experienced, in assembling custom-made IEDs.'

'Not an amateur then?' DS Hulme reasoned.

'Not necessarily. Apparently, you only have to enter "IEDs" in your search engine and you'll find all manner of official descriptions of how they're constructed. And you don't even need a background in chemistry and electricity to follow the instructions on the Dark Web.'

'What about the components?' Carter asked. 'Would we be able to find out where they came from?'

Benson shook his head. 'All items are readily available online or from shops all over the country. Our best hope will be that they manage to identify manufacturers' serial numbers on what's left of the electrical components, otherwise it'll be like hunting for a needle in a haystack.'

'How about the mercury fulminate? Is that a controlled substance?' Carly Whittle wondered.

Amit Patel raised a hand. 'You can make your own,' he said. 'All you need is mercury, ethanol and nitric acid. Plus, big cohones. It's incredibly sensitive to heat, shock and friction. '

'And you know this because . . .?' said Carter.

The analyst looked embarrassed at having become the centre of attention. 'I took science A-Levels,' he said.

'So how do we know you didn't make this device?' DC Franklin joked.

'Because he doesn't have cohones!' said another.

Caton walked between the carousels until he towered over DC Mark Gadd seated at his desk.

'The fact that you've only been with us a fortnight, detective constable,' he said, 'has no bearing on your inability to comprehend what "crossing the line" means. One more remark like that, and you're back to Division faster than you can say sorry. Understand?'

'Sorry, Boss . . . I mean . . . yes, Boss,' Gadd replied.

'And you, DC Franklin,' Caton said, 'should know better than to encourage other smart alecs.'

'Sorry, Boss,' Franklin intoned. 'Won't happen again.'

'It had better not,' Caton said.

He moved back towards the front of the room.

'Mr Wallace, how difficult would it be to track down sales of mercury, nitric acid and ethanol, do you think?'

'Extremely time-consuming and potentially fruitless, Boss, until we have named suspects. I'm thinking internet sales across a raft of different sites, agricultural suppliers, chemical suppliers to schools and colleges, swimming pool supplies, the Dark Web . . .'

'Horticultural products,' Amit Patel added, 'even antique and bric-a-brac shops who might have sold the odd mercury-based barometer.'

'There is one complication,' Doug Benson said.

Caton clocked the hesitation in his voice. 'Go on.'

'The nature of the device has attracted attention from our colleagues in Counter Terrorism Policing North West. I've been told to expect a visit.'

There were groans around the room. Caton knew well the disruption and frustration such involvement was likely to entail, and the underlying tribalism of close-knit units across the force.

'Until an act of terrorism has been discounted,' he said. I expect everyone to cooperate fully with our colleagues. Is that understood?'

He waited for the chorus to die down.

'For now,' he said, 'let's just concentrate on the actions we've already agreed. DI Carter will task you. All reports through DI Hulme, please.'

He looked at the faces in front of him. Most of them eager, a few still underwhelmed. It was a shame that it took a corpse to motivate some people.

'Do we have an operational name yet, DI Hulme?'

'Yes, Boss. *Sentinel*,' Jimmy Hulme replied.

'Right,' Caton said, 'Operation Sentinel it is. Let's go!'

Chapter 16

Castlefield, 3 p.m.

'Are you sure it's okay to park here?' Carly Whittle said.

They had just arrived at Castle Street next to Dukes 92, overlooking the Castlefield Basin. Henry Powell unclipped his belt and reached behind his seat to grab the bag containing his tablet.

'It's fine. People do it all the time. If the wardens booked everyone, the restaurants wouldn't have any customers.'

Carly wasn't convinced but, since the pool car was out in Henry's name, he'd be the one that ended up paying the fine. She retrieved her bag from the footwell and exited the car.

A young woman was standing on the balcony of one of the apartments opposite sipping from a mug. Behind some of the full-length windows Carly glimpsed people seated at desks, presumably working from home. A gust of wind swept through the Basin causing the narrowboats on the Bridgewater Canal to rock and creak as they strained at their moorings. Carly wondered what it would be like to live on one of these boats. Probably a damn sight cheaper than the rent on her apartment in the Northern Quarter.

'Are you coming?'

Head down, arms pumping, Powell was already twenty metres away. Carly set off after him. She found him around the corner of the building, standing with his back to the entrance to Albert's Shed.

'This is more like it,' he said, nodding in the direction of the old Merchant's Warehouse on the opposite side of the

The End Game

cobbled roadway. The two-hundred-year-old three-storey redbrick building had retained all of its original features. A sandstone parapet ran along the edge of the roof. Iron-barred, half-arched windows rested on sandstone lintels. The two upper storeys sported drawbridge loading bays. The use of floor-to-ceiling toughened glass on the stairwells was the only nod to modernity.

'In what sense?' Carly asked.

'As in, more befitting a modern IT company.'

'I wouldn't have thought there was much to choose between the two,' she said. 'Incidentally, what's with the power walking? Have you gone all weight conscious on me?'

He pretended to be hurt. 'Are you implying there's something wrong with my weight?'

'No, just wondering if there's a logical explanation, or if you've flipped?'

'If you must know,' he said, 'I missed my early morning training session for the Manchester Marathon.'

'Good for you,' she said. 'You can put me down for 10p a mile.'

'Gee, thanks, Sarge,' he said. 'Are you sure you can afford two pounds sixty?'

She laughed and walked off towards the Merchant's Warehouse. 'That's assuming you make it to the end,' she said.

He powered past her and stopped at the entrance, his hand hovering over the call button on the intercom. 'How do you intend to play this?' he asked.

Carly was secretly pleased at his deference to her rank. It wasn't always the case with male colleagues, and it hadn't been with Henry at first. But he'd been a quick learner. Theirs was now a comfortable and, in her eyes, successful partnership.

'With a straight bat,' she told him. 'They're in the same business. They're taking a keen interest in acquiring MancVG. Even if they're not involved, odds are they'll already have heard about it on the grapevine.'

'Makes sense,' he agreed. 'Should we see them one at a time or altogether?'

The End Game

'That might depend on them, but my preference would be all together to start with. Less chance of them tipping the wink to each other, and it won't feel as formal, like they're under suspicion. This way we might catch them off guard, and we can observe how each of them responds to the same questions, and to each other for that matter.'

'You're the boss,' he said, pressing the buzzer.

'Don't you forget it,' she said.

The curl at the corner of her lips betrayed the solemnity with which she'd said it.

***

Five minutes later, they were shown into a small meeting room and told that the directors would be with them shortly. When the door had closed behind the receptionist, Henry pulled a chair aside, crouched down, and peered under the table.

'What are you doing?' Carly said.

'Checking for bugs,' he whispered. 'It's an IT firm. Can't be too careful.'

As he withdrew, he banged his head against the underside of the table. 'Ouch!' he said, vigorously rubbing the offending spot.

'Serves you right,' she told him. 'If you're going to check the lights next, I hope to God there's a defibrillator handy.'

He grimaced. 'Don't be silly.'

She pulled a chair out and sat down. 'It's not me playing big boys' games.'

She waited for him to settle himself, then asked, 'What do we know about them?'

'Not a lot, just what's on Companies House. All three are shown as directors. Draper Junior and White each hold forty per cent of the shares, Draper Senior twenty per cent. They have fixed assets of just over a quarter of a million pounds. Net current assets – intangible assets, cash and debtors, less creditors – get this, comes to eighty-seven million! Harry Draper, Matt's father, is a self-made

The End Game

businessman with a chain of cash and carry stores across the region. His accounts look less transparent to my unskilled eye, but he's worth at least ten million in his own right, not including his dividends from Castlefield Digital Creations.'

'Doesn't sound as though they need to go around trying to extort money from a competitor?' Carly mused. 'Least of all by bombing their premises. What do the newspapers have to say about them?'

'There are articles going back to when they set up the company. Draper, Junior and White were proclaimed part of the new wave of ex-Manchester University IT entrepreneurs. There've been reports every couple of years charting a meteoric rise to riches. A couple of awards ceremonies. Donations to local charities with a whiff of PR about them. That's about it,' he paused, 'except . . .'

'Get on with it, Henry,' she said. 'They could be here any minute.'

'Matt Draper's father, Harry Draper, has a previous for affray.'

'Affray?'

'There was a mass punch-up in a pub in Burnage. He was one of three arrested. He pleaded self-defence and was still found guilty. Given six months in prison, suspended for two years, and a fifteen-thousand-pound fine towards costs and damages.'

'When was this?'

'Two thousand and two.'

'Twenty years ago. Nothing since?'

'Nope.'

'What about social media?'

'Nothing you wouldn't expect. Their company presence is straight marketing. The female, Charlotte White, has the more sophisticated public presence. Most of her references are to the company, or charity work. The only personal stuff suggests she's addicted to novel diets, and ten thousand steps a day.'

'Sounds like you've found a soulmate.'

He ignored her and pressed on.

'Matt Draper, on the other hand, comes across as a bit

of a jack-the-lad. Lots of photos with adoring ladies, or flash gits in clubs and hip bars in the city, or beside a two-hundred-thousand-pound sports car.'

'Flash gits?' she said. 'I don't think I know that one. Is it part of the new gender self-identification lexicon?'

'Harry Draper,' Henry continued smoothly, 'like many of his generation, doesn't have a social media presence of his own. He appears occasionally on his son's social pages holding a bottle of beer at a celebration or a barbecue. Other than that, it's just the odd mention in the *Manchester Evening News* related to his cash and carry business.'

The door opened.

'Here we go,' Carly said.

Chapter 17

A man and a woman, both in their late twenties to early thirties, entered the room. The woman closed the door behind them.

Of African or African Caribbean heritage, she was tall and athletic, with broad shoulders. Her pair of striking turquoise-rimmed designer glasses had large asymmetric lenses that graduated from dark at the top to clear at the bottom. Over a plain white T-shirt, she wore a tailored black trouser suit nipped in at the waist, the cuffs and collars turned back to reveal a multicoloured print. She moved confidently across the room on five-inch-high heels and sat down opposite Carly Whittle.

The man looked as though he'd spent a night on the tiles. His fair shoulder-length hair was unkempt, his two-day-old beard more stubble than designer. He wore a plain white hoodie that drowned his thin frame except where it bulged at the waist. His faded blue jeans and scuffed white trainers didn't do a lot to help the overall impression. He hesitated a moment before seating himself at the head of the table. His eyes flicked between the two detectives. He appeared uncertain about how to proceed. His colleague decided for him.

'My name is Charlotte White, and this is Matt Draper,' she said, then paused. 'And you are?'

'Detective Sergeant Carly Whittle.'

'Detective Constable Henry Powell.'

White placed a smartphone on the table and clasped her hands in front of her.

'And why exactly did you ask to see us?'

The End Game

Carly employed her stock-in-trade disarming smile.

'We're hoping you might assist us with an ongoing investigation in connection with another Manchester-based video game company.'

'And which company would that be?' White responded. Deadpan. No trace of irony.

'MancVG.'

White's eyebrows rose a notch. 'Really?'

Carly was unable to detect even a hint of surprise behind those shaded lenses. Draper, on the other hand, looked distinctly unsettled. He had placed one hand over the other and was pressing them into the table in an attempt to disguise the tremor that had overtaken them.

'Are you alright, Mr Draper?' Carly asked.

'Fine,' he said. 'Had one of those nights. I'll get over it.'

'Assist you how exactly?' White said.

'We have a few questions regarding your relationship with MancVG,' Carly told her.

'Relationship? I wasn't aware that we had one. Were you, Jack?'

Draper's laugh was forced and unconvincing. 'No way,' he said. 'Have you met them?' He laughed again. The tremor crept up his right arm.

'Really?' Carly pretended to look at her notes. 'We've been led to believe that you're seeking to buy MancVG. Isn't that right, DC Powell?'

Henry pretended to check his own notes. 'That's right,' he said. 'For fifteen point three million pounds?'

'That's privileged information!' Draper protested. 'How the hell did you get hold of that?'

Charlotte White held up a commanding hand towards him.

'It's fine, Matt,' she said. 'The officers have a job to do. The sooner they get it done, the sooner we can return to ours.' She turned to Carly Whittle. 'Offering to buy out a competitor does not constitute a relationship.'

'A business relationship, surely?'

'I don't think so. We don't do any business with each other, nor have we ever. It's simply an offer to buy their company, not to go to bed with them.' She ignored her

The End Game

colleague's snigger and continued. 'Perhaps it would help if you could explain what this has to do with your investigation?'

'I assumed you would have heard,' Carly said.

'Heard?'

'Earlier this morning there was a fire at the premises of MancVG. Arson is suspected.'

White raised her hand to forestall the protest on the tip of Draper's tongue.

'And you suspect we may have had something to do with that?' she said.

Unemotional. No sense of incredulity.

'We have no evidence to suggest that you were involved,' Carly told her, 'but we do have a responsibility to explore any links with MancVG and eliminate as many of them as quickly as possible. I'm sure you can understand that?'

'Do we need a solicitor present?' Matt Draper said.

'I don't know, do you?' Carly responded.

'Since we're not involved, we have no need of legal representation,' Charlotte White said. 'Whatever you need to know in order to eliminate us, as you put it, just ask.' She leaned forward a little. 'But before you do, perhaps you could explain how setting fire to a business we wish to acquire would in any way make sense?'

'Depending on the amount of damage,' Henry Powell said, 'it could potentially lower the value of the company and make it cheaper to purchase. It could also frighten the owners into selling. We see it quite a lot.'

Charlotte White gave him an appraising look, as though just discovering his presence and being pleasantly surprised.

'I hadn't thought of that,' she said. She turned back to Carly Whittle. 'Please,' she said, 'ask away.'

'Mr Draper,' Carly began, 'where were you last night? Between midnight and four o'clock this morning?'

'That's easy,' he said. 'I was at . . . er . . . last night you said? What, that's Sunday night?'

Charlotte White drummed her fingertips on the table. The first emotion she had shown since entering the room.

The End Game

'Yes, Matt,' she said, 'last night – that was Sunday night through to this morning, between the hours of midnight and 4 a.m.'

He nodded and smiled in a way that made Carly wonder if he was still intoxicated rather than hungover.

'That would be unlikely,' he stated.

'Unlikely?'

'I'm guessing it's that nightclub, Unlikely,' Henry told her, 'in The Printworks.'

'That's right,' Draper responded. 'Me and some mates. We had a great time, as ever.'

'What time did you leave, Mr Draper?' Carly asked.

'When they chucked out.'

'Which would be?'

He shrugged. 'Twoish?'

'And then what did you do?'

'Went home.' He grinned. 'Work in the morning.'

'How did you get home?'

'Walked. Tried flagging down a taxi but they wouldn't take us.'

'Us?'

'Me and Dickie Bee. We live in the same apartments.'

'Where exactly?'

'Castlegate Apartments. City Road. Got a lovely big balcony overlooking the Basin.'

'I can see why you'd want to acquire MancVG,' Henry Powell said. 'Just a two-minute stroll to work.'

Carly gave him one of her looks.

'Do you have a partner who can confirm when you arrived home, Mr Draper?' she said.

'No, I'm between partners. The last one left me during lockdown. Bitch! Can you believe it?'

Carly could.

'I'll need this Dickie Bee's details,' she said, 'so he can corroborate your story.'

Draper sniffed, then wiped his nose on the sleeve of his hoodie. 'It's not a story,' he muttered.

'Ms White,' Carly began.

'Charlotte, please – I find "Ms" rather ambiguous, don't you... Carly?'

The End Game

Carly gritted her teeth and took a moment. 'And where were *you* between midnight and 4 a.m. this morning . . . Charlotte?'

'Tucked up in bed with my husband, Winston. And before you ask, there's no one else who can corroborate that.' She smiled. 'We don't do threesomes, Carly, in case you were wondering?'

Henry Powell clocked the expression on his DS's face, and jumped in.

'What does your husband do for a living?' he asked.

'Is the answer likely to be germane to your investigation?' she said.

Henry smiled. 'We won't know until we've heard it, Charlotte.'

'Ouch!' she said. 'Or is that touché?'

'Definitely touché,' he said, with a smile.

She smiled back. 'Winston is a partner in a law firm on St John's Street. Next time you come calling, I'm sure he would be happy to join us.'

The door opened and a man in a hurry burst in.

'What the hell's going on!' he demanded.

Chapter 18

'We've been helping these police officers with an investigation,' Charlotte White told him. 'Apparently MancVG have had a spot of bother.'

'Nothing to worry about, Dad,' Matt Draper said.

His father pulled out the seat next to his son and plonked himself down. 'I'll be the judge of that.'

Harry Draper was pushing sixty and built like a former rugby league player who had let himself go. He sported a beer gut and his shoulder-length hair was dyed a curious shade of brown. His teeth were whitened to the point where they might as well have been artificial. He turned to Charlotte White.

'Why isn't Winston here?'

'Because this has nothing to do with us. We have nothing to hide.'

'I've told you before,' he growled, 'where the police are concerned, you can't be too careful, even if you're innocent.'

'Is that based on personal experience, Mr Draper?' Carly said. She instantly regretted it, but it was too late to take it back. He fixed her with a malevolent stare.

'Yes, darlin', as it 'appens. So, what kind of bother are we talkin' about?'

'Someone started a fire at their place in Ancoats,' his son told him.

Harry Draper laughed. 'There you go then,' he said, lounging back in his chair. 'That'll be them after the insurance.'

'Is that based on personal experience too?' Henry Powell asked.

The End Game

Carly shot him a look, but she needn't have bothered. Harry Draper wasn't the least bit fazed. He clapped his hands slowly.

'Nice one,' he said. 'But if that's the best you can come up with, you may as well both do one.'

'We're not going anywhere, Mr Draper,' Carly told him. 'Not until we've established your whereabouts between midnight and 4 a.m. this morning.'

Draper smirked. 'Give yer 'ead a wobble,' he said, folding his arms across his chest. 'I don't need to tell you diddly squat.'

'That's true,' Carly acknowledged, 'but if you feel unable to help us, we'll have to find out for ourselves. Of course, that would mean a great deal of time and effort asking around, wouldn't it, DC Powell?'

'Yes indeed, Sarge,' Powell replied.

'And I guess it would make us wonder what Mr Draper has to hide. Who knows who we might have to involve?'

'Absolutely, Sarge,' Henry agreed. 'Trading Standards, HMRC, National Crime Agency . . .'

Draper Senior sat up and banged the table. His cheeks had reddened, and his neck strained against the collar of his shirt.

'That's bobbins, an' you know it!'

'Ooh . . . we seem to have touched a nerve, Detective Sergeant,' Carly observed.

'Just tell them, Harry,' Charlotte White said. 'We don't need the hassle and nor do you.'

In the silence that ensued, it was impossible to discern which way he was going to jump. Just when Carly thought they had lost him, he breathed out, and sat back in his chair.

'I was at home in bed with the wife.'

'Was there anyone else in the house?'

He folded his arms. 'If there was, they had no right to be.'

'I'll take that as a no.'

He smirked. 'Take it however you want, darlin'. It makes no odds to me.' He turned back to Charlotte White. 'How bad was this fire?'

'I've no idea,' she said. 'This is the first we've heard of it.'

He leaned forward, hands on the table, staring Carly in the eyes.

'What are we talking,' he said, 'slap on the wrist, or terminal?'

'Firstly, Mr Draper, please stop calling me darlin'.'

'What should I call you?'

'Sergeant, or officer.'

The son sniffed. 'Or Carly,' he said.

'And secondly,' Carly said, 'what possible difference does it make to you how bad the fire was?'

'None at all. Just curious, that's all.'

'What you may not appreciate, officer,' White said, 'is that while we would like to acquire the company, compared to us, MancVG is a minnow. And in terms of global video game production, we're minnows too. There'd be no benefit to us in removing them as a competitor. On the contrary, a weak and damaged infrastructure would make any acquisition out of the question.'

'Surely, it's the copyright to their games you're really after,' Henry Powell said, 'that and their customer base? The building is probably rented, and you could easily rent more computer servers if you needed them. And then there's the insurance.'

'Only if they're insured against arson,' Harry Draper said.

'Are you, Mr Draper?' Carly asked.

His eyes flared. 'None of your business.'

'I'm only asking,' she said, 'because who's to say that the perpetrator won't target other video game producers in Manchester?'

The three directors stared at each other, and then at her. Now she had their attention.

'Are you serious, Sergeant Whittle?' Charlotte White demanded.

Carly shrugged.

'I'm only saying it's possible.'

'Then we need protecting!' said Harry Draper.

Carly smiled again. 'You must have read about the cuts in policing over the past two decades,' she said. 'No, your best hope of protecting your company and yourselves,

The End Game

assuming that does turn out to be necessary, is to cooperate fully with our investigation.' She eased her chair back from the table. 'Thank you for agreeing to see us today. We'll check the information you've given us, and be in touch.'

'Hang on!' Harry Draper protested.

But she was already heading for the door, with Henry Powell playing catch-up.

Chapter 19

'Nice one!' Henry said.

They were walking back down Castle Street towards the car.

'Which one in particular?' Carly asked.

'When you let them believe they might be next. Pure genius.'

'It certainly grabbed their attention.'

'Had them wetting themselves more like, which is telling in itself.'

'That's why I did it,' she told him. 'Their reactions suggest that either none of them have anything to do with this attack on MancVG, or at least one of them is a very convincing liar.'

'Well, Draper Junior certainly isn't, and as for the father, "What a piece of work is a man."'

'Please tell me you're not going start quoting Shakespeare in your reports?'

Henry grinned. 'If I do, Harry Draper will be right up there with Claudius, Macbeth, and the Merchant of Venice. But let's face it, all of them are liars, including Lady Macbeth.'

Carly stopped by the passenger door. 'I presume you're referring to Charlotte White?'

'Obviously,' he said. 'When you told them you'd assumed they'd have heard about the fire, it was clear that Draper had, but neither at that moment, nor at any time during the meeting, did her tone and body language give anything away. She's a cool customer. I wouldn't want to have to do business with her, let alone cross her.'

The End Game

'I agree,' Carly said. 'She obviously wears the pants in the boardroom. The brains of the operation too, especially now that the son appears to be intent on frying his own. She was right though. It doesn't really make a lot of sense, attacking a business that they wanted to buy.'

'I thought I made out a pretty convincing case,' he said.

'Yeah, but you didn't really mean to, did you?'

'Actually, yes, I did.'

'Think about it, Henry,' she said. 'The arson attack, maybe. But using an elaborate form of extortion to make them shift funds to a charity that's not only trying to stop in-game purchases, but also forcing them to publicise the fact. Are they really going to do that when their own firm relies on in-game purchases?'

'When you put it like that,' he said.

They opened their doors and climbed in. Henry clicked his seatbelt into place.

'And you're right about the son,' he said, 'I clocked it as soon as he sat down. Eyes all over the place, runny nose, sniff, sniff, sniff, early signs of damage to his septum. It's no accident he was wearing a *white* hoodie.'

'Skittish hardly covers it,' she agreed.

He looked at her. 'Skittish? He was more wired than a prisoner with electrodes on his . . .'

'Stop!' she shouted. She turned to face him. 'Henry, what the hell was it you did in the Forces?'

He grinned. 'Nothing like that, it's just one of those aphorisms that came with the job.'

She shook her head. 'Well, can I suggest that you save them for your veterans' reunions? Not everyone is going to be as tolerant as me.'

'Tolerant?' he said. 'If you're tolerant, Sarge, then Putin's a bloody pacifist!'

Chapter 20

Salford Quays, 3.15 p.m.

Becky Kerson stared out of the window of her office on the third floor of Imperial Point.

It was a glorious afternoon. The Millennium Bridge shone silver and blue, its reflection shimmering on the waters of the Manchester Ship Canal. Her eyes were drawn, as they often were, to Broadbent's sculpture on the far bank. A cluster of steel sheets weathered brown, each of which represented a dock worker's union card. At the top of every sheet, a glass circle representing a porthole, set in a ring of stainless steel, held an image of one of the 'casuals' who had worked on these docks.

Casual, because every day there was a queue to join in the hope of securing one of a limited number of jobs. Becky's grandfather had been one of those men. One day he'd be shovelling iron ore into buckets, the next he'd be moving bales of cotton or crates of bananas. On the days they stopped hiring before he'd reached the head of the queue, he had to return home empty-handed, and the family went without – sometimes, he'd told her, for weeks at a time.

He had thought those days long gone, and good riddance. She wondered what he'd have to say now about the one point five million people in insecure work. Zero hours contracts; low wages; casual, seasonal and agency workers. Every one of them denied the rights and the protections that come with being employed, and no safety net for them or their families when they were unable to work, or the work dried up.

The End Game

She sighed. It wasn't as though any of it affected her. Business was booming. She lived in a fabulous house. Jake had more money than he knew what to do with, even if he *was* turning into a snowflake . . . in more than one sense of the word. But she had never forgotten her grandpa, or what her mother had told her about the impact of those wage-less weeks on her life as a child. Which explained why all of Becky's staff were on permanent contracts, including the part-timers.

She returned her attention to the penthouse on her monitor screen. A three-thousand-square-foot duplex penthouse in the NV Buildings on Salford Quays. Three double en-suite bedrooms, galleried reading room, library, kitchen to die for, and no less than three terraces looking out across the water towards the Manchester skyline. Oh, and two parking spaces! Asking price? Just £850,000.

Becky had two reasons to be interested in this property. It was sure to sell in under a week. Netting her a cool eighteen K from the seller, and a finder's fee of eight point five K from one of the buyers on her uber-rich client list. Not bad for a week's work. The second reason was that she quite fancied it for herself. Her apartment on the Quays was pokey, and with the commission rolling in, she both deserved it and could afford it, with or without Jake's money. But she'd have to decide today. Odds on, she wasn't the only agent on the buyer's books.

The intercom squawked.

'Yes, Hannah?'

'Becky, there's a policeman here asking for you. A Detective Chief Inspector Caton.'

Becky swore under her breath.

'Please show him in,' she said. 'Oh, and Hannah, ask the chief inspector if he'd like a drink. I'll have my usual.'

Chapter 21

'I hope this is convenient, Ms Kerson?' Caton said.

'That depends on how long it's going to take?' she replied. 'I have a viewing in forty-five minutes, and it's on the other side of the Quays.'

'This should take no more than ten minutes,' he assured her.

She smiled and pointed to a plush velvet two-seater couch.

'In that case, please, Detective Chief Inspector, do sit down.'

'Mr Caton will do fine,' he said. He looked around the room and glanced over his shoulder at the view through the windows. 'This is very nice,' he said. 'What is it you do exactly?'

'I manage property sales on the Quays and in Media City, for purchase or as buy-to-let investments. My clients are mainly foreign investors: Middle Eastern, Russian, French and Chinese.'

She sat down opposite him in a matching armchair. Red bob-cut hair surrounded a pleasant oval face. Dressed smartly in a tailored black business suit over a white blouse, she was tall, considerably taller than her partner Jake, even without her six-inch heels. She seemed unperturbed by his presence, and her hazel eyes regarded him with mild curiosity.

'So, to what do I owe the pleasure?' she asked.

'Business, rather than pleasure, I'm afraid,' he told her. He woke up his tablet and rested it on his thighs. 'It has to do with an incident at a company in Manchester with whom Mr Gorlay and his fellow directors have a connection.'

The End Game

She raised her eyebrows and her lips parted. 'Incident?'

He observed her closely. 'I assumed Jake would have told you?'

She shook her head. 'When was this?'

'In the early hours of this morning.'

'That explains it then,' she said. 'I've not seen or spoken to Jake since we both left for work this morning. I assume he hadn't been told by then.'

Unless he already knew, thought Caton. 'And was Jake with you all night?' he said.

She frowned. 'You're not suggesting that Jake had something to do with this?'

'I'm not suggesting anything. It's just routine. A process of elimination.'

'Well, he was with me all night,' she said. 'We went to bed around midnight. We were asleep by one in the morning. Neither of us stirred until around eight o'clock.'

The door opened and a young woman entered with a tray bearing a glass of yellowish milk, a glass of water and a plate of wrapped chocolate biscuits. She placed the tray on the coffee table.

'Thank you, Hannah,' Becky Kerson said. 'Please see we're not disturbed, but don't let me run over twenty minutes.'

'Absolutely,' Hannah said, and left the room.

They leaned forward in unison and picked up their drinks. Kerson nodded at the glass in Caton's hand.

'Water?' she said.

'Hot water,' he told her. 'I was out training this morning and got back to an unexpectedly large breakfast. According to the Chinese, hot water kick-starts the digestive system, increases blood circulation, helps detox your body and reduces the likelihood of cramp.'

'I'll take your word for it,' she said, 'but I think I'll stick to soy.' She put her glass down. 'You mentioned an incident? What kind of incident?'

'There was a fire in Ancoats that we're treating as suspicious...' He paused. '... At the premises of MancVG.'

Becky Kerson's face registered alarm. 'My God!' she said. 'Was there a lot of damage?'

The End Game

'Enough to disable several servers. But otherwise, the premises are undamaged, and the company is operating normally.'

She sat back. 'Thank heavens – but I don't see how I can help you.'

'We're asking everyone connected with your partner's business if they can think of anybody who might wish to damage the firm or its reputation?'

She shook her head. 'No. Absolutely not . . .' He saw her pupils widen. 'Except . . .'

'Go on?'

'There's a firm, in Castlefield I think, that's been trying to buy Jake and the others out. Could it be them, do you reckon?'

'That's interesting,' he said. 'What do you think they'd have to gain by setting fire to the business?'

'I don't know. Applying some pressure? Trying to force them to sell?'

Caton pretended to make a note on his tablet, then looked up. 'What about personal vendettas?'

'Personal?'

'Yes. Can you think of anyone who may have a grievance with the company, with one of the directors, or with your partner?'

She seemed genuinely confused. 'Are you serious?'

'Absolutely. For instance, how about you, Ms Kerson?'

'Me?'

'Do you have a grievance against your partner Jake, for example?'

He expected her to be outraged, but she surprised him by laughing.

'You *are* joking,' she said. 'Why on earth would I have a grievance against Jake? That's insane.'

'Because of his peccadillos, Ms Kerson?'

She began to laugh again. It turned into a cough that had her reaching for her milk. It was a good thirty seconds before she was able to speak.

'I've always been aware of what you choose to call Jake's peccadillos,' she said. 'Let's be honest, they run the gamut of one-night stands, mild flirtations and quite

The End Game

lengthy affairs. Jake can't help himself. And given how much money he has, neither can the women in the clubs he frequents. He's a sex addict, Chief Inspector. That became clear to me pretty soon after we met in one of those clubs, but in me, he's found a soulmate willing to live with the fact, not least because an open relationship suits me too.' She smiled. 'That's why I have my own apartment here on the Quays. Jake and I have three simple rules: we are both completely honest with each other about our extra-partnership relations, we take appropriate precautions to respect each other's sexual health, and we spend weekends and holidays together.'

She looked at her watch.

'Time is pressing, Mr Caton,' she said. 'So, if you have no more questions?'

Caton closed his tablet and stood up. 'I'm grateful for your time, Ms Kerson,' he said, 'and thank you for being so frank.'

She stood up. 'There was no point in wasting my time or yours. You'd have found out eventually and then we'd have had to do this all over again. Besides, I have nothing to be ashamed of or to hide.' She walked over to the door and opened it. 'I hope you find the bastards who torched Jake's offices and soon,' she said. Her face clouded over. 'Do we need to worry about the house in Cheshire?'

'I hope not,' he replied, 'but I have officers checking the security system with your husband.'

She put a hand to her face. It was the first time that her composure had slipped. 'Should I be worrying about my apartment, or this office?'

'We have no reason to suspect that this has anything to do with you or your company,' he told her, 'but you will also be getting a visit from one of my officers to advise you on staying safe. I'll make sure you get a phone call first.'

Caton waited until he'd exited the building and then called Nick Carter.

'I've just left Gorlay's partner, Becky Kerson,' he said. 'She claims they were both tucked up in bed all night and she's not heard from him since he left this morning.'

'Do you believe her?'

'Yes, but he could still be involved, although I agree that wouldn't make any sense. Where are you at the moment, Nick?'

'I'm on Deansgate. Outside the firm of accountants where Gorlay's former mistress Mylene Terry works.'

'In that case,' Caton said, 'I'll go ahead and talk to her husband. Don't worry, I won't let on about his wife's relationship with Gorlay. I'll just check his alibi. It'll be interesting to see how he reacts when I turn up at Central Park.'

'Won't it just,' Carter said. 'Text me when you're done, Boss. We can compare notes when I've finished with the wife.'

Chapter 22

Manchester Deansgate, 3.30 p.m.

Mylene Terry had an office on the first floor. Carter could see why Jake Gorlay had fallen for her. Late twenties, light brown hair, green eyes, full mouth, wonderful complexion, and a body that was a tribute to the gym she frequented.

'Come in, officer,' she said, 'and take a seat.'

She sat facing him on a swivel chair, crossing her feet at the ankle.

'Is this about the fire in Ancoats?' she asked.

'What makes you think that, Mrs Terry?' Carter said.

'Well, it's obvious, surely? It was on the radio and the midday news. I manage that company's accounts. I just assumed that you would wish to speak with me.'

'Why?' he said, flustered.

'Well, because I assumed you'd want to know about the business – how it might be affected by the fire, if it was insured.'

'Has anyone from the company contacted you today, Mrs Terry?' he said.

A blush began somewhere beneath her emerald blouse and slowly spread up and across her neck. He watched her as she consider how best to respond and recognised the moment when she decided to tell the truth.

'The chief executive officer called me.'

'Jake Gorlay called you?'

'Yes.'

'When was this?'

'Around midday.'

Carter nodded. Immediately after Gorlay had been interviewed.

'To warn you that we know about your relationship with him, and that we were likely to want to speak to you.'

It wasn't a question, and she didn't bother to refute it. The flush spread to her cheeks.

'That's what I really wanted to speak with you about,' Carter told her. He switched his tablet on. 'When did your relationship with Jake Gorlay begin, Mrs Terry? The personal one, that is, not the professional one.'

She uncrossed her legs and folded her hands in her lap. 'Three years ago. The first Wednesday following Easter.'

'That's very precise,' he said.

'It was memorable.'

He looked up. 'Would you care to elaborate?'

'Not really. Not unless you can prove its relevance to your investigation?'

He couldn't.

'I understand that you met frequently at Mr Gorlay's apartment in the Northern Quarter?'

She failed to hide her surprise that he was so well informed. 'Yes.'

'Including during lockdown?'

She hesitated.

'You can answer that,' he told her. 'We're not doing retrospective fines any more.'

'Then, yes, we did. But only once a week, and never at weekends.'

Carter didn't see what difference that made but decided not to pursue it. 'When did Mr Gorlay tell you that he wanted to finish the relationship?'

'Four weeks ago.'

'And how did you take it?'

She looked down at her feet and lowered her voice. 'I wasn't happy. Obviously.'

'That's something of an understatement, isn't it, Mrs Terry?'

She raised her head. 'I don't understand?'

Carter scrolled through his interviews until he found the right one.

'*"She all but trashed the apartment . . . It cost me four grand to replace the stuff she broke. But it was worth it to get rid . . .*

The End Game

What makes a woman turn from a lovely, thoughtful, romantic being into a raging beast?"'

'Clearly not happy, either of you,' Carter said.

Her entire face was red now, and her hands clenched. He saw for himself how little it took to tip her over the edge.

'You don't understand,' she said. 'I gave him three years of my life! He led me on with promises. I thought he was going to leave that bitch. She doesn't love him. Do you know, he told me she knew all about me and him, but she didn't care? She's just a gold digger! He promised me he was going to leave her, but he had no intention of doing that, did he?'

'We've been told you found it difficult to accept that your relationship with Mr Gorlay was over,' Carter said.

'What do you mean?'

'Frequent phone calls to the office asking where he is. Unscheduled visits asking to see him. I have to say, it sounds a lot like stalking, Mrs Terry.'

'That's ridiculous!' She slumped back in her seat.

'Does anyone else know you were Mr Gorlay's mistress?' Carter asked.

'I resent that word. This is the twenty-first century, Detective Inspector. Ours was a mutually advantageous relationship.'

'But not ended by mutual agreement?' he observed. 'Did your husband know about your affair?'

Her eyes flared. 'No. Definitely not.'

'He didn't even suspect?'

She gripped the arms of her chair. 'No. And he mustn't find out. Please. There's no reason he should, is there?'

'I don't know,' Carter replied. 'How do you think he'd react if he was told?'

The colour fled from her cheeks. It was a stark reply.

'Badly, I'm guessing,' he said. 'Moving on . . . Can you tell me, Mrs Terry, your exact whereabouts between midnight last night and four o'clock this morning?'

'I was in town, celebrating a friend's thirtieth birthday.'

'And she'll vouch for that?'

'There were seven of us – take your pick.'

'Where was this exactly?'

The End Game

She named a cocktail lounge on Bridge Street, and a couple of clubs off King Street. 'We met at nine in the evening for cocktails and then went clubbing.'

'What time did you leave for town?'

'Must have been just after three,' she said. 'The taxi dropped me off around half past.'

'Was your husband home?'

'Yes.'

She had hesitated a fraction too long.

'You don't seem too sure.'

'We have an agreement that if either of us is out really late, then we'll sleep in separate rooms. Derek's car was on the drive, and the bedroom door was shut.'

She saw a question forming on his lips.

'Oh! And I set the downstairs alarm when I came in. I would definitely have heard him if he'd come in after me.'

'I assume there's a delay before it sounds. What was to stop him simply cancelling and resetting the alarm?'

'It emits a really annoying beep before it goes off. I would certainly have heard it.'

'Even after six hours on the lash?'

'Yes.'

'We have an address for you in Kingston Road, Didsbury,' Carter said. 'Is that correct?'

'Yes.'

'According to the times you've given me, Mrs Terry, at three in the morning it took half an hour by taxi from King Street to Didsbury. I would have put that at closer to fifteen minutes, even with all the traffic lights against you?'

Her only response was to shrug.

Carter scrolled back over his notes.

'Well,' he said, 'I think that's it for now, Mrs Terry.' He stood up. 'If you could just jot down the name of the taxi firm you used, and the contact details of your friends?'

'All of them?'

'Don't worry,' he said, 'we won't retain any of them unless they prove germane to our investigation.'

She stood, crossed to her desk, and began to write on a notepad next to the landline. She tore the page out and

The End Game

handed it to him but didn't let go. 'Please,' she said, 'don't tell my husband.'

'You do realise,' Carter told her, 'that he's bound to wonder why we need to talk to him?'

She blanched again as she let go of the note.

'Probably best if you tell him yourself,' Carter said. He paused in the doorway. 'Do you have CCTV at home, Mrs Terry?'

'We do,' she said. 'Two cameras in the eaves, and one in the doorbell.'

'Excellent,' he responded. 'Thank you for your cooperation. Do take care.'

Chapter 23

4 p.m.

'How did it go?' Caton asked.

'Interesting,' Carter replied. 'She is so not over Gorlay.'

'Enough to hire a hitman?'

'Why a hitman – what's to stop her doing it herself?'

'Are you telling me you think her capable?'

Carter chuckled. 'No, Boss. But if I'd just assumed that she wasn't, you'd have called me sexist and queried my professional objectivity.'

'I'll give you that,' Caton responded. 'In the interests of professional objectivity, does she have an alibi?'

'She claims she has six friends who can all verify that she was celebrating in town from nine till three this morning.'

'Convenient. That still leaves her a window of opportunity.'

'Except that she claims a taxi picked her up and dropped her off at home around half past three.'

'Did you ask her if the husband was there when she got home?'

'Come on, Boss – 'course I did. His car was there and the alarm was off, but she slept in a spare bedroom and she didn't actually see him. The good news is, they have CCTV. I'm on my way back to base to get DS Hulme to task the team to check it out, as well her alibis.'

'Good work, Nick,' Caton said.

'There's one thing you might want to consider when you're questioning the husband,' Carter told him. 'She's clearly terrified of him. She's desperate for him not to find out.'

The End Game

'She should have thought about that before she took up with Gorlay.'

'Obviously. I told her there were no guarantees, and she should tell him herself.'

'It suggests that he's the jealous type,' Caton observed, 'If he did know . . .'

Carter finished the thought. '. . . Then he had a motive to bomb Gorlay's offices. But why those extortion demands? Why not target Gorlay directly?'

'To throw us off the scent?' Caton mused.

'Seems a bit excessive.'

'Don't forget what Amit Patel told us,' Caton cautioned. 'Derek Terry is a police-performance analyst and he's an Army Reservist. He'd have garnered enough knowledge of police work, forensics and crime scene investigations to come up with something like this. He's also bright enough to know that we'll find out about his wife and Gorlay and come knocking at his door.'

'Hell of a risk then,' Carter observed. 'If it is him, it would give a whole new meaning to the phrase "jealous type".'

'Just a thought,' Caton said, 'if she really is that terrified, perhaps we should get someone round to their house before he gets home?'

'You're going to tell him then, about her affair?'

'Not if I can avoid it. But we have to assume that he's bright enough to put two and two together – if he doesn't already know.'

'If he does, and it is him, wouldn't he play it cool rather than give the game away?'

'And if he doesn't?'

'Point taken,' Carter said. 'If you let me know what time he's due to clock off, I'll arrange for our guys to be checking out the CCTV when he gets home.'

'Got to go. This is him now,' Caton said. 'I'll see you back at base.'

Chapter 24

Central Park, 4.45 p.m.

Caton observed Derek Terry as he walked across the mezzanine. Tall, with an athletic build, he moved with confidence. His side-parted hair had been cut high and tight, and then tamed with paste. His eyes were alert, his expression relaxed. Caton stood up.

'Mr Terry?' he said.

Terry nodded.

'Yes, sir. You must be DCI Caton. My boss says we can use his office – unless you want to do it here?'

The mezzanine was deserted. There was plenty of space between the breakout pods, but Caton had no idea how heated the conversation might become.

'The office would be fine,' he said.

Terry led the way around the mezzanine and into a large administrative space. Heads turned as his colleagues watched the two of them weave their way between the work carrels to a small office at the far end. Terry held the door open for him. Caton chose to sit on one of the two padded bentwood chairs rather than the imposing executive leather one behind the desk. Terry took the seat opposite.

'You haven't asked why I wanted to see you, Derek?' Caton said.

'I didn't think it was my place to,' Terry replied, 'but I have to admit, I'm intrigued.'

Caton nodded. 'It's to do with a suspicious fire last night at a digital media company in the Northern Quarter.'

Terry looked confused. 'I don't understand,' he said. 'What makes you think I might be able to assist

The End Game

your investigation?'

'You weren't aware of this fire then? It's been all over the news today.'

The data analyst shook his head. 'I was in early. Head down all day. You wouldn't believe the workload.' He smiled. 'Then again, you probably would. I'm working my way through thousands of unrecorded crimes. Trying to collate them so they can be prioritised.'

'The fire was at the premises of MancVG,' Caton said.

Terry frowned and shook his head again. 'Never heard of them.'

'Your wife is their accountant.'

'Right,' Terry said. 'So that's why you wanted to see me. Well, I can't enlighten you, I'm afraid. Neither of us take our work home with us. You could call it a pact.'

'Very wise, Derek,' Caton said. 'Nevertheless, I'd appreciate it if you could answer a few questions for me. It's just routine. For elimination purposes, you understand? I'll be making a few notes if that's okay?'

'Certainly,' Terry responded. 'Fire away.'

'Can you tell me where you were last night between midnight and four in the morning?'

Terry smiled. 'That's easy. Mylene was out on the town with the girls celebrating a mate's birthday. I went to bed around eleven o'clock and binge-watched *The Lincoln Lawyer* on Netflix till just after one. Then I went to sleep. I woke up when my alarm went off at seven.'

'Do you know what time your wife arrived home?'

'I haven't a clue,' Terry said. 'I was just leaving when she came down for breakfast.' He grinned. 'I got the impression she'd had a heavy night though.'

Caton took a moment. Terry had become increasingly cocky, and he was sorely tempted to burst his bubble. On the other hand, with little to gain and a lot to lose for the wife, it was probably too early to press his buttons. He decided to tread a middle path.

'Have you ever met any of the directors of MancVG?' he asked.

Terry slowly folded his arms and shook his head. 'Not that I know of.'

The End Game

There was an acronym for light detection and ranging, LiDAR, that DS Hulme had appropriated for the syndicate. It had now become liar detection and recognition. It only took two tells to set Caton's off, and right now his LiDAR was flashing.

'You've never met Jake Gorlay, their chief executive, for instance?'

Terry frowned and passed a hand across the right side of his hair, smoothing it down.

'Gorlay?' he said. 'Jake Gorlay?' He shook his head. 'Can't say that I have.'

'Your wife has never mentioned that name?'

'No,' Terry said, a little too quickly. 'Why, is it important?'

'Probably not,' Caton told him. 'Don't worry about it.' He made a note on his tablet. 'Do you work shifts, Derek,' he said, 'or is your job nine to five?'

'It's normally quarter to nine till four thirty,' Terry replied. 'Although I often work an hour or so overtime; it depends on what time Mylene is due home.' He grinned. 'Wouldn't want to be first home – I'd have to get dinner ready.'

Caton made a point of switching his tablet off and closing the cover.

'You're in the TA, I gather,' he said. 'That must be exciting?'

'It is,' Terry replied with enthusiasm, 'especially if we're on manoeuvres with the Regular Army. I've been abroad a fair few times.'

'Really? Where?'

'Norway and a number of European countries. Keeps me fit, and you'd be surprised what you learn.'

'I can only imagine, Mr Terry,' Caton said. 'How many years have you been with the Army Reserve?'

'Seven, and in that relatively short time I've risen to the rank of corporal. I command my own section, a challenge that I'm really enjoying.'

'Congratulations, Mr Terry,' Caton said. He stood up. 'Thank you for your help.'

'Not at all,' the analyst replied, 'though I'm not sure

The End Game

how helpful I've been.'

'You'd be surprised,' Caton told him. 'Don't worry, I'll see myself out.'

***

He waited until he was back in his car and called DS Hulme.

'Jimmy,' he said. 'I need someone to go and talk to Derek Terry's TA commander. Who's available?'

'DC Powell's at his desk,' Hulme replied. 'With his army background he'd make a great fit.'

'Perfect,' Caton said. 'I know it's late, but tell him to give them a ring and see if he can set up a meeting. We need to know about Terry's personality and the skills and specialisms he's developed with the Army Reserve – especially anything to do with explosives. If there've been any concerns about his behaviour. And if they have any issues with equipment going missing. Oh, and Powell has to keep this all as lowkey as possible. We don't want any of it getting back to him. Not till we're ready.'

'That's a tall ask, Boss,' Hulme observed.

'I know,' Caton replied, 'but if anyone can do it, Henry can.'

Chapter 25

Deepdale Road, Preston, 6.40 p.m.

Henry experienced an uncomfortable feeling of déjà vu as he drove past the stadium. He had been here twice to watch his beloved Wrexham play Preston: in the league cup and then in the Auto Windscreens Shield. They had lost both times. Neither had come as a great surprise. Their recent record against the Lilywhites was shocking. They hadn't won a single game since October '97.

The barracks stood next to the stadium. Instantly recognisable as an MOD building, it was a bland, uninspiring, squat three storeys of brick and stone surrounded by spiked railings. He pulled up beside the signboards attached to the railings. A full-size photo showed a young soldier looking through the scope of an SA80.

Henry stared at the image. But for the colour of his skin, that young soldier could easily have been a photo of himself when he joined the regiment. It seemed a long time ago now, and yet there wasn't a single engagement with hostiles that wasn't indelibly imprinted on his brain. None of those memories, however, came back to haunt him in the night. He was able to lock them in a box to which he held the only key, and which he opened rarely and briefly, and only then to remind himself of comrades who had been killed or suffered life-changing injuries. And of how fortunate he himself was.

Henry drove through the first set of gates, waited for the CCTV to relay his number plate, and the gates to swing open. He drove up to the reception entrance, parked in a guest space, and went inside. While he waited, he flicked through the promotional leaflets.

The End Game

He was so busy considering what skills, motivation and mindset the regiment might have imbued in Derek Terry, and how that might relate to Operation Sentinel, that he failed to notice an adjutant approaching. She stopped in front of him.

'DC Powell?' she said.

He looked up. 'I'm sorry,' he said. 'I was miles away.'

Her smile was perfunctory. 'The Major is ready for you now,' she said.

'You were lucky to catch us, DC Powell,' said the officer, offering his hand. 'My name is Major Osborne, and this is CSM Inman.'

The brusqueness of his manner left no doubt that this was an inconvenience.

Henry shook hands with them both, reflecting on how habit had nearly led him to salute the major instead.

'Please,' said Osborne, 'take a seat.'

'I appreciate you finding the time, Major,' Henry said. 'As a veteran, I understand how precious your time is.'

'Who were you with?' the major asked.

'The Queen's Dragoon Guards,' Henry told him.

The major nodded. 'The Welsh cavalry,' he said.

His company sergeant major leaned forward. 'How long did you do?'

'Seven years. Including a tour in Iraq and two tours in Afghanistan as part of the Brigade Reconnaissance Force. The second, in 2014, was my final tour overseas.'

The CSM raised his eyebrows. 'Herrick 20,' he said. 'My brigade deployed with the BRF on Herrick 12. Hairy doesn't cover it. You have my respect.'

The major tapped his watch. 'Thank you, CSM,' he said. 'To business, I think. Mr Powell, I understand that you asked to see us regarding Corporal Terry. What is your enquiry in relation to?'

'Mr Terry is one of a number of persons of interest assisting us in the initial stages of an ongoing investigation,' Henry told them.

'I see,' the major said. 'Does this investigation have anything to do with his role in the Army Reserve?'

'Not so far as I'm aware at this moment,' Henry told him.

'Then I don't see how we can help you.'

'Perhaps if I were to put my questions, Major,' Henry said, 'that would become clear.'

'Very well,' Osborne said. 'I suggest that you address them to CSM Inman. He's likely to be best placed to answer.'

He lounged back in his chair and folded his arms.

'Thank you, Major,' Henry said. 'Mr Inman, perhaps you could begin by telling me a little about Corporal Terry's personality?'

Inman frowned. 'Personality?'

'That's correct,' Henry replied. 'I seem to remember the armed forces having adopted the acronym OCEAN when assessing the personality of recruits, as well as serving soldiers and staff?'

'That's true,' Inman responded. 'However, I was wondering how this relates to your investigation.'

'Just answer his question, CSM,' the major said softly.

Inman sat up tall. When he responded, it was with formality, as though reporting to a superior.

'I've always found Corporal Terry to be direct, frank and truthful in his responses and conscientious in carrying out his duties. He tends a little more towards introversion than extroversion and is less likely than most of his colleagues to engage in banter.' He paused. 'As to his agreeableness, he has on occasion exhibited a quick temper when those in his section have either been slow, or have failed, to meet his expectations. Regarding neuroticism, other than the occasional irritability aforementioned, he has shown no signs of anxiety, depression or self-doubt. On the contrary, when leading his men, he is supremely confident, if a little overfond of his authority.'

'Thank you, Mr Inman, ' Henry said. 'That's extremely helpful. I wonder if I could ask if you have ever had to reprimand Mr Terry about his temper?'

Inman took a moment or two to reply. 'On one or two occasions,' he said, 'although more to advise than admonish. I pointed out that this was not the first two weeks of basic training and that motivating and encouraging soldiers under your command is rarely achieved by hounding them.'

The End Game

'Hounding?' Henry said. 'That's a very strong word?'

Inman shrugged. 'As I said, it was only one or two occasions.'

Henry pretended to make a note, then looked up. 'Am I correct in assuming that Corporal Terry will have gained all of the skills necessary to deploy as a rapid-force light infantryman?'

'Naturally,' said Major Osborne, making no attempt to hide his impatience. 'And as a former infantryman yourself, I assume there's no need for us to go through all of those with you?'

Henry smiled. 'None whatsoever,' he said. 'Could you, however, tell me if Corporal Terry has had any training in relation to the construction and deployment of improvised explosive devices?'

That had both soldiers sitting up in their seats. They exchanged glances.

'IEDs?' the company sergeant major said.

'You assured us, Detective Constable,' the major protested, 'that this had nothing to do with his role in the Army Reserve?'

'Perhaps I should have qualified my answer,' Henry replied. 'What I meant was that our investigation has nothing to do with his or anyone else's role per se in the armed forces, and there's certainly no motivational link as far as we can tell. However, the particular skills developed within such a role could indeed prove relevant.'

Osborne shook his head. 'That's splitting hairs,' he said. 'Despite which, I can assure you that there is no way that he or any of his company would have been taught how to construct an IED. We leave that to Special Forces. Am I right, CSM?'

'Yes, sir,' Inman agreed. 'He would have been instructed in how to search for, recognise, avoid and report IEDs, but certainly not construct one. Mind you, these days anyone can find out how to do that on the web.'

'Now, if you're quite finished, Detective Constable,' the major said, 'we have somewhere we need to be.'

Henry made a point of closing his tablet. He stood up, hesitated, and said as though it had just occurred to him, 'I do have one final question for the CSM. In your opinion, Mr Inman, is Derek Terry someone likely to hold a grudge?'

Inman frowned, thought about it and said, 'I'm not aware of anything that would lead me to believe that he is.'

'In that case, ' Henry said, 'thank you both very much for making time to meet with me today. And for your frank responses.'

Major Powell opened the door for him. 'CSM Inman will show you out,' he said, 'but first, I have a question for you, Detective Constable. In light of the nature of your questions regarding Corporal Terry, should we be worried?'

'I'm not in a position to say, Major,' Henry told him. 'As I said, it's early stages, and Mr Terry is one of a number of persons helping us with our investigation, but I think it unlikely that you would need to be concerned.'

Chapter 26

Naval Street, Ancoats, 6.30 p.m.

'What the hell is that godawful stink?' Jake Gorlay asked.

'Ylang ylang essential oil,' Louie said, pointing to a diffuser on the desk. 'Nuan's put these all around the office to get rid of the smell of smoke.'

'Think I preferred the smoke,' Jake growled. 'Where is she anyway?'

'Left for the night. Said she needs to have a good shower and get changed. She and her partner have a market-dinner reservation at Street Urchin.'

'Street Urchin?'

'That trendy seafood restaurant on Great Ancoats Street.'

'Plate glass windows and what looks like a bathing hut by the entrance?'

'That's it. You should take Becks there. She'd love it.'

Jake's smartphone pinged. It was a text.

'Please God, not another one.' He read it and relaxed. 'It's alright,' he said. 'Different number.'

He opened the text and immediately cursed.

'The bastard's got another phone!'

'The first one was a burner,' Louie said. 'He's probably got dozens of them.'

'Some Job's comforter you are,' Jake told him.

'What does it say?' Louie asked.

Jake read it out.

The End Game

ENDGAME Level Two

Your failure to complete Level One means that you must now donate £500,000 to the End In-Game Purchases charity within 24hrs of receiving this text. Within the same time frame, you must release a statement on all social media declaring your support for ENDIP, your intention to remove all in-game purchases from your own video games and call upon the rest of your industry to join you in this mission.

WARNING: Failure to complete this task will result in a Level Two personal loss sanction.

I am The Boss.

'The bastard!'

He hurled the phone across the room. It landed on a sofa and bounced onto the floor.

Louie hurried across the room. 'That's evidence,' he said.

He picked up the phone, took a screenshot, and checked the photo.

'Personal loss,' he said. 'What does that mean?'

Gorlay held out his hand. 'What am I, a bloody mind reader? Give me my phone.'

'What are you going to do?' Louie asked.

Gorlay snatched the phone from him.

'What d'you think? Call Caton and find out what the hell the police think they're doing to stop this!'

Chapter 27

Nexus House, 6.45 p.m.

'Calm down, Mr Gorlay,' Caton said. 'I appreciate how upsetting this is, but becoming abusive is not going to help.'

'Well, you tell me what is!' Gorlay responded. 'Because from where I'm standing, with my effing business smouldering all around me, you lot seem to be doing naff all.'

'For your information,' Caton told him, 'we have followed every lead that you and your fellow directors gave us. That includes interviewing all of the directors of Castlefield Digital Creations and several other potential persons of interest. I have officers scouring hours of CCTV and other digital media. We're working to track down the location of the burner phone used to communicate with you. And we're trying to identify the sources of the components of the device used to set fire to your premises. Furthermore, I have officers continuing to check the security at your properties, and your fellow directors' properties.'

'Very impressive,' Gorlay said in a voice laden with sarcasm, 'and what have you got to show for it?'

Caton hesitated a fraction too long.

'Like I said, naff all!' Gorlay said mockingly.

Caton thought that close to the truth, but he wasn't going to admit it. 'We're making progress,' he said.

'And while you're stumbling around in the dark, what are we supposed to do about this latest demand? And what the hell does "personal loss" mean?'

'I have no idea, Mr Gorlay,' Caton admitted, 'but my advice remains the same. Do nothing. In the meantime, please forward me that text. And try not to worry.'

He ended the call and turned to face his deputy SIO.

'How did he react when you told him not to worry?' Carter asked.

'His mask has well and truly slipped. Whatever veneer of civility university may have given him is out of the window. Suffice to say, if I'd been recording it, I would have had to delete most of it. Either that or bleep the expletives.'

'It's understandable,' Carter said, 'especially when you're being threatened with "personal loss". That could mean anything from having your car nicked to having your partner killed or your fingers chopped off.'

'Boss!'

DS Hulme scooted his chair away from his desk and stood up. 'I've been sent a link from the passive media team. CCTV footage from one of the houses opposite Derek Terry's address shows his car leaving home at 1.30 a.m. and returning an hour and a half later, at 3.15. It also captured his wife being dropped off by taxi, at 3.22. Not only that, but his car was caught on an ANPR camera on Oldham Road, within a quarter of a mile of the MancVG offices, at 2.59 at night, at which time he claimed to be at home. That means she was telling the truth about when she got home, whereas the husband lied about where he was that night.'

'He was cutting it fine if he only got home seven minutes before his wife,' Carly Whittle observed. 'She only had to put her hand on the bonnet of his car, and she'd have known he was telling porkies.'

'We need to have another word with Mr Terry,' Caton said. 'Let's see what DC Powell has to tell us about his visit to Preston, and then pay Mr Terry a visit early doors before he starts his shift.'

The door to the incident room opened, and Henry Powell walked in. Nick Carter and Carly Whittle began to laugh; Jimmy Hulme clapped his hands. Henry stopped dead in his tracks.

'My ears are burning,' he said.

'Only because you arrived dead on cue,' Caton reassured him. 'Sit yourself down and tell us what you've got. Somebody fetch him a drink – it's no fun in rush hour on the M60.'

The End Game

'In essence, what we have, Boss,' Powell said, 'is someone who is conscientious in his duties, supremely confident, quick-tempered, and fond of exercising his authority to the point of hounding soldiers under his command on at least two occasions.'

'In my experience,' Carter said, 'when someone says, "one or two occasions", they definitely mean three or more.'

'Beyond that,' Caton said, 'what impression were you left with, DC Powell? What was the subtext?'

'My overall impression, Boss,' Powell said, 'was that they weren't all that surprised to discover that Terry might have overstepped the mark in some way – that is until I mentioned IEDs. And when I asked the company sergeant major if he thought Terry was the type to hold a grudge, he had to think about that. And when he answered, he was a little too careful not to commit himself one way or the other.'

'As though he'd not considered it before, but now you'd mentioned it, he could see how that might be the case?'

'Exactly, Boss.'

Caton looked at the progress board. 'We have colleagues trying to get a location on the burner phone from which the most recent threat and instructions were sent to Gorlay. Passive media analysis is ongoing. I'm still waiting to hear if HQ are prepared to provide any resources for protective observation on the homes of the three MancVG directors. There's nothing more we can do this evening. I suggest we all go home. DS Whittle and DC Powell, I'd like you to be at the Fletcher Moss car park on Millgate Lane, the one by the Alpine Tea Room, at six o'clock sharp tomorrow morning.'

'Very convenient, Boss,' DS Hulme quipped.

'The Boss just happens to live a hundred metres down the road,' Carter said, 'meaning he'll get an extra half an hour in bed.'

'More importantly,' Caton said, 'the Terrys live only a hundred yards away on Kingston Road, back-to-back with Millgate Lane. We can check out the cameras on the lane while we're walking round there.'

'Does Terry know you two are neighbours, Boss?' Carter asked.

'No,' Caton said, 'and that is how I'd like it to stay!'

Chapter 28
Day Two
Saturday 3rd September

Didsbury, 6.10 a.m.

'What time does the tea room open, Boss?' Henry Powell asked. 'Perhaps we could call in for breakfast when we're done?'

'Eight o'clock,' Caton replied, 'and unless we discover a body in the garden you can forget that.'

Carly Whittle was several paces ahead of them. She stopped opposite a tall wooden gate. 'This must be the back of their garden, which makes that the roof of their garage.'

'With all these high walls and trees,' Henry Powell observed, 'even if there are any cameras at the back of these houses, they're not going to show anyone coming or going on the lane.'

'True,' Caton acknowledged, 'but they're going to hit an A-road at both ends – Wilmslow Road at this end and Parrs Wood Road at the other. That means speed cameras and ANPR cameras. If they had really wanted to avoid detection, they'd have had to leave on foot and pick up their transport some distance from here.'

They resumed walking.

'With this epidemic of electrically assisted pedal cycles and scooters, it's getting easier for ne'er-do-wells to avoid every kind of traffic camera,' Powell observed.

'Ne'er-do-wells?' his DS said. 'I've never heard you use that expression before.'

'That's because just about all the alternatives I could use are now frowned upon, Sarge,' he responded. 'Isn't that right, Boss?'

'You could try criminals, felons, lawbreakers, offenders,' Caton suggested.

'And you accuse me of being a walking thesaurus,' Powell joked.

'Among other things,' Carly muttered.

They turned right onto the main road, and immediate right onto to the road where the Terrys had their house.

'Just to be clear,' Caton said, 'Derek Terry may not be a police officer, but his training and his work will mean that he's going to be far better informed about his rights and ours than most members of the public. Let's not give him the opportunity to play the barrack-room lawyer.'

'Very appropriate, Boss,' Henry Powell said.

Caton stopped. 'Come again?'

'With him being Army Reserve, Boss. Barrack room?'

Caton continued walking. 'Focus, Detective Constable,' he said, 'focus!'

He turned to his DS. 'Carly, I want to keep the two of them apart. If the wife is there, I'd like you to talk with her on her own.'

'Anything specific you want me to ask, Boss?'

'Just get her to go over her movements that night one more time, and find out if she believes the husband knows about her affair with Gorlay.'

'Yes, Boss.'

They stopped outside a substantial, well-maintained Victorian semi-detached house. A neat front garden with a hedge fronting the road, a trim lawn, and flowering perennial shrubs in the borders. Derek Terry's car was parked on the road in front of the house, his wife's car was on the drive. The curtains had been drawn in all of the windows.

'Early risers,' Carly observed.

As though to prove it, the front door opened. Derek Terry, dressed for work, mobile phone in hand, stood in the doorway.

The End Game

'Looks as though he was expecting us,' Henry Powell said under his breath.

They walked up the gently sloping drive.

'This is a surprise?' Terry said. 'I was just checking my emails and you popped up on my phone.'

He registered three blank expressions and pointed to the video doorbell.

'It's set to alert us if people are anywhere near my car, or the drive.'

'That's extremely sophisticated, Mr Terry,' Caton said. 'Must be annoying though?'

Terry shrugged. 'Well, you can't be too careful.'

He stared at their faces, seeking a clue as to why they were there. Finding none, he stepped back into the hallway.

'I suppose you want to come in?' he said.

Chapter 29

They were shown into the front room. There was a three-seater sofa against one wall, a two-seater in the bay window, and two bookcases on either side of an original fireplace. An antique floral fire screen filled the space where the fire would have been. A large-screen TV hung on the wall above the mantlepiece. Through an arch in the third wall, they could see an open-plan kitchen-diner.

'My wife is in the bathroom,' Terry said. 'Will you need to speak with her?'

His tone suggested that he'd prefer they didn't.

'That won't be necessary, Mr Terry,' Caton told him. 'Not unless she comes down before we've finished. It's you we've come to see.'

Terry waited for more. Caton kept him waiting. Terry hovered by the bay window.

'You'd best sit down,' he said, pointing to the larger of the sofas.

Henry and Carly placed their rucksacks on the floor beside them, and the three of them sat down.

'Can I get you a drink?' Terry asked. 'I was putting the kettle on when I got the alert.'

'No, thank you,' Caton said. 'Why don't you sit down, Mr Terry? We have a few questions for you.'

Terry went over to sit on the two-seater in the bay window. With the early morning sun low in the sky, it made it harder for them to clearly see his face. He opened his tablet, and deliberately took his time reading the relevant statement.

'Yesterday,' he said, 'when I asked you where you were between midnight and four in the morning the night before

The End Game

last, you told me that you'd gone to bed around eleven o'clock and binge-watched *The Lincoln Lawyer* on Netflix till just after one. You then went to sleep and were woken by your alarm at seven in the morning.'

He looked up.

'That isn't true, is it, Mr Terry?'

Terry's pupils contracted, dilated, contracted again. Although miniscule, the changes were enough for Caton to see the man's mind working furiously. He reckoned that Terry had anticipated the question but was still deciding which web to spin: the one with an outright lie, a partial truth, or the whole truth.

'I was about to turn the light off and go to sleep,' he said, 'when I saw a set of Mylene's keys on the dressing table. I assumed she'd forgotten to take them. That meant she'd have to wake me up to let her in, so I rang her phone but there was no reply. I decided to go and give them to her.' He paused. 'Excuse me a moment,' he said.

He stood up, went over to the door, listened for a moment and padded back to his seat.

'Sorry about that,' he said. 'I thought I heard Mylene calling me. Where was I?'

'About to set off for town to find your wife. How did you know where she'd be?'

'Since Covid, there aren't that many late-night clubs in town,' he said. 'There are a few around King Street and in the Northern Quarter that she and her friends are fond of.' He shrugged. 'I thought it was worth a go.'

'How many did you try?'

Terry hesitated.

'Three . . . or four.'

'Well, if you let us have the names of these clubs, I'm sure that the doormen will remember you?'

'I guess,' he replied, 'although there were quite a few people coming and going.'

'No matter,' Carly Whittle said. 'They all have CCTV on the doors. It's a condition of their licences.'

There was a flicker of disappointment on Terry's face.

'Did you find your wife, Derek?' Caton asked.

'No,' he said, 'I didn't.' He shook his head. 'It was a

The End Game

daft idea. I shouldn't have bothered.'

Caton pretended to check his notes. 'You spent a long time looking. What time did you arrive home?'

He was reading Terry's face like a book now.

'Er . . . I'm not sure. Two thirty? Two forty-five, maybe?'

'We have your car arriving back at three fifteen precisely,' Caton told him. 'I assume you were driving it?'

Terry gritted his teeth.

Caton smiled. 'Silly me, your video CCTV will tell us that,' he said. 'When your wife returned home, did she have to ring the bell to get in?'

'No. She must have had her spare set.'

'Dear me,' Caton said. 'All that wasted effort rushing round town in the middle of the night. You must have been exhausted.'

He checked his tablet again. 'Incidentally, you've just told us that you searched for your wife in the vicinity of King Street in the city centre, and also in the Northern Quarter. Is that right?'

Terry stared at the other two detectives, hoping to work out if this was a trap. 'That's correct,' he said.

Caton looked up. 'Anywhere else?'

'No.'

'Then can you explain what you were doing on Oldham Road, close to Ancoats, at two fifty-nine?'

Terry had to think about it.

'When I couldn't find Mylene in one of her usual haunts I thought I'd try Ancoats,' he said. 'It was a long shot.'

'The thing is,' Caton said, 'before we came to see you, we searched online for late night clubs and bars in Ancoats. What do you think we discovered?'

'I've no idea.'

'It turns out there are none.'

Terry shrugged. 'Like I said, it was a long shot.'

Caton closed his tablet and stood up. The others stood with him.

'I need you to hand over your mobile phone, Mr Terry,' he said.

Terry's right hand moved instinctively towards his trouser pocket and pressed against it, as though to protect its contents.

'Why?' he said.

Caton sighed. 'I would have thought that was obvious. We need to verify your account and establish your actual whereabouts the night before last.'

'I don't have to hand it over,' Terry said.

'That's true,' Caton acknowledged. 'But if you're innocent of any wrongdoing, I can't see why you wouldn't want to prove that as soon as possible. Of course, there is an alternative.'

'Which is?'

'I can arrest you, seize your phone, and search your premises.'

Terry bristled. 'On what grounds? You haven't got a warrant.'

'I don't need one,' Caton told him. 'We have you in the vicinity of a serious and ongoing crime around the time said crime was committed and you have twice lied to us about your whereabouts. That amounts to reasonable suspicion that you might be involved in this ongoing crime. It is within my power to arrest you for questioning, to seize your phone and any computerised devices and, in the light of ongoing threats, to search your premises for property and material relevant to the crime in order to prevent damage to property and injury to life or limb.' He turned to his colleague. 'Am I right, DS Whittle?'

'Absolutely, sir,' Carly replied. 'Authority to search under code B of PACE, section 17, and to use appropriate force to do so under subsection 2.12.'

'There you have it, Mr Terry,' Caton said. 'The alternative is that you hand over your phone, come with us voluntarily while we examine it, and then I don't have to arrest you.'

Terry took his phone from his pocket. 'I want it back,' he said. 'I've got my bank cards, GP appointments, and Covid pass on there. Everything.'

Everything was precisely what Caton had been hoping for. He took the phone and handed it to Carly Whittle.

'Don't worry, Mr Terry,' he said. 'You can have it back once we've finished examining it.' He smiled. 'Unless, of course, it turns out to contain evidential material.'

Chapter 30

Nexus House, 10 a.m.

'Boss!'

Caton looked up from the map that he, Nick Carter and Carly Whittle had been studying. Duggie Wallace was seated at his desk, holding up a printout. Terry had been left to kick his heels in an interview room while Duggie connected his phone to an extraction device for a full data download.

'Come on,' Caton said, 'let's go and see what pearls Duggie has for us.'

Duggie handed Caton the A4 sheet. 'It's the geolocation analysis. It tells us he travelled from home to the Northern Quarter, where he parked in a multistorey at 1.50 a.m. He then walked to the vicinity of Gorlay's apartment block, where he hung around until 2.51, when he returned to his car. Then he crossed Great Ancoats Street, drove down Jersey Street, turned left onto Murray Street, left again onto Blossom Street, back up to Oldham Road where he was caught on the ANPR, and then straight home.'

'He didn't stop anywhere in Ancoats?' Caton asked.

'Nope.'

'All this tells us,' Carter reminded them, 'is where the phone was, not where Terry was. It's perfectly possible that during all that time when the phone was stationary, from 1.50 until 2.51, he'd hidden the phone at that location, walked the quarter of a mile to Naval Street, planted the device, made the call, and returned to retrieve his phone before making his way home.'

'It's equally possible,' Carly Whittle said, 'that he has an accomplice, and gave the phone to them to create a

The End Game

fictional narrative while he was somewhere else entirely.'

'Talk about criminal minds,' Caton said, 'I hope you two never take up crime – you'd be a nightmare to catch.'

'Assuming, although plausible, neither of those are true,' Carter said, 'why did he drive back into Ancoats? That would just increase the chances of him being picked up on any one of the CCTV cameras down there.'

'He did say he was pursuing a long shot that the women might have gone there,' Carly pointed out, 'and Blossom Street is where most of the bars are located.'

'True,' Carter said, 'but they're all closed by midnight.'

'If he is our perpetrator,' Caton mused, 'maybe he wanted to see how the fire was doing? He only had to look right as he drove up Bengal Street and he'd have had a clear view down the length of Naval Street to MancVG's offices.' He shook his head. 'But it makes no sense to take all those precautions to avoid detection and then brazenly drive by when he knows emergency services, including the police, are going to be there.'

'Not with uniform's current response rate,' Carter joked.

'You'll want to see this, Boss,' Wallace said.

He eased his chair back to give them a clear view of the monitor screen.

'These are all from his photo library. He's done us a favour by creating a folder specifically for these.'

Caton leaned closer. They were photographs and videos of Mylene Terry. In most of them she was alone, or with female friends. But in a handful, she was with Jake Gorlay. They showed her leaving her car, opening her car and getting in. Arriving at and leaving Gorlay's apartment. One shot caught the two of them leaving a bar in the city centre.

'He's stalking her,' Carter said.

'Legally speaking, he may not be,' Caton reminded him. 'How far back do these go, Duggie?'

Wallace selected the first of the images and clicked on it. He pointed to the date on the menu bar. 'Four months ago,' he said.

'Twelve weeks before Gorlay said he'd ended their affair,' Caton said.

'And this is the most recent,' Wallace told them, 'taken two days ago, the night of the bombing.'

It was a close-up of the exterior of an apartment. All the blinds were closed. The absence of even a glimmer of light suggested that the rooms were in darkness.

'That looks like Gorlay's apartment,' Carter said.

'What time was it taken?' Caton asked.

'At 2.20 a.m.,' Wallace replied.

'That fits the timescale, Boss,' Carly said.

Caton straightened up.

'It also gives him a convenient explanation of why he was in that area,' he said, 'and a bloody good motive for the campaign of extortion, and the attack on the MancVG office.'

'There's nothing on his phone to suggest that he sent any of those threatening text messages, Boss,' Duggie Wallace told him, 'and nothing in his internet search history that relates to the company, or to improvised explosive devices.'

'The perpetrator is using burner phones,' Caton pointed out, 'and, given his job, Terry is well aware of police forensic procedures and data analyses. We need to seize his computer devices and search his property. And thanks to you, Duggie, we have every justification to do so.

But before we do, let's hear what he has to say for himself.'

Chapter 31

'I was embarrassed,' Terry said, 'that's why I lied. I'm sorry.'

On the table in front of him was a copy of the photo he had taken of Gorlay's apartment on the night of the explosion. He pushed it away as though seeking to distance himself.

'Sorry doesn't quite cut it, Derek,' Caton told him. 'This is your last chance to be completely honest with us. To try to convince us that you had nothing to do with the attack on the premises of MancVG.'

That wasn't true, of course. He would have other opportunities to do so, but it didn't hurt to ramp up the pressure, and Caton was banking on the fact that the evidence they had found on his camera had knocked him off balance. Terry placed the palms of both hands on the table.

'Look,' he said, 'it's no big deal, and I was stupid not to have told you from the off. The truth is that I was looking for my wife, not to give her the keys, but because I needed to be certain that she wasn't still cheating on me. I lied to you, because I didn't want her to find out, that's all.'

'That's all?' Caton said. 'We're investigating an extremely serious crime, including potential threat to life. Lying to the police and attempting to hide something that gives you a motive in relation to this crime is not a trivial matter, Mr Terry. Given your current role with GMP, you must have known that.'

'I do,' Terry replied, 'and I can only repeat that I'm sorry and I'll try to put it right by telling you the truth.'

'Very well, ' Caton said. 'Go ahead.'

The End Game

Terry leaned forward. He looked and sounded earnest. 'I began to suspect that Mylene was cheating on me. Just little things – hesitations, over-elaborate accounts of what she'd been doing, patterns of absence from the office when I'd rung her at work to check. I decided to find out for definite. I began following her. That's when I discovered she was having an affair with that bastard Gorlay. When I confronted her, she confessed, not that she had any alternative. Not with the videos and the photos, and the lies she'd told me about where she'd been. She said it had been going on for about six months. That she regretted it. That they both did. And it was already over.'

'When was this?' Caton asked.

'About a month ago.'

'Carry on.'

'Well, I wasn't convinced, so I carried on checking up on her.'

'Did you find out if she was telling the truth?'

Terry shrugged. 'I didn't find out one way or the other. That's why I was still following her.'

'Tell me about the night before last, in as much detail as you can,' Caton said.

'After Mylene left, I watched the TV, like I said. Around twelve thirty, I decided to ring one of her friends to see where they were up to. It was really noisy at her end. She said she'd not seen Mylene for quite a while, but maybe she'd gone to freshen up, or gone outside to cool down. Did I want her to ring me when she turned up? Give her a message? I said no, not to tell her I'd rung – she'd think I was checking up on her. Her mate laughed, and we ended the call. I reckoned I knew where she was, I just needed proof. I drove to the multistorey car park in the Northern Quarter, parked up, and walked down to where Gorlay has his apartment. I stood in a ginnel between two shops where I had eyes on the entrance, the exit from the underground car park, and the front of the apartment.'

'What did you see?' Caton asked.

He shrugged. 'Nothing. The blinds were drawn. No lights on and no sign of life.'

'It was night-time. What did you expect to see?'

The End Game

'One of the windows at the front belongs to the through-lounge and kitchen-diner. The other is the master bedroom. On two previous occasions there were always lights in at least one of the rooms, and sometimes shadows on the blinds.'

'How did you know how the apartment was configured?'

Terry shifted in his seat. 'I'd had a look on the online property sites. There was one for sale in those apartments and another for rent. They were all set out the same way.'

'Carry on.'

'It got late, so I decided to ring her, tell her I couldn't sleep, and I'd pick her up if she wanted.' He grimaced. 'I expected to see a light come on, but it didn't. Then she answered. I could hear the other girls laughing in the background. She told me the party was still going strong and not to worry, she'd get an Uber. And not to wait up for her – she'd no appointments in the morning so she'd sleep in till lunchtime.'

'Let me get this straight,' Caton said. 'You'd wasted half the night hanging around Gorlay's apartment. You had confirmation that your wife was still with her mates. Why didn't you give up and go straight home? Why take a detour through Ancoats?'

'I don't know,' he said. 'When I came out of the car park, I just happened to be facing that way. I'd never been over there that late at night. I just wanted to see if any of the bars were still open.' He sat back and folded his arms.

He'd sounded convincing to Caton, except for that last part. It would have been feasible but for the fact that it was common knowledge that all the bars close at midnight.

'Thank you for finally telling us what we had already discovered,' Caton said. 'I am now going to apply for a warrant to search your premises. In the meantime, I need you to stay here. You can then accompany me to your house to assist us with the search.'

Terry jerked forward, his hands pressing against the edge of the table. 'I've just told you why I was there,' he said. 'You don't have...'

'Let's not go through that all over again,' Caton said holding up a hand to silence him.

He pushed his chair back and stood up.

'I've already explained that a clear motive, together with your presence in the vicinity of a serious crime is more than sufficient grounds for a warrant.'

***

Assistant Chief Constable Gates was not so sure.

'It's a stretch, Tom,' she said. 'Is that why you've come to me? Because you didn't want to risk applying for a warrant yourself?'

'Not at all, Ma'am,' he replied, 'I came to you because you asked me to update you at regular intervals. And, with respect, I don't see it as a stretch. He's lied to us twice, he has a motive, he has military skills that at the very least give some understanding of IEDs, and he's clearly stalking his wife . . .' He could have kicked himself. '. . . Well, strictly speaking, that's not true.'

'No, it isn't,' she said. 'Since his wife was unaware that he was following her, it can hardly have been causing her alarm or distress. He can also claim that his behaviour was reasonable, given that his wife had already admitted to having an affair. After all, if he'd employed a private detective that would have been lawful.'

Caton knew all of that, and having just corrected himself, he didn't appreciate the lecture. He decided to let it go. All he wanted was for her to give the go-ahead. She steepled her fingers and tapped the tips together. It was an annoying habit of hers. He had never worked out if it meant that she was thinking or was simply a way of making him sweat. She placed her palms on the desk.

'Very well,' she said. 'You can go ahead. But make sure it doesn't come back to bite us.'

'Yes, Ma'am.'

He turned and walked to the door.

'And, Tom,' she added, 'you'd better find whoever's behind this before it gets any worse.'

The End Game

Caton didn't need telling.

'Yes, Ma'am,' he said.

Tempted though he was, he closed the door oh so gently behind him, while allowing himself the childish indulgence of whispering . . .

Yes, Ma'am, Yes, Ma'am, three bags full.

Chapter 32

Swettenham, Cheshire, 9 p.m.

Shelley was late. Very late. Not that anyone would know.

The sun had set two hours ago, so it was lucky that Mr Gorlay had solar lights lining the drive up to the house. Mind you, she'd been doing this for so long that she was confident she could find her way in the dark.

She shone her torch on the panel beside the gates, entered the access code, and waited for them to swing open. The gravel crunched beneath her feet as she strode towards the house. A reassuring clunk told her that the gates had closed behind her.

She climbed the sandstone steps, turned the key in the lock, opened the door, and stepped into the hallway. The light came on automatically. She opened the door to the large downstairs cloakroom, entered the code to disable the alarm, stepped back into the hall and called out.

'Buddy, I'm here! Shelley's here!'

Her voice echoed as it travelled along the hall and up the staircase to the floors above. Then, silence. That was weird. Buddy always began barking as soon as she entered the house. She tried again.

'Buddy, it's me!'

She listened intently. Still nothing. She felt the hairs on the back of her neck stand up. She could feel her heart beating in her chest. She called him a third time, stepped back into the cloakroom, and from the umbrella stand selected Mr Gorlay's favourite walking stick, the shepherd's crook with the large ram's head carved in bone. She tiptoed down the hall towards the kitchen-diner and eased the door open. The lights came on automatically.

The End Game

Shelley's eyes were drawn towards the stainless-steel knife block on the marble island. She was relieved to find it full. The door to the utility room where Buddy had his basket, food and water was ajar, as it ought to have been, given that Buddy had the run of the kitchen when alone in the house. She slid her hand down the shaft of the walking stick and gripped it tight.

'Buddy?' she said softly.

Her voice trembled. There was no reply. She edged towards the utility room, raised the stick high, and prodded the door open with her foot. The dog basket was empty. The water bowl was half full. The food bowl had been licked clean. No Buddy. Shelley steeled her resolve and began to search the rest of the house.

Five minutes later, she was satisfied that the dog was not in the building. Had Mr Gorlay or Becky had taken him to work? If so, it would have been the first time and surely they'd have told her? She took out her mobile phone and called Jake Gorlay.

'Shell,' he said, 'what's up?'

'It's Buddy,' she said.

'What about him?'

'I'm sorry, Mr Gorlay,' she said hesitantly, 'but I was a bit late tonight. I wondered...'

'Forget that,' he said. 'What's going on?'

She could tell by the tension in his voice that he could sense there was something wrong. It also meant that Buddy was not with him.

'It's just . . . that he isn't here,' she said. 'I wondered if...'

The air turned blue. She had never heard him swear like this before. The anger in his voice was such that she had to hold the phone away from her ear. But she heard the last thing he said before he ended the call.

'So that's what he meant by "personal"! The bastard!'

Chapter 33

10.30 p.m.

Caton was not happy. The search of the Terry home and outbuildings had proved fruitless. There was nothing to link him to the attack on MancVG's premises. No evidence of bomb-making equipment in the house or the garage at the rear where his motorbike was stored, along with a stationary bike and some home gym equipment. No burner phones. They were still waiting for the analysis of Terry's computer, laptop and tablet, but he wasn't holding out much hope. And, to cap it all, Caton had just arrived home when Jake Gorlay called.

It was far from the first time that he'd needed to turn on his heel and go straight out again. It wouldn't be the last. Kate's patience had worn thin years ago. Since the last Covid lockdown, she had entered that stage of weary acceptance that bordered on indifference. That worried him far more.

Gorlay's house was close to the Swettenham Arms, an iconic sixteenth-century inn, now a gastropub. Caton had eaten in the inn perhaps a dozen times, most of them with Kate before Emily was born, and then with the two of them, combining lunch with a visit to the Quinta Lovell Arboretum which ran from the rear of the pub down to the River Dane.

As he drove into the car park of the pub, he saw Carly sitting on the bonnet of her car.

'Why did you ask me to meet you here, Boss?' she asked.

'You're a detective,' he replied. 'Why do you think?'

The End Game

'Because neither of us have had our dinner yet, and this is your way of rewarding a loyal colleague?'

'In your dreams.'

'Because you don't want us destroying any potential tyre mark evidence with our wheels?'

'Much better,' Caton said. 'Come on, the house isn't far.'

They crossed the car park, turned left down Church Lane, and walked alongside the parish graveyard. Caton glanced at the gilded clock face on the illuminated church tower.

'At this rate we're going to miss supper too,' he said.

'What's that lovely smell?' Carly asked.

'It isn't me,' he replied.

'You don't say?'

'Behind the pub they have a lavender field,' he told her. 'A late summer evening such as this is the perfect time to enjoy it. And I'm told they've added a sunflower meadow since I was last here.'

'That's a shame,' she said. 'I'd love to have seen those sunflowers, but they go to sleep when the sun goes down.'

'Lucky for some,' he said.

Gorlay's home was a large converted Georgian farmhouse, the entire façade lit from beneath the eaves. The gates were open. They trudged up the drive to where a black BMW SUV with personalised plates was parked up by the steps.

'JAK1 MANC,' Carly observed. 'Modesty is not his strongest suit.'

'Ditto frugality,' Caton said. 'You and I could probably have bought a car for what that plate cost him.'

'Speak of the devil,' Carly whispered.

Gorlay was standing in the doorway. His expression was thunderous, a perfect match to his voice. 'Finally!' he boomed. 'What kept you?'

Caton refused to dignify that with a reply. The two detectives climbed the steps, brushed past Gorlay, and entered the hall. Gorlay was not prepared to give up that easily.

'I suppose the kidnap of a pedigree French bulldog doesn't merit a speedy response from GMP?'

Caton turned to face him. 'As I understand it,' he said, 'we don't yet know what's happened to your dog.'

The End Game

'Buddy!' Gorlay said. 'His name is Buddy.'

'Has Buddy gone missing before?'

Gorlay appeared fit to burst. 'No, he bloody hasn't! And he is *not* missing. He's been kidnapped!'

'Strictly speaking, Mr Gorlay, it's dognapped,' Carly Whittle said.

Gorlay turned towards her.

'I take it you've searched the house thoroughly?' Caton said, eager to avoid a confrontation.

Gorlay glared at him. 'What the hell do you think?'

'In situations like this, people sometimes panic. They look in the obvious places, but not everywhere.'

'I'm not *people*,' Gorlay retorted, 'and I don't bloody panic. Of course I searched the house, not that I needed to. Buddy has the run of the ground floor where the motion sensor is tuned to ignore him. But it'll pick up an intruder and all hell will break loose. I'll get a text alert, and the security monitoring station alerts the local nick. The upstairs is fully alarmed. And before you ask, yes, the alarm was on. Our dog walker switched it off when she came in.'

'You checked all of the doors and the windows?' Caton asked.

'The windows were all closed, and the doors were locked. I've checked all of the internal and external CCTV footage. I tell you, nobody's broken in. It's an effing mystery!'

'A locked-room mystery,' Carly observed.

Gorlay glared at her again. 'Duh!' he said.

'Is your dog walker here?' Caton asked.

'Shell? She's in the library. I'll take you.'

Chapter 34

'Library' was a stretch. Three of the walls were covered floor to ceiling with faux bookshelves filled with genuine leather book fronts. The giveaway was wooden door handles behind which, no doubt, there were secret cupboards and a well-stocked bar. A couple of computer monitors sat on the antique desk in the bay window. The dog walker was perched on a sofa, legs tucked up beneath her.

'Shell, this is the police,' Gorlay told the girl. 'Tell them what you told me.'

She uncurled her legs and sat up. She looked pale and anxious and had clearly been crying.

'I'm sorry Mr Gorlay,' she said.

'Not again,' he replied brusquely, 'just tell 'em.'

'Thank you, Mr Gorlay,' Caton said. 'We'll take it from here.'

Gorlay was ready to object until he saw the stern look on Caton's face. 'I'll be in the kitchen ,' he said. 'I suggest you get a shift on.'

Caton waited until the door had closed.

'I'm DCI Caton and this is DS Whittle,' he said, 'and you are?'

'Shelley – Shelley Jones.'

'Okay, Shelley,' he said. 'I can see you're upset, but don't worry, you're not in any trouble. We have a few questions and then you can go home.'

'I'd like to stay and look for Buddy,' she said.

'That's understandable,' Caton told her, 'but we've sent for a dog handler, and they'll stand a better chance of tracking Buddy down if he's still in the vicinity. If we do find evidence that someone's taken him, this will become a crime scene and then we'll have to get a team of crime scene investigators down here. I'm afraid you'd only be in the way.'

She looked close to tears. Carly sat down on an arm of the sofa.

'Shelley,' she said, 'the best way you can help us find Buddy is to answer Mr Caton's questions – do you understand?'

The girl nodded and wiped her cheek with the sleeve of her hoodie. 'Yes,' she replied, 'it's just hard . . . not knowing where he is, what's happened to him.'

'We get that,' Carly said.

'You're Buddy's regular dog walker?' Caton said. 'Is that right?'

She looked up at him. 'For the past three years, ever since he was a puppy.'

'You have a regular routine?'

'Yes. Tonight, I was running late . . . It's usually around eight-thirty in the evening.'

'You don't walk Buddy in the morning?'

'Not unless Mr Gorlay and Becky are both away. Then I come about 8 a.m. and walk him for twenty minutes or so around the fields.'

'And who walked him this morning?'

'Mr Gorlay.'

'Presumably he'll have locked up and set the alarm?'

'He must have. I switched the alarm off as soon as I stepped into the hall. It beeps for twenty seconds before it goes off. I definitely deactivated it.'

'Go on.'

'I sensed straight away there was something wrong. Buddy always starts barking the moment I set foot in the house, he's so pleased to see me. I called out his name, then I went to get him—' she looked at Carly Whittle, and then back at Caton '—but he wasn't there.'

'What did you do then?' Caton asked.

'I searched the house, then I went out into the garden and called his name. He always comes when I call him.

That's when I rang Mr Gorlay.'

'Did you notice anything out of place at all?' Carly asked. 'In the house, the grounds, any vehicles you'd not seen before in the village?'

Shelley shook her head.

'No. There was nothing.'

She began to sob.

Chapter 35

'What do you think, Boss?'

Gorlay had gone to see the dog walker out, and they were standing in the vast kitchen.

'I've never read or experienced a locked-room mystery that didn't have a simple answer,' Caton said. 'You just have to find it.'

'That must be where they keep the dog.' Carly pointed to a room on their left, its door ajar.

'Buddy,' he reminded her, tongue in cheek.

She shook her head. 'Don't you start.'

She walked over to the utility room and pushed the door fully open. Caton peered over her shoulder. It was box-shaped, two metres square. Along one side stood a ceiling-height fridge-freezer, a washing machine and a spin dryer. On the opposite wall was a small sink and a draining board. On the floor against the back wall lay a black and anthracite portable dog kennel with a solid roof and three sides of padded fabric. The mesh blind had been rolled up, revealing a dog bed in the interior. Beside the kennel was an empty stainless steel food bowl and a plastic cube drinking fountain. Higher up on the same wall, around four feet from the ground, was a small rectangular uPVC window. The window was open in ventilation mode, angled inwards leaving a tiny gap at the top and left-hand side.

'There you go,' Caton said. 'Mystery solved.'

'What are you talking about?' Gorlay asked.

Neither of them had heard him enter the kitchen. Caton stepped into the utility room and turned sideways so that Gorlay could see. He pointed to the window.

The End Game

'Was this how you left the window this morning?'

Gorlay frowned. 'Yes. So what? A cat couldn't get in through that space – Buddy certainly couldn't get out, and as for a human...'

'Is it locked?' Caton asked.

'There are three lugs engaged in the bottom of that frame.'

'I can see that,' Caton said. 'But is the handle locked?'

'I'm not sure.'

'Let's find out,' Caton said. 'DS Whittle?'

Carly took a latex glove from her pocket and put it on. She used the thumb and index finger of her right hand to lever the handle downwards, pushed the window completely closed, and then tucked her fingers behind the handle and fully opened the window.

'Hang on,' Gorlay protested, 'that's all well and good from the inside, but there's no way anyone could reach in to open it from the outside.'

'Do you have your mobile phone with you, Mr Gorlay?' Caton asked.

'Why?'

'Humour me,' Caton said.

Gorlay reached into his back pocket and took out his phone.

'Search for "how to open a window at ventilation position from the outside",' Caton said. 'I'm willing to bet that everyone's favourite video site will have an answer for you.'

While Gorlay was entering the details, Carly removed her glove, took out her own phone and began a similar search.

'There's something here, but there are ads first,' Gorlay said. A few beats later, he shook his head. 'Oh no!'

'I've got it too, Boss,' Carly said. She held her phone so they could both watch.

The video showed a pair of uPVC windows in what looked like a kitchen. They had identical handles to the one that Carly had just opened. The righthand window was cantilevered inward just as Gorlay's had been, leaving narrow gaps at the side and bottom. On the outside, a male in his mid-thirties stood with one foot on the sill. He began by threading a cord with his right hand through the gap in

The End Game

the top of the window. Tied to the end of the cord was what appeared to be a piece of cloth with a pocket attached. He fed the cord through the opening until the pocket was level with the top of the upturned handle, then jiggled and lowered the cord until the handle was inside the pocket. Keeping the cord taut, he slid it away from him along the top edge of the window, and then down the righthand side almost to the bottom. With his left hand, he attached another cord to something in the gutter at the top of the frame and pulled the window towards him until it closed completely. Finally, he pulled the cord in his right hand to draw the handle down, pushed the window wide open, leaned in, and roared like a tiger, much to the amusement of the small boy on the inside.

Gorlay looked up.

'It's not the same,' he said. 'That window's two and a half times the size of this one. Even if someone were to open it like that, they'd couldn't get in.'

'They wouldn't need to,' Caton told him. 'Does Buddy have a collar?'

''Course he does.'

'And how strong is that kennel?'

Gorlay was puzzled by the question.

'Very,' he said. 'It's got a steel frame.'

'Well,' Caton said, 'this is what I suspect your enterprising dognapper did. First, he opens the window in the manner shown in that video; second, he calls your dog. If Buddy hasn't already been alerted by the sound of the window opening, he patters in, and finds an arm dangling a treat, or a juicy piece of meat just out of reach. Being enterprising, he climbs up onto the drinking fountain and from there hauls himself onto the roof of his kennel. But the treat is still out of reach. He makes himself taller by stretching his paws up the wall. As he takes the treat, a second hand grasps his collar and hauls him up and through the window. Look closely and you can see the scratch marks where he's scrabbled for purchase.'

Gorlay inspected the wall and then grunted. He turned to face Caton. 'But how come the window was closed and the lugs engaged?'

The End Game

'The thief secures your dog with a lead, then simply reverses the process by which he opened the window. Except that this time he only needs the cord attached to the handle. He ensures that the handle is horizontal, then he pulls the window to, pushes the top so it's at the semi-open position as he found it, and then uses the cord to pull that handle up, at which point the sock, or whatever else he's used, slips off and away. As does he.'

Gorlay stood for a moment, disconsolate. Then he pulled himself together. 'We don't know for certain that's what happened,' he said.

'Let's go and find out,' Caton said.

Chapter 36

Gorlay led the three of them around the side of the house along a raised resin-bonded gravel path. Each of them carried a torch. As they neared the window to the utility room, Caton told him to stop.

'If this is how it was done,' he said, 'there'll be trace evidence. Please wait here, Mr Gorlay. DS Whittle, you're with me.'

Caton stepped down from the path onto the lawn and walked slowly forward, eyes on the grass, until he was a metre or so from the window. Carly drew level with him.

'D'you see anything, Boss?'

Caton crouched down, tilted his head to the side until it was almost level with the surface of the path, and shone his torch across the surface. He straightened up and stepped back.

'See for yourself.'

She bent down. 'You were right,' she said.

'What is it?' Gorlay asked. 'What have you found?'

'There are two faint footprints and one partial footprint under the window,' Caton told him. 'When was your lawn last mown?'

'Saturday,' Gorlay told him.

Caton nodded. 'That figures. There are also some fragments of grass.' He shone his torch across the width and height of the side elevation of the house. 'I don't see any cameras or lights here?'

'That's because there aren't any,' Gorlay responded. 'All the CCTV and motion sensors are on the front and rear of the house where all the entries and exits and large

The End Game

windows are. I didn't think we needed them here and neither did the security firm.'

'Well, your dognapper has clearly done his or her research,' Caton said.

'There are also slight scuff marks that look as though something else was under that window,' Carly said. 'Probably what was used to get the extra height needed to get a foot or knee on the window ledge.'

Caton turned and shone his torch across the lawn. It lit up a wrought-iron bench five metres away on the grass.

'There's your something else,' he said.

'That's not been moved,' Gorlay told him. 'That's where it's always been.'

'Something else we've learned about our thief then,' Caton said, training the torch beam along the ground between the window and the bench. 'He's tidy as well as clever. There are footprints and drag marks where he brought it over here and then returned it.'

'Not so clever,' Gorlay observed. 'He must've known we'd find them?'

'Except that nobody did, not until now,' Caton reminded him. 'Returning the window to its original position gave him an extra few hours' head start.'

He turned and shone his torch across the lawn towards the far perimeter.

'What's out there?'

'A nine-foot-high twin-mesh metal perimeter fence,' Gorlay replied.

Caton thought he heard the sound of a car.

'Beyond that?'

'There's a road. But how are you going to get yourself over a fence like that carrying a twenty-six-pound bulldog?'

Caton didn't answer. Stepping back onto the path, followed by Carly Whittle, he brushed past Gorlay and walked towards the front of the house.

'Hang on!' Gorlay said. 'Where are you going?'

'To have a look for ourselves, Mr Gorlay,' Caton said, 'and then find your dog. Keep everyone away from there – it's a crime scene. I'll be sending a CIS team to gather evidence.'

The End Game

'Becks is going mental,' Gorlay shouted as the two detectives disappeared around the corner. 'If *you* can't find Buddy, I'll hire someone who can!'

***

It was more of a lane than a road, with barely enough clearance for two cars side by side, but they discovered a small passing place cut into the bank supporting the fence. Consisting of a sturdy wire mesh, it stood two and a half metres high. The vertical wires protruded four centimetres over the top of the fence.

Carly clambered up the bank and tried to get a grip on the wires, as well as somewhere to place her feet.

'I can see what he meant,' she said. 'It's almost impossible to find a stable handhold, and there's nowhere to put your feet.'

She jumped down next to Caton. 'As for cutting a hole in it, I'm guessing you'd need some pretty hardcore tools.'

Caton shone his torch up and down the fence.

'Forget the wire,' he said. 'Look at the steel posts.'

They were box-shaped, capped in black plastic. The horizontal wires of the fence were bolted to the post by a four-centimetre vertical strip of steel.

'Everyone forgets the posts,' he said, 'but all you have to do is loop a climbing rope around the top of the post, lean back, and walk up it. When you're close enough, you get one foot on the top, haul yourself up, and jump down the other side, taking the rope with you. I've seen it done in a training video on burglaries at Sedgeley Park.'

'Sounds like the kind of training you might get in the Army Reserve,' Carly said. 'How would you get the dog over?'

By way of an answer, Caton put on a pair of latex gloves, climbed up the bank, and slowly started to make his way along beside the fence, training his torch along the top as he went. Two posts to the west, he stopped. He took a closer look, then turned and shone his torch on the ground and the tree behind him. He placed his torch in his mouth,

The End Game

took out his mobile, and took photos of the top of the post and the tree trunk, then bent to take another one close to the ground. He stood, put his phone away, and retrieved his torch.

'What you do,' he said, with a hint of triumph in his voice, 'is bring a sling with you. When you return, you climb back over the way you came, put something curved over the top of the post—' he bent down, picked something up from the ground, shone the torch on it, and held it up '— like this burst football . . . secure your end of the rope around this tree, haul the dog up, then reach up and lift the dog over and down. Then you remove the rope, put the dog on a blanket in the boot with some treats laced with GHB to keep it quiet, unless of course you'd already done that to the meat, and then drive away.'

He bent down and placed the football where he'd found it.

'Better let CIS deal with this. I've messed up some of the footprints up here, but, in my defence, there are more by the post and the tree, and we do have the ones under the window and on the lawn.'

Caton walked back to where Carly was waiting, jumped down, took his gloves off, and held them up.

'Have you got an evidence bag handy?' he asked. 'Mine are in the car.'

'And mine has got *my* gloves in,' she said.

He couldn't see her face because of the dark but he could tell she was grinning. They began to walk back to the Swettenham Arms.

'Why the photos?' she asked.

'There are rub marks on the tree trunk from the rope,' he told her, 'and what look like dog hairs on the mesh beside the top of the post. There's also a small strip of cloth hooked over one of the wires protruding from the top.'

Now it was Caton who was grinning.

'I hate to burst your bubble, Boss,' Carly said, 'But now all we have to do is find out who those footprints belong to.'

Chapter 37
Day Three
Sunday 4th September

Nexus House, 8 a.m.

'We lifted excellent boot prints from the path, the garden, the fence post, the windowsill, and partials from the wrought-iron seat,' Duggie Wallace told his colleagues at the syndicate briefing. 'They all appear to have been made by the same pair of boots. There were no fingerprints on the burst football, fence posts or the window, suggesting that the intruder wore gloves. We are therefore expecting that those lifted from the chair will prove to belong to the residents or their gardener.

'We already have confirmation that all of the fragments of hair retrieved from along the top of the window frame and the fence were fine short hairs typical of a French bulldog. They were also fawn-coloured, as was the missing dog.'

He looked up from his notes.

'French bulldogs tend to shed their undercoat in the summer to help keep themselves cool. Jake Gorlay's partner had insisted on having the dog's details placed on the local canine DNA database. Some of the hairs that were caught on the wire mesh had roots attached so we should know for certain if they're our dog by the end of today.'

Duggie checked his notes again.

'Coloured fibres were found on the window frame, in the bark of one of the trees, and embedded in the surface of the punctured football. Those on the window frame were a

The End Game

different colour from the rest, but all of them consisted of synthetic polyamide.'

'Nylon,' Henry Powell said. 'Climbing ropes.'

'Possibly,' Wallace said, continuing with his report. 'A small strip of cloth retrieved from one of the vertical steel wires at the top of the fence appears to be camouflage material such as you'd find in clothing from an army surplus store. Soil, grass and pollen samples have been collected from the garden and on either side of the fence.' He looked up. 'If and when we do have a suspect, we'll have a fair bit to go at, forensically speaking.'

'Terry will have plenty of access to camouflage clothing,' DC Nair observed.

'Unfortunately,' the crime scene manager responded, 'not only did we draw a blank on the search of his property, but there was nothing on any of his devices to link him to Operation Sentinel.'

'Nothing?' DS Hulme asked.

'Only photos and data from his phone proving that he's been following his wife. There's nothing sus on his laptop, tablet or PC. No web searches related to video games, in-game betting, MancVG or any of its directors, arson, bomb-making or dognapping. No online store searches for, or purchases of, any of the materials that the perpetrator might have used or that have been recovered. There's plenty of stuff related to his role in the Army Reserve, including online videos, but nothing that relates to this investigation.'

'I asked DI Carter and DS Whittle to pay Mr Terry another early morning call,' Caton told the room, 'in order to check his whereabouts yesterday evening. I also asked them to check his boot size.'

He turned to his case manager.

'Jimmy, where are we up to with tracing the perpetrator's routes to and from Gorlay's house?'

Hulme stood up. 'Cheshire police are conducting a door to door around Swettenham village. They are also looking through any passive media on the properties and the local roads. They've also put an appeal out for any motorists who might have screen-cam footage. It was a

The End Game

stretch persuading them when I mentioned dognapping, but once I'd told them the full story, they were surprisingly cooperative.'

'What about buses or trains, Sarge?' Amit Patel called out.

'The nearest train stop is Plumley Moor. It's a forty-minute walk each way from there. The nearest bus is a twenty-minute walk. Besides, our perpetrator was hardly going to risk using public transport bristling with CCTV.' Duggie raised a hand. 'And before you ask, I've requested the bus and train companies to check their footage, just in case.'

'Thank you, Jimmy,' Caton said. 'Now . . .'

The door opened, and Carly Whittle entered, followed by Nick Carter.

'Just in time,' Caton told them. 'Come and tell us what you've got.'

'Don't hold your breath, Boss,' Carter replied. 'When we explained why we were, there they thought we were taking the proverbial. They insisted we search the place from top to bottom, inside and out, to see for ourselves that they hadn't got the dog. Then Carly asked the wife to step into another room and we interviewed them separately. Terry said he was at work from eight in the morning till five in the evening, which we'd already verified. Then he says he went straight home. He claimed he did a workout in the gym in their garage, and then cooked pasta for when his wife came home. The CCTV footage confirmed that his car was definitely on the drive all that time, but because we still have his mobile here, there's no way of tracking his movements.'

'After work, Mrs Terry was at her gym on the Quays,' Carly Whittle added. 'She arrived home at six forty-five. They both confirmed they'd had a flaming row because of the questions we'd been asking her. She said she'd suspected he was having an affair, and this confirmed it. She threw her dinner at him.' Carly grinned. 'There were still stains down one of the walls. She said he accused her of having the affair with Jake Gorlay and admitted that he knew for a fact because he'd been following her.'

The End Game

She shook her head.

'Thank God they have a choice of bedrooms each with their own flat-screen TVs. There was still a bad atmosphere when we came knocking.'

'I agree,' Carter said. 'I had the feeling it would have kicked off all over again if we hadn't been there.'

'Did you check his boot size?' Duggie Wallace asked.

'He had two pairs, plus his army boots. He's got dainty feet for a tall man. Size eight and a half.'

'The prints we lifted were size eleven,' Wallace told them.

'They were clean as a whistle, his boots, too,' Carter said, 'soles as well as uppers. But there's no way he could have gone to Swettenham and back in that timescale unless the two of them are lying.'

'But if they are,' Carly said, 'he could have slipped through the gate at the end of the garden and taken his motorbike from the garage onto Millgate Lane. But then he'd have needed another vehicle he could use to put the dog in.'

There was suppressed laughter from the back of the room.

'Would you like to share it with us?' Caton said.

Heads turned. One of the new DCs stood up.

'I'm sorry, Boss,' she said, 'I had this sudden vision of a French bulldog riding pillion on a motorbike.'

Now everyone was laughing. Caton found it impossible not to smile.

'You need to stay off the magic mushrooms,' he said.

Chapter 38

Naval Street, Ancoats, 9.15 a.m.

'You might want to steer clear of Jake,' Louie told Nuan. 'He's angrier than I've ever seen him.'

'It's hardly surprising,' she said. 'His dog has been stolen.'

Louie lowered his voice. 'I don't think it's that. Buddy was Becky's idea. It's her dog, not his. I think he's more bothered that his privacy's been invaded.'

'You two!' Jake shouted from the other end of the room. 'What are you whispering about?'

'Nothing important,' Louie replied.

'In that case, get down here so we can talk about what is!'

They went to sit side by side on the sofa, hands resting on their knees, like a pair of naughty children. Jake paced up down behind them.

'I'm sorry about Buddy, Jake,' Nuan said.

'Not as sorry as I am – Becks is in bits. And now this!' He threw his mobile phone onto the sofa beside her.

'What is it?' Nuan asked.

'See for yourself.'

She picked up the phone.

'It's a screenshot of another message,' she told Louie.

'I got it half an hour ago,' Jake told them. 'I've already informed DCI Caton. He's on his way here, for what good it'll do.'

'What does it say?' Louie asked.

Nuan read it out.

The End Game

> ENDGAME Level Three.
>
> Your failure to complete Level Two means that you must now donate £750,000 to the End In-Game Purchases charity within 24hrs of receiving this text. Within the same time frame, you must release a statement on all social media declaring your support for ENDIP, your intention to remove all in-game purchases from your own company's games and call upon the rest of the industry to join you in this mission. Compliance will result in the restoration of your personal loss.
>
> I am The Boss.

Nuan looked over her shoulder at Jake. 'He's saying you'll get Buddy back.'

'Never mind that,' he told her, 'read the next bit!'

She frowned and turned back to the screen.

> WARNING: Failure to complete this task will result in a Level Three multiple material loss sanction.

'What's he going to do next?' Jake demanded. 'Burn our houses down?!'

'It's time we put a stop to this,' Louie said. 'We'll have do as he says.'

'I agree with Louie . . .' Nuan began.

Jake shouted her down. 'No bloody way! Nobody tells me what to do. And who's to say that once we fold, he won't keep upping his demands?'

'But what about Buddy?' Nuan said.

'What about him?' Jake retorted. 'He's a dog, for God's

The End Game

sake. Becks will get over it, especially when I get her another one. And how do we know he isn't already dead? The guy hasn't sent any proof of life.'

His pacing had speeded up. Louie and Nuan were flicking their heads from side to side to keep up with him. On hearing these last words, however, they stared down at the coffee table.

'It's too late anyway,' Jake continued. 'It was made clear from the outset that bartering is not allowed, and all sanctions – once applied – are irreversible. The dog's gone, and there's nothing we can do to get him back.'

Nuan was tempted to remind Jake that there was a way to get Buddy back. He simply had to change his mind and do as The Boss demanded. But even she could tell it would fall on deaf ears.

Jake stopped pacing and stood at the end of the sofa. His colleagues turned to look up at him.

'And another thing,' he fumed, 'no way do any of us ever refer to this arsehole as The Boss. From now on, it's The Turd!'

'Mr Gorlay?' Harriet the temp's timid voice emerged from behind the potted palm.

'Get out here where I can see you!' Gorlay ordered.

She stepped nervously into view. 'I'm s . . . s . . . sorry,' she stammered, 'but the p . . . police are here.'

'Finally!' Gorlay said. 'Well, don't just stand there, show them in. And don't offer them a drink – they won't be staying long.'

They waited in sullen silence. Footsteps approached. Gorlay shook his head.

'Someone needs to teach that girl the difference between singular and plural,' he growled. 'Inspector Gadget is on his own.'

Caton sensed the atmosphere as he entered the breakout space. 'Should my ears be burning?'

'It's your pants should be burning,' Gorlay told him. 'Why did you slope off last night? And where's my dog?'

'We're working on that . . .' Caton began.

'Then you need to work harder, and faster,' Gorlay retorted. 'Did you get the message I forwarded?'

The End Game

'Yes, Mr Gorlay,' Caton replied.

'And?'

'We're doing everything we can to trace the source.'

'Well, it's not happening, is it? Why don't you bring in the National Cyber Security Unit, or GCHQ?'

'Because this is neither cybercrime, nor a threat to national security. They won't touch it, I'm afraid.'

Gorlay's face was beginning to redden. Caton was concerned that he might give himself a stroke. For a millisecond he wasn't sure if that might not be a blessing.

'Arson! Dognapping! And now he's talking "multiple material loss" – whatever that's supposed to mean. What if he's going to blow up our homes? How bad does it have to get before you lot take it seriously? We need protection!'

Caton had a lot of sympathy for him, for them all. He wondered how he would react if it was his home, his family, under this kind of threat. But Gorlay's attitude wasn't helping.

'I assure you we're doing everything we can,' he told them. 'I've already applied for directed surveillance of you, your families and your homes but, given the vagueness of the threat, the number of people and properties involved, and the fact that there's no immediate threat to life or serious harm, I can't guarantee we'll get it.'

'In that case,' Gorlay responded, 'I'll sort it myself!'

That set alarm bells ringing in Caton's head. 'What does that mean?'

'I'm going to call in a private security firm.'

'Please don't do that,' Caton said. 'It would make our investigation so much harder.'

'That's your problem,' Gorlay said. 'If you can't sort this mess, what choice do we have? In fact, why waste any more time.'

He strode past the coffee table and brushed past Caton.

'Where are you going, Jake?' Louie asked.

'To let slip the dogs of war!' Gorlay shouted back.

'That's from *Julius Caesar*,' Nuan said, 'although Jake has forgotten the most important part.'

'What's that?' Louie asked.

'"Cry 'Havoc!'"...' Caton said. '"*Cry 'Havoc!' And let slip the dogs of war.*"'

Chapter 39

Nexus House, 10.20 a.m.

Caton was pulling into the car park when his phone rang. It was Jimmy Hulme.

'Boss, the dog's dead.'

Caton sighed. 'Go on,' he said.

'The body was discovered by a female motorist in the middle of Ashton Road in Bredbury. She carried it to the verge and rang the police. They reckon it had been struck by a vehicle, and then driven over at least a couple of times by other vehicles before the woman stopped.'

Caton knew the answer but asked anyway. 'Are they sure it's Gorlay's dog?'

'There was a brass name tag on his collar, but he was so badly damaged they say the only way to identify him for certain will be from his chip.'

'Bredbury,' Caton said. 'That's, what, fifteen miles from Gorlay's house?'

'Seventeen.'

Caton pursed his lips. 'The questions are, how did the dog come to be there? Was it involved in an accident after escaping? Was it released, and died trying to find its way home? Or was it killed, and then dumped in the road to make it look like an accident?'

'Only a post-mortem will rule the last of those in or out,' Hulme said. 'DI Carter's already requested one. But I was thinking . . .'

'Go on,' Caton said.

'Given the severity of the other charges our unsub is facing, what difference will it make if he was killed first?'

The End Game

'It'll tell us something about the perpetrator. The more we know, the better.'

'Problem is,' Hulme said, 'because of where the dog was found, there's bugger all chance of working out how it got there. It's all industrial estates and farmland. And there's no way we'll get the resources to recover and analyse passive media from God knows how many miles of town and countryside for a dead dog.'

Caton knew he was right. 'Presumably this is what was meant by "personal loss",' he said, 'the burglary and the dog.'

'In a way, that's a relief,' Hulme said.

'What does that mean?'

'Well, let's face it. It could have been a hell of a lot worse.'

'That's true,' Caton responded, 'but try telling that to Gorlay and his partner when you tell them what's happened to their beloved Buddy?'

'No need, Boss – the woman who found the dog has already done that. There was a phone number on the dog's identity tag.'

'That's all I need,' Caton reflected. 'Gorlay will go berserk, and he'll want to know why he had to hear it from a member of the public.'

He was silent for a moment while he pondered their next move.

'I'll need to talk to ACC Gates about issuing an Osman warning,' he said.

'I doubt they'll need us to tell them they're at risk,' Hulme said.

'We still have to go through the motions.' Caton paused. 'Hang on, I've got a call waiting . . . it's Gorlay.'

'Sorry, Boss,' Jimmy Hulme said. 'I'm off. Good luck!'

Caton decided to get in first. 'I'm so sorry, Jake,' he said.

'When were you going to tell me?!' Gorlay yelled. His voice reverberated from the four in-car speakers.

Caton lowered the volume. 'I only found out myself a few...'

'And how come my Becks was told first...?!'

Caton leaned his head against the headrest, closed his eyes, folded his hands in his lap, and let Gorlay rant on.

'She's distraught – in bits! She's blaming me because we've not gone along with this lunatic and given in to all of his demands. And she's terrified. She says there's no way she's staying in that house on her own. I told her she can come and stay at the apartment in town . . .'

That'll rule out the girlfriends for a while then, thought Caton.

'...only she won't have it. She says she's going to stay at her parents' house until you've caught the bastard.' Gorlay paused for breath. 'Are you there, Caton?'

'I'm still here,' Caton replied.

'Good, because I warned you that if you couldn't sort this I would, and I will! In fact, I'm already on it. And you can rest assured that I'll be making a formal complaint about you to the Commissioner of Police!'

'That would be the Chief Constable,' Caton said. 'I believe you're thinking of the Metropolitan Police.'

'Are you taking the piss?' Gorlay said.

'No, Jake, really, I'm not. Believe me, I understand how serious this is, which is why I'm about to seek approval to give each of you an Osman warning.'

'What the hell does that mean?'

'It consists of a formal warning that there is a clear and present threat to life. It comes with advice to be on the lookout for suspicious behaviour, and to consider relocating, albeit temporarily, everyone connected with you and your fellow directors.'

Gorlay's laughter was brittle. 'Bit bloody late for that, don't you think?' he said. 'What we need is protection. I've been looking it up. What about the UK Protected Persons Service?'

'That's a no go, I'm afraid,' Caton told him. 'That service is for witnesses, subjects of honour-based violence, and people helping with the investigation of serious crime.'

'Like a CHIS?'

Caton sighed internally. *Line of Duty* had a lot to answer for. It had undermined the reputation of the police and turned people like Gorlay into amateur detectives.

'Yes. Like a covert human intelligence source. The National Crime Agency will not deem the UKPPS appropriate in this case. However, I'm confident that after what happened to Buddy, together with the latest threat, I'll be given authorisation for directed surveillance.'

'You're too late, Detective Chief Inspector,' Gorlay said. 'You've missed the boat!'

He ended the call, leaving Caton to ponder what that meant, and how much trouble it was going to cause.

Chapter 40

Naval Street, Ancoats, 11.30 a.m.

'Perhaps I should begin by introducing myself,' Linslade said. 'My title is Director of United Kingdom Corporate Security Services Inc. We were established in 1968 and have a track record of over fifty years of successful service, not just in the UK but around the globe.'

Louie and Nuan were impressed. They had been involved in hundreds of video conferences in the past two years and had yet to come across someone as striking in appearance and manner as Alex Linslade. In his late forties, square-jawed, with blond, artfully tousled hair, and wearing a high-end corporate suit, he looked every bit the ex-Lieutenant Colonel in military intelligence and former security manager with a global bank as boasted on his CV.

'We provide extensive personal and corporate services,' he continued, 'including static and mobile surveillance and observation; hard-wired and wireless, covert camera systems; vehicle tracking; computer-based tracking software; computer and IT-based crime investigation, including extortion and fraud. And we have unrivalled expertise in tracing missing persons, as well as providing personal protection.'

He paused to check that they were following the narrative. Happy with what he saw, he carried on.

'In the main, our investigators and security consultants have a background in financial and/or IT services, the Armed Services, and the police. We employ over one hundred former detectives, not just from police forces but also from HM Revenue and Customs, the Border Force, and

The End Game

even the National Crime Agency. Furthermore, we provide a dedicated case manager to work with each client to ensure that their needs are being met.'

Jake Gorlay leaned in towards the webcam. 'Forget the hard sell, Alex,' he said. 'I've read all this on your website. You know from our telephone conversation what our problem is – just tell us what you think you can offer that the police can't.'

Alex Linslade took it in his stride. 'We don't like to see ourselves as in competition with the police,' he replied, 'or to be duplicating their efforts. But we do have an advantage in that our resources can be mobilised much faster.' He smiled. 'We're not restricted by red tape, bureaucracy or competing demands. Put simply, if you can afford it, we can supply it.'

'And in our case,' Gorlay said, 'where exactly do you see the *it*?'

'I would suggest that we identify and cover any gaps in your CCTV at your workplace and at yours and your fellow directors' homes and provide overt and covert human surveillance of both your workplace and your homes. We can install trackers on your vehicles. If any of you feel personally threatened, we can also provide discreet tracking devices for you and those closest to you, including panic buttons. And if either you or the police believe that you may have identified the perpetrators, we can utilise our specialist investigators to help track them down. We can also request, through you, sight of the police forensic report on the explosive device and then request a more detailed analysis by the Defence Science and Technology Service's Forensic Explosive Laboratory at Porton Down near Salisbury. That could tell us more about the skill background or likely contacts of the perpetrator.'

'Won't the police do that anyway?'

'Not necessarily. They may not have the operational budget to cover that.'

Gorlay turned to his colleagues. 'No bloody wonder the police aren't getting anywhere, not if they're that bootstrapped!' He turned back to the screen. 'What about tracing the phone being used to send us these messages?'

Linslade shook his head. 'Now that is one area where the police are better placed to do that within the law, although I understand that your extortionist appears to be using a different single-use burner phone each time, and then disposing of them. And since he only uses text messages, there's no possibility of real-time call tracing. If the police are telling you that the phones are untraceable, then they almost certainly are . . .'

He spotted that Gorlay was about to speak and held up a hand.

'...I do have people who can trawl the Dark Web to look for any link between BlackOp users and your perpetrator. They can also trawl the web and social media platforms for people that may have been taking a particular interest in you and your company.'

Nuan Lau leaned in towards the screen. 'The police are already doing that,' she said.

'Then it's entirely up to you if you want to pay for more "eyes on" in that regard.'

'I think we've heard enough, Alex,' Gorlay said, without checking with either of his colleagues. 'Can you give us five while we discuss your offer?'

'Of course,' Linslade replied. 'I'll go grab myself a coffee, but I'll be right here for the next twenty minutes. After that, you have my number.'

The screen went blank, and they were informed that Linslade had left the meeting.

'I think...' Louie began.

Gorlay placed a hand on his arm. 'Not here,' he said. 'With all that technology, for all we know they could listening in right now – give themselves a heads-up in the negotiations.'

The three of them retreated to the break-out area.

'It's a no-brainer,' Jake said. 'The police haven't got a clue, literally.'

'I'm not sure I agree, Boss,' Louie said.

Jake turned on him. 'Well, let's see if I make your mind up for you,' he said. 'What's your problem with this?'

'For a start,' Louie said, 'we don't have any idea what this is going to end up costing. He's only sent us outline

The End Game

estimates for the surveillance equipment he thinks we might need, and the hourly rates and day rates for everything else.'

'He's right, Jake,' Nuan said. 'It's five hundred pounds a day plus expenses for a single surveillance operative, and a thousand pounds a day for an investigator. To watch this office and all of our properties around the clock seven days a week, as well as watching our backs, will take at least sixteen operatives working in shifts, and double that if they insist on working in pairs. Furthermore, we have no idea how many investigators he might say he needs to deploy. It would be the equivalent of an open cheque.'

Emboldened by Nuan's apparent support, Louie chipped in.

'If it dragged on more than a couple of weeks, it would have been cheaper to pay the two hundred grand the extortionist was demanding at Level One.'

Jake regarded them both with icy disdain. 'You're missing the point,' he said. 'The reason we're going private is to prevent it from dragging on. Besides, it's not just about the money, is it?'

Louie frowned. 'Isn't it?'

Jake flared up. 'No, it bloody isn't! It's a matter of principle! *Nobody* gets away with doing this to us.'

He began pacing up and down the room. Louie and Nuan sat in stunned silence. He stopped and turned on them.

'Besides, we have no idea how far this mad bastard is going to go. It could cost all of us a bloody sight more than money. It could cost us our lives! Do either of you want to put a price on that?'

Nuan was tempted to point out that this was precisely why they should do as The Turd demanded and put a stop to it right now. Despite her emotional agnosia, even she was able to sense that not doing so would be a very bad idea. That fact was even clearer to Louie. Nevertheless, he plucked up enough courage to suggest a compromise.

Five minutes later, Jake Gorlay was back in front of the video screen. Louie and Nuan had decided to leave him to it.

'Alex,' he said, 'my fellow directors and I have decided on a phased approach. How about if we go initially with the

The End Game

CCTV upgrade, and the tracking devices on our vehicles, along with the trawl of the Dark Web?'

'That sounds like a sensible plan,' Linslade replied. 'I'll email you with a firm quote and a contract to sign straight away. In the meantime, I'll set the wheels in motion.'

'One other thing,' Gorlay said. 'I wondered if we might ask you to use your military connections to run a check on someone the police are looking at. Name of Derek Terry? Apparently he's in the Territorials.'

'That would be the Army Reserve,' Linslade told him. 'The Territorials are no more.' His smile was reassuring. 'Worry not, I'll take care of that myself.'

Chapter 41

Nexus House, 3.00 p.m.

'We do have one development, Boss,' Nick Carter said.

There were just three others standing in front of the progress board: Jimmy Hulme, Duggie Wallace and Caton himself.

'We have doorbell CCTV footage from one of Terry's neighbours showing Terry arriving home at half past five last night, and then nothing until he left for work this morning, after we'd finished searching his house. As for him leaving on his bike via Millgate Lane, he doesn't appear on any of the local cameras. The only way he could have avoided them would have been by taking a detour through the park.'

'That would mean him having to lift his motorbike over the locked gates, there and back,' Jimmy Hulme pointed out. 'I know he's fit, but he's hardly The Rock.'

'Who?' Wallace asked.

'Dwayne Johnson, holder of multiple world wrestling titles,' Carter told him. 'Keep up.'

It put Caton in mind of a case fourteen years earlier when the perpetrator had used a specially modified ramp to wheel his first victim over the locked gates of a Central Manchester park. That perpetrator was still alive in a prison hospital, but in a permanent minimally conscious state. As this could not be described as an end-of-life situation or even a terminal condition, the state was not legally able to switch off his life support. The irony was that Caton had actually watched him attempt to kill himself.

'Boss?' Carter said. He sounded concerned.

'Sorry,' Caton said, 'I was thinking.'

'We'll be the judge of that,' Carter quipped. 'Anyway, I was asking if you still have Terry down for this one?'

'I always kept an open mind as far he was concerned,' Caton replied, 'but it's certainly looking unlikely that he was involved in the firebomb or the dognapping. That doesn't mean he's not involved at all.'

'Whether he is or not,' Carter said, 'we do know that he's been a very naughty boy! Tell him, Duggie.'

'The analysis of the hard drive on Terry's computer,' the intelligence officer said, 'revealed that he's been using a colleague's log-in to access ANPR records relating to his wife's car and Jake Gorlay's car.'

'Inappropriate and unauthorised access to information, and use of a colleague's personal password without their knowledge. That's gross misconduct on both counts,' said Jimmy Hulme. 'He'll be suspended and then given the boot.'

'And the Army Reserve will have to be informed,' Carter said. 'They're sure to kick him out too.'

'God knows how he'll react to this,' Caton said, 'or his wife. We know he has a temper. There'll be duty of care issues for both of them.'

'Not our responsibility, Boss,' Carter said. 'That's down to the Professional Standards Branch.'

'We'll need to warn them before we tell his line manager,' Caton said. 'Leave that to me. But so far as Operation Sentinel is concerned, he remains a person of interest. Is that clear?'

'Yes, Boss!' they said in unison.

'Good. Now, as I understand it, the only people who we're aware of having a potential personal motive are Terry and Gorlay's girlfriend, Becky Kerson. We have nothing evidential on either of them?'

'That's correct, Boss,' Jimmy Hulme said. 'Plus she's lost her beloved dog, which pretty much rules her out.'

'What about corporate motive? Where are we up to with Castlefield Digital Creations?'

Duggie Wallace raised a hand. 'Harry Draper, the father,' he said. 'His contacts include associates with criminal backgrounds who are known to Serious and

The End Game

Organised Crime Branch. Their activities include robbery, extortion, handling stolen goods, money laundering and the importation and distribution of drugs. It's feasible he could be paying them to lean on MancVG. Fortunately, Serious and Organised Crime have been running a surveillance operation on these associates, and they have a CHIS. If any of them are involved, it's likely they'd have heard something.'

'That doesn't mean they'd tell us,' Carter said. 'They like to keep their cards to their chests, especially if there's a CHIS involved. They don't want to risk their targets discovering they've got an inside man.'

'Or woman,' said Jimmy Hulme.

Carter couldn't tell if he was joking. 'Or woman,' he said.

'Send me the details,' Caton said, 'and I'll go and see their boss.' He scanned the board. 'Duggie,' he said. 'You were looking for political activists working to put an end to in-game purchases?'

'That's right, Boss,' Duggie said. 'We found several well-organised campaigns, including the intended recipient of the payments being demanded by our unsub. So far, all of them appear to be exactly what they claim to be – peaceful, if vociferous, pressure groups. And all of their named activists have come up clean on the Police National Computer. The chief executive of the End In-Game Purchases charity is on her way here as we speak. She was horrified to learn that her organisation might be linked with a criminal venture, and she can't wait to help us. She hopes to be here by half four this afternoon.'

'Good,' Caton said. 'What about people who might have been seriously affected by in-game purchases?'

Wallace grimaced. 'I've a list as long as your arm,' he said. 'You'll be surprised how many there are. There's even a social media support group. The problem is that while people are happy to share their stories in these groups, they don't always use their real names or provide contact details. But I have been able to link some of them to specific events in news items.'

'How long is the list?' Carter asked.

'One hundred and ninety-eight incidents so far, covering bankruptcy, theft to cover debts, serious mental illness, missing from home, suicides.'

'Right,' Caton said, 'star the most serious, prioritise anywhere there's an obvious military connection, and send me the list.' He turned to his deputy SIO. 'Nick, you and I had better go and prepare for this interview with . . .?'

'Ms Rea,' Duggie said. 'Poppy Rea.'

Chapter 42

4.50 p.m.

Poppy Rea was impressive. In her mid-forties, with short black hair, a square face, and standing at a little over five foot tall, she wore a crisp white shirt and black pinstriped suit that struggled to contain her highly toned physique.

She strode, tight-lipped, down the corridor with an air of impatience. Behind her trailed a man in his early twenties. Tall and slim, with long curly hair, he was dressed like a student. Caton assumed him to be of North African heritage, in all likelihood the Horn of Africa.

Caton showed them into the meeting room. Before he had a chance to introduce himself and Nick Carter, Poppy Rea leaned forward.

'I was surprised and curious when your Mr Wallace said you wanted us to assist you with an investigation,' she said. 'When he told me it was connected with a criminal enterprise that, for some inexplicable reason, is using our organisation's name to extort money from people, I was shocked and horrified. Naturally, I can't wait to prove that the charity has nothing whatsoever to do with this, and to help you put these people behind bars.'

'Thank you,' Caton said. 'How would you prefer me to address you?'

'As Poppy,' she said. 'I find it's much simpler without titles or pronouns and avoids unnecessary embarrassment or offence.'

'Poppy it is then,' he said. 'I am DCI Caton, and my colleague is DI Carter, but in both cases "Mister" will be fine.'

The End Game

He turned his attention to the young man on her left, expecting an introduction. When none was forthcoming, he pressed on.

'To be clear, Poppy,' he said, 'there is nothing at all to suggest that your organisation is involved in any way, other than as an unwitting beneficiary.'

'Of course there isn't,' she said. 'Why would there be? We'd have nothing to gain.'

'Except a great deal of money for the cause.'

She glared at him. 'And a prison sentence! And the removal of our charitable status! Why would I risk any of that?'

Caton held up both hands. 'I understand,' he said, 'and I'm not suggesting for a moment that you would. However, among the thousands of social media responses to your website and publicity videos posted by passionate supporters, there are some that could be described as bitter and vengeful.'

'Have you any idea why I became involved?' she asked. 'Why all of us became involved?'

'No.'

'Because we've all been directly affected by video gaming. There are mothers and fathers whose children became addicted to these games, and there are some whose own lives were all but destroyed by this addiction.'

She looked across at Nick Carter and then back to Caton, to see if they had the faintest notion of what she was talking about.

'Have you any idea of the harm the monetisation of these games has caused... *is* causing?'

'That's not strictly...' Carter began.

Caton placed a hand on his arm. 'I think we should hear this,' he said.

Her expression softened a fraction. 'Very well. I don't wish to waste your time, so why don't you tell me what you know about in-game purchases.'

'As I understand it,' Caton said, 'within many of these games, the player will come across mystery boxes...'

She nodded. 'Loot boxes and bonus buys.'

'...where they can purchase virtual items that will help

The End Game

them to progress faster within the game. Items such as weapons or shortcuts that might give them better protection.'

'Or change the appearance of their avatar,' Carter said.

'They're called skins,' she told them. 'And then there are power-ups, which help improve the gaming experience: changes to the time limits in which to complete each task; the ability to engage in real time with other people playing the same game. On the face of it, these elements appear harmless, and of course the players have the option to ignore them altogether, but in reality that's almost impossible to do.'

'Because?' Caton asked.

'They're specifically designed to entice the players like a bait on a hook. And there's often a lucky dip or mystery element that appeals to children, and to the kind of born risk-takers you'll find in any bingo hall or booking shop, online or otherwise. The immediate gratification that comes from securing something that will give you an edge in overcoming the challenges in the game, the advantage it gives you over other players, the possibility that this will make you a winner, or help you improve on your previous bets – these are the equivalent of sport-enhancing drugs to an athlete. And once the bait is taken, they reel you in. And since you feel no pain, only excitement and empowerment, you keep going back for more until you're well and truly hooked, just like with any drug or addiction.'

She stopped and stared at Nick Carter.

'You seem to be having some difficulty in hiding your scepticism, inspector,' she said. She turned to the young man who had been sitting silently beside her.

'Tell them, Ali,' she said.

Chapter 43

'My name is Ali Hassan Mahamoud,' he began, tentatively at first, but growing in confidence as his story unfolded.

'I am twenty-three years old. I was born in Somalia. Twenty years ago, in 2002, I was brought by two of my uncles as an asylum seeker to the Netherlands. In 2006 I was granted EU citizenship. I came to the UK in 2014 and went to Manchester University to read Business Studies and Economics. During lockdown, in isolation in our rooms, a group of us became hooked on a particular video game, competing against each other, and others, on the internet. I would spend hours playing into the night. I began making in-game purchases to give me an edge, an advantage. At first it gave me a buzz. But then I found myself falling behind my fellow gamers and slipping down the championship tables. I raided more and more loot boxes. I was spending up to seventy or eighty pounds a night. When that made little or no difference to my performance, or my standings, I became depressed. By the end of the second term, I'd squandered most of my student grant. I failed my first year.'

He paused and took a sip from a water bottle he had brought with him.

'I was forced to resit, although the university waived the resit fees because of the disruption caused by the pandemic. I failed the resit and dropped out. I did not tell my uncles, and I was too embarrassed to go home. When I confided in a friend, he told me about EIGP. I was introduced to Poppy.'

He turned to her and smiled. She nodded and smiled back.

The End Game

'Poppy arranged counselling,' he said. 'I received CBT and group therapy. I am now free of my addiction, although I know I can't expose myself to any form of gambling, and I no longer engage in video gaming. Poppy spoke to the university on my behalf. They told her that I was far from the only student whose studies had been affected in this way. They agreed to allow me to resit my first year.'

He paused and took a deep breath.

'Without the help of Poppy and EIGP, I truly believe I would have taken my life.'

'Ali is now working with us,' Poppy Rea said, 'helping to warn other students online, on campus and in local schools, including primary schools, because these games can normalise gambling among very young children. We have several parents in our organisation whose children maxed out their credit cards to the tune of over a thousand pounds – children under ten years of age. And there are instances of young children and teenagers running away from home because they've been stealing from their parents to feed their obsession and are too ashamed or frightened to tell them.'

'I understand that there have been incidences of suicide and attempted suicide among video gamers?' Caton said.

'Too many!' she responded. 'Research tells us that more than sixty thousand eleven- to sixteen-year-olds are addicted to some form of gambling, primarily as a result of addiction to video gaming.' She became increasingly impassioned. 'As many as ten per cent of suicides in the UK are related to gambling! That's over six hundred and fifty deaths per year. Gambling addicts are twenty-five per cent more likely than any other kind of addict to commit suicide. There have even been examples of young children killing themselves, simply because they lost a game to which they had become addicted. So you'll understand why, in May 2017, "gaming disorder" was included as a behavioural addiction in the World Health Organisation's International Classification of Diseases.'

She took a breath to calm herself.

'I'm sorry,' she said, 'I know I've gone on at length, but if you're looking for someone who has a reason to support us, and at the same time bring video game purchases and gambling to an end, you won't be spoilt for choice.'

'I do understand now,' Caton said, 'and it's not going to make our investigation any easier.' He paused while he thought about how best to put what he had to say next. 'Our strong advice to the directors of MancVG is that they should not give in to these demands, but I'm afraid, Poppy, that the police have no control over what they decide to do. So, and please don't take this the wrong way, I'm obliged to advise you that acceptance of any donations to your organisation made under duress will leave you open to prosecution as an accessory.'

'There is no way,' she said, 'that any registered charity is going to accept donations that are the result of criminal activity. In any case, everything goes through the banks, and every year we have two separate audits, plus Charity Commission checks. I'll see to it that any such donations are immediately returned, providing you can assure me that they're associated with your investigation.'

'Please don't do that,' he told her, 'just acknowledge receipt of the funds, and place them in some kind of holding account until you hear from us. That way the perpetrator will believe that his or her demands have been met, they won't retaliate against the company, and we'll have more time to track them down.'

'Very well,' she responded. 'After all, whatever the outcome, this will still shine a light on the negative aspects of online gaming.'

Caton eased back his chair and stood to signal an end to the interview.

'Thank you for coming in,' Caton said to his visitors, 'and please don't hesitate to contact me if you think of anything that may assist our investigation.'

He turned to the young student.

'And thank you for sharing your story with us, Ali. I can't begin to imagine how difficult that must have been. Good luck with your studies, although after all you've come through, and the manner in which you've conducted yourself today, I know you'll smash those exams this time round.'

The End Game

'Thank you, sir,' the young man replied. '*Allah yubarik fik w bieamalik.*'

'May God be with you, and with your work.'

Chapter 44

When Carter returned from showing them out, he found Caton standing in the corridor outside the incident room, watching their visitors as they crossed the car park.

'Does this mean you're going against standard policy, Boss?' Carter said.

'How do you mean?' Caton asked.

'Advising them to go along with his demands, and then telling the charity to squirrel the money away until we've got our perpetrator?'

'Well, it's an option we should have considered sooner. Policy says we advise against handing over any money, but where the victims go ahead and pay, we follow the money as far as we can. This, however, isn't your average extortion. We know exactly where the money is going to end up, and since the recipients know they'll have to give it back, we can retrieve it whenever we want.'

'The perp must have thought of that?'

'Not necessarily, but if he has, that might explain why he's also insisting on the public statements, and the removal of the in-game purchases. I'm beginning to think this is more about those demands than it is about the money.'

'Then why demand the money transfer in the first place?'

'I have no idea, other than it would still be helping the cause. The whole thing smacks of desperation, Nick. Experience tells us that desperate people aren't only dangerous but also irrational. We have to think like them, outside of the box.'

Poppy Rea unlocked her car. She rested her hand on the roof of the vehicle for a moment and gazed back at the building, then opened the door and ducked inside.

The End Game

'What did you make of her, Boss?' Carter asked as the car drove off towards the exit.

'She's passionate about what she's doing. Determined to protect the victims she's trying to help. Uncomfortable about the position in which the perpetrator has placed both her and the charity.'

Carter grunted. 'That's no excuse for her manners. More *Stroppy* than Poppy if you ask me.'

He turned and opened the door to the incident room.

'That's exactly what you need to be in a job like hers,' Caton told him. '"Those who conquer others are strong; those who conquer themselves are stronger." Lao Tzu, Chinese philosopher, sixth century BC. Except that he used the masculine pronoun.'

'"He who is slow to anger is better than the mighty",' Carter responded.

That stopped Caton in his tracks. 'Where did that come from?'

Carter grinned. 'Proverbs – as in the Bible? No idea who, or when, but "he" was obviously pre-woke, like your guy. It was on a poster a man was waving at those climate activists in Piccadilly Gardens. One of their women used a loudhailer to shout back at him: "Those who are slow to anger have lost before they start." Also from the Bible, I think. I thought that was mint.'

'Don't tell Gorlay,' Caton said, 'it'll only encourage him. Speaking of which, I'm going give him a call, and see if he's calmed down. I'd like you to get together with DS Hulme so you can update each other. When I join you, I want to know exactly where we're up to.'

***

It took less than five minutes for the three of them to discover that there had been no meaningful progress since they had last met.

'Right,' Caton said, 'Gorlay isn't for budging. He's also employing a private global surveillance and investigation agency.'

His three colleagues groaned in unison.

'Exactly,' he said. 'But when it all goes belly up, we can't afford to be accused of simply issuing Osman warnings and then walking away and leaving them to it. I've decided that while I wait to hear back on our request for directed surveillance, I'm going to arrange drive-by surveillance on their properties. What are we looking at exactly?'

'Are we talking just the directors and their families?' Jimmy Hulme asked.

'I think so. There's no evidence of a threat outside that circle,' Caton replied, 'and besides, we'll be stretched as it is.'

'In that case,' Hulme said, 'Gorlay has the place in Cheshire, the one in the Northern Quarter, and his partner has a pad on the Quays. Ellish lives with his parents in Barlow Moor, and Lau has an apartment overlooking New Islington Marina.'

'You're forgetting Lau's partner and her son,' Caton said. 'They live on a houseboat on the marina.'

'We can hardly drive by that,' Carter pointed out, 'or the place on the Quays.'

'No, but whoever's covering Lau's apartment can park up and walk down to the marina from time to time,' Jimmy Hulme pointed out. 'Ditto the place on the Quays.'

'Two cars, each with two upfront working in shifts,' Caton said, 'should be enough to cover the Manchester properties every hour from 9 p.m. till six in the morning. As for the mansion in Swettenham, I'll see if I can sweet-talk my contacts on the Cheshire Force to have a patrol car drive slowly past, as and when they can – more as a disruptor than anything else.'

'That'll leave plenty of opportunity for the unsub,' Carter said.

'Can't be helped,' Caton replied. 'It's better than nothing, and we'll have been seen to have acted proportionately. Besides, if Gorlay is serious about employing a private firm, that'll let Command off the hook in terms of providing directed security.'

'Only one problem with that scenario, Boss,' Jimmy

The End Game

Hulme said. 'Our lot could end up tripping over this firm's operatives and vice versa.'

'Looking on the bright side though,' Nick Carter said, 'that'll make it crowded for the perpetrator too.'

Caton checked the MIR wall clock. 'I'm going to talk to Cheshire,' he said, 'then I'll nip home, grab some dinner, and get my head down for a few hours. I'll come back later and join the night detective.'

'That'll be DS Whittle,' Jimmy Hulme told him. 'I'll stay on here till she relieves me.'

'In which case,' said Carter, 'I'll get off home too. I'll come in early in the morning.'

'It's going to be a long night,' Caton said. 'We can't get any surveillance in place before the morning, and I have a nasty feeling that our unsub won't be holding back until we do.'

Chapter 45

Millgate Lane, Didsbury, 6.55 p.m.

'Emily's been running a temperature all day,' Kate said. 'Doctor Jimmy thinks it's a strep A infection. He's given her antibiotics, and I put her straight to bed.'

Caton's heart began to race. 'Is she alright?' he said.

'She's fine. Apparently, we caught it early and he said we just need to make sure she's hydrated and keep an eye on her.'

He threw his jacket over the newel post and put his hand on the banister. 'I'll just go up and check on her.'

Kate reached out and held his arm. 'You'll do no such thing. You'll only end up disturbing her. Come and have your dinner. I've put Alexa by Emily's bed, and an Echo on the kitchen table. If Ems so much as stirs, we'll know.'

Reluctantly, he followed her into the kitchen.

'Wash your hands and sit,' she said. 'Fortunately for you, when you rang to say you were on your way, I'd not eaten yet, so we can have this together. It'll make a nice change.'

Caton chose to ignore the barb and concentrated instead on washing his hands in the sink. He rinsed, then looked around for a towel. Seeing none, he reached for the tea towel. Kate spun round and rapped his knuckles with a wooden spoon.

'Ouch!' he said, rubbing the back of his hand. 'I'd forgotten you had eyes in the back of your head.'

She lifted the hand towel from the back of the chair beside her and lobbed it at him. 'Here,' she said, 'And hurry up, it's going cold.'

The End Game

In the centre of the table was a large bowl of spaghetti bolognaise. Beside it was a wooden bowl full of mixed salad leaves dressed with olive oil, balsamic vinegar and parmesan shavings. Next to that stood a bottle of Valpolicella Ripasso. No further encouragement was required.

Table cleared, dishwasher loaded, they sat facing each other. Glass of wine in hand, replete after a comforting meal, this was Caton's favourite time of the day. More so, as Kate had been at pains to remind him, because it was an increasingly rare occurrence. Kate took a sip, savoured the wine, and placed her glass on the table.

'Unsub,' she said. 'Unidentified subject. It's so American, Tom. What's wrong with "suspect"?'

'Because we can't call them suspects until we know who we're talking about. The two are separate, until they merge and become one. Then we use "suspect".'

'Got it,' she said. 'So, what is it you *do* know, or think you know, about this person?'

'I have no idea if we're looking at one person, a conspiracy, or a common enterprise,' he replied.

'Regardless of which it is,' she said, 'in matters of coercion there's almost always one person pulling the strings. Let's start by working on that assumption. You tell me what you know about that person. And to keep it simple, let's just assume it's a man because it usually is. Tell me what you think you know about him. One attribute at a time.'

Caton swirled the wine in his glass, ordering his thoughts as the liquid settled. 'He's intelligent.'

'How do you know?'

'Because of the way in which he issues his threats and has tailored them to his intended victims. And because the tactics he's using to convince them that he's serious show meticulous research and psychological insight.'

Kate nodded her approval. 'Okay, and?'

'He has considerable experience . . .'

'In blackmail or extortion?'

'That's for you to decide,' he said. 'I'm referring to the manufacture and placement of an improvised explosive device, his ability to avoid CCTV and other passive media surveillance, and his use of burner phones.'

The End Game

Kate arched her eyebrows. 'Surely, anyone able to use a computer, watch a crime series, follow criminal proceedings on the news or in the papers, and use their eyes when checking out somewhere they intend to commit a crime, could manage all of that?'

'In theory. But to put it all together in the way he's done requires a lot more than knowledge. It takes intelligence and cunning, and a degree of confidence that only comes with experience.'

'That's two other things you know about him...' Kate said, '...or them. Despite what I said, this could be a single puppet-master and several others, each with their own skills to bring to the party.'

'Is that likely?'

She shrugged. 'I'll reserve judgement. What else have you got?'

'He's mobile. It's just over twenty miles from the city centre to Swettenham, which is where Gorlay's Cheshire mansion is, and he must have used something like a van to put the dog in.'

'The Swettenham Arms!' Kate declared. 'When are you going to take us back there? We could go for lunch next Saturday. Emily loves the arboretum and the wildflower meadow. Harry could come too.'

'Just as soon as you've helped me put Operation Sentinel to bed.'

She tutted and shook her head. 'That could be classed as coercive control.'

'I don't think so,' he retorted. 'As I recall, you volunteered to help.'

Kate took another sip of wine. 'Fair enough,' she said.

She put her glass down again. He could tell from her expression that she was going into lecture mode.

'When you first told me about this case,' she began, 'I had a quick look at what the research has to say about extortion. Most studies place blackmail, extortion and coercive control in a domestic setting, and the use of threats to deter others from a course of action, under the same lens.'

'I don't follow,' Caton said.

'These are all forms of coercion, Tom. No different

The End Game

from that used in diplomacy: essentially, it's all about threats and ultimatums. Think Putin and Ukraine.'

'I'd rather not.' He raised his glass and took a mouthful of wine.

'They all involve,' she continued, 'the use of threats to influence another person's choice of action. It takes the form of a game, albeit a hostile one. Have you heard of the term "payoff matrix"?'

'No.'

She grinned. 'Consider it a gift. You can use it to impress next time you're at one of those Command meetings where they spray the acronyms around. The payoff matrix consists of the person issuing the threats – let's call him the controller – and a victim. The victim is presented with just two choices: to comply or to resist. If the victim chooses to resist, the controller has two choices: to accept and withdraw, or to punish the victim. The controller's challenge is to make the threat plausible. In other words, to convince the victim that the sanction can and will be carried out if they resist. That is because most threats are by their very nature implausible.'

'How so?' Caton asked.

'If you think about it,' she said, 'most threats appear irrational in that they carry a considerable risk for the controller. The risk of being caught, and the cost of executing the threat. So, to convince the victim that the threat is credible, he'll use one or more of the following methods: firstly, convince the victim that he – the controller – has no choice but to carry out his threat; secondly, convince the victim that to comply would be the rational choice; thirdly, by introducing ever more threatening forfeits for non-compliance; and, finally, by appearing to be irrational.'

Tom nodded. 'Like Putin.'

'Exactly. He wants people to believe that he has right on his side, that his cause is just, and at the same time appear sufficiently unstable for his victims and their allies to believe that he is capable of anything, however irrational.'

'I can relate all of that to our unsub,' Caton said. 'He calls himself "The Boss", so that's your controller. The fact that his demands involve supporting a charity and discarding what many would regard as unethical business practice, gives him the moral high ground; he's using progressively more costly forfeits; the whole enterprise will certainly be costly for him when we catch him; and nobody would describe his actions as rational. To some extent, it's working.'

'How do you mean?' Kate said.

'I believe he's already split his victims into two camps. Gorlay is adamant that he's not going to submit, whatever the cost, and I get the sense that both of his fellow directors would rather comply and move on.'

Kate nodded. 'I'm not surprised. The unsub does present a compelling and apparently unselfish motive. And in this case, there may even be a payoff for the victims, in terms of marketing themselves as an ethical enterprise – an initial loss of capital versus higher revenue over time.'

'That's what one of his directors intimated,' Caton said. 'But I can hardly be seen to be encouraging them to surrender to a serious criminal, whatever his motives.'

Kate drained her glass and stood up. 'That's your key, Tom: find out why he's wedded to this cause. What's really driving him. That's when you'll be able to turn your unsub into your prime suspect.'

Chapter 46
Day Four
Monday 5th September

Barlow Moor, 3.50 a.m.

'This is not what I signed up for,' grumbled Detective Constable Gadd. 'I was told I'd be working on the juiciest investigations from that backlog of unrecorded crimes, not driving round and round the city in ever-decreasing circles.'

'Tell me about it, mate,' DC Franklin responded. 'Mind you, it's a relief from sitting staring at a screen, trying to tell one stray dog from another.'

'Hang on!' said Gadd, placing one hand on the dashboard. 'We may have something here. Pull in behind that Beamer. Not too close in case he decides to reverse into us and speed off.'

'You've been watching too many police documentaries, you,' Franklin said as he pulled into a resident's parking space, leaving a Mini Clubman between their unmarked car and the BMW.

'Is that one or two upfront?' Gadd asked. 'I couldn't tell because of the passenger headrest.'

'Two, I think. They weren't there on our last pass.'

Gadd was already entering the BMW's registration number into the Police National Computer. The result was almost instantaneous.

'The model and colour's right,' he said. 'Registered owner, Wilfred Owen; address in Richmond, Surrey. No markers on it.'

The End Game

'Wilfred Owen? Wasn't he one of those war poets?' Franklin said. 'We did him for O-Level.'

'Lucky him,' said Gadd. 'I'm calling it in. I'll make sure backup's on hand just in case.'

Franklin waited until he'd finished the call. 'What do you reckon,' he said, 'shall we wait for backup or check them out?'

'Let's do it,' said Gadd. 'What is it they say – your car's your coffin? Besides, why else do you think Caton authorised Tasers?'

Gadd took the pavement, Franklin the road. They had their IDs in their left hand, their right hand resting lightly on their Taser. They had both drawn level with the front seat headrests when the driver saw Franklin in his mirror. His head whipped round. Franklin stepped slightly away from the door and showed his ID. Gadd tapped on the passenger window and did the same. A woman in her late thirties stared back at him. Franklin gestured for the driver to lower his window.

'Good morning, sir,' he said, 'may I see your driving licence? And could your passenger please show my colleague some identification?'

'Certainly, officer,' the driver replied, seemingly unperturbed.

He reached inside the left breast pocket of his leather jacket. Franklin's right hand stiffened around the Taser. The driver handed him a driving licence.

'James McIntyre,' Franklin read. 'Is this your car, sir?'

'Yes,' the man replied.

'Then can you explain why your name is not the same as that given by the DVLA as the registered owner of this vehicle?'

McIntyre smiled. 'That would be Wilfrid Owen,' he said. 'All of our vehicles, for security reasons, show the registered owner as one of our directors. In this case, I am the registered keeper.'

'"Our" cars?' Franklin said.

'United Kingdom Corporate Security Services Inc.,' Gadd said, waving the ID the passenger had handed him.

The End Game

'And thank you, officer, for blowing our cover. Now we'll have to do a switch with one of our other teams.'

Franklin silently cursed his colleague for not having mentioned the registered keeper entered on the police database.

'You blew your own cover when you failed to inform our FMIT that you were watching these premises,' Franklin told him as he handed back the driving licence. He gestured to his colleague. 'Come on, Mark,' he said, 'let's leave these clowns to it.'

As the two detectives returned to their car, McIntyre and his partner got out of their vehicle. McIntyre began stretching his cramped limbs, and his colleague reached for her vape.

'Corporate Security Services?' Franklin observed as he pulled his door to and began to buckle up. 'Wouldn't pay them in brass washers.'

That was when the bomb went off.

Thirty metres away, on the opposite side of the road, the bonnet of Louie Ellish's parked car now lay across the windscreen. Smoke and flames billowed from the engine compartment.

'I'll call the fire service!' Franklin shouted over the sound of multiple alarms, 'and then I'll call it in.'

'I'll get the fire extinguisher from the boot,' Gadd said, as he exited the car. 'Much good it'll do.'

Chapter 47

Princess Road, City Centre South, 4.01 a.m.

Caton was on his way to Barlow Moor when Carly Whittle rang.

'Boss,' she said, 'there's just been an explosion in the garage under Gorlay's apartment block. One of the security firm's private detectives rang it in. He's called the fire service. What do you want me to do?'

'I'll take it,' he said. 'I'm the closest. You get down to Barlow Moor and secure the scene. Before you do, call DCs Powell and Nair and get them over to Gorlay's place.'

'What about Nuan Lau – someone should warn her?'

'As far as I'm aware, she doesn't have a car. And those apartments have CCTV all over them. You call her. Tell her to keep her head down and her wits about her. I'll get over there as soon as I've finished at Gorlay's.'

He was approaching the Greenheys junction.

'Got to go,' he said. 'Stay in touch.'

The lights were on red. Caton switched on his blues and twos and did a tight U-turn onto the northbound carriageway. Mercifully, the roads were almost empty, just the occasional white van delivering wholesale into the city centre. Within three minutes he was in the Northern Quarter, pulling in behind a fire tender.

***

Uniformed officers were trying set up a cordon on either side of the apartments, while simultaneously urging

The End Game

anxious residents, some in hastily donned coats, others still in dressing gowns and pyjamas, to move back. As Caton approached, he could see hoses from another fire appliance snaking down the slope into the garage basement, from where a cacophony of car alarms shattered the early morning calm.

On the pavement immediately opposite the apartments, Jake Gorlay was haranguing two men. They wore identical black zipped leather jackets over matching chinos and black leather trainers. It didn't take a genius to recognise a pair of corporate private investigators. It wouldn't have surprised Caton if they'd also worn black shades and an FBI logo on their backs.

'I don't believe you!' Gorlay shouted. 'I arrived home at eleven oh five. If you'd been here like you say, I'd have seen you, and you'd have seen who blew my bloody car up!'

'As for the first, Mr Gorlay,' the taller of the two men replied calmly, 'it's our job to remain inconspicuous. And as for the second, we've already told you that nobody entered that garage from the street after you'd parked the car. Furthermore, nobody left the garage after your car disappeared and the roller door came down.'

Caton approached them, holding up his ID.

'Detective Chief Inspector Caton,' he said, addressing the two men. 'And who exactly are you?'

'These jokers are supposedly the expert private investigators I'm paying megabucks for!' Gorlay said. 'Come to that, Caton, where were your lot when I needed them?'

'Roger Lever, United Kingdom Corporate Security Services Inc.,' the taller man told Caton, reaching in his jacket for his ID.

'Marshal Knobbs,' the other one declared, holding up his own photo card.

Gorlay laughed. 'Marshal must be some kind of joke,' he said, 'but Knobbs, I get.'

'What time did the explosion take place, Mr Lever?' Caton asked.

'Four o'clock on the dot,' the man replied.

Almost certainly simultaneous then.

The End Game

'I think you'll find you owe Mr Lever and Mr Knobbs an apology, Mr Gorlay,' Caton said. 'Yours was not the only car targeted this evening. A similar explosion damaged Mr Ellish's car – two devices, several miles apart, at exactly the same time. Unless there was more than one perpetrator, I think we can rule out radio-controlled signals. Both devices could have been planted well in advance and detonated by a timer or a mobile phone notification.'

Despite the glare of the sodium streetlight, Gorlay's face visibly paled and his shoulders slumped.

'You're saying I've been driving around with a bomb under my car? It could have gone off anywhere and blown me to smithereens!'

Caton took Gorlay's arm and steered him away from Lever and Knobbs.

'I need you to stay here,' he said, 'and think about every location where your car was parked unattended, for however short a period, over the past twenty-four hours. One of my team will be with you shortly.'

'You're mad if you think I'm staying here,' Gorlay replied.

'You're probably safer here now than at your place in the country,' Caton said. 'Besides, the sanction referred to "multiple material loss", which seems to have been achieved. There's no suggestion that your life or physical safety is at risk.'

'You reckon?' Gorlay responded. 'What if they'd got it wrong. What if it had gone off when I was doing eighty on the motorway?' He began to walk away. 'I'm off to a hotel,' he said, 'and one of you—' he pointed at one of the private detectives '—can make sure no one's following me!'

'I'll need those locations for your car,' Caton shouted after him.

'I'll text them!'

'And I'll need to know your whereabouts. We'll need to meet with you and the other directors in the morning.'

Jake flicked his hand in the air. 'Whatever,' he said.

As Caton walked back to his own car, he received a call from Carly.

'Boss?'

The End Game

'How bad is it?' he asked.

'Ellish and his parents are fine. Just a bit shocked as you'd expect. Franklin and Gadd saw it happen. They were just leaving. The bloke and the woman from the private security firm Gorlay hired to watch the house came off worse. They'd just got out of the car to stretch their legs when the bomb went off. The blast was contained under the engine compartment of Ellish's car, but the security guy tripped over the pavement and twisted his ankle, and his partner cut the roof of her mouth on the stem of her vaper.'

Caton couldn't help but smile at the thought.

'I know,' Carly said, as though reading his mind. 'I had trouble keeping a straight face when they told me. According to Franklin, the car looks like it's a write-off because it'll have destroyed the engine, gearbox and transmission. What's it like where you are, Boss?'

'Much the same but without the histrionics. Except for Gorlay. He threw his toys out of the pram and left. Can you ask Ellish to give you a list of everywhere that car's been in the past twenty-four hours?'

'Already on it,' she said.

'And tell Ellish we'll be beefing up the surveillance, regardless of what that security firm is doing.'

'Will do. Hang on, Boss, SOCO have just arrived, and a white van. Right... it's the bomb squad. I'd better go.'

'Stay away from that car until they've checked it for secondary devices,' he told her, but she had already gone.

Chapter 48

New Islington Marina Apartments, 6.35 a.m.

Caton pressed the bell and waited. He detected voices coming from inside, stepped back a foot or so and raised his ID closer to the spyhole. He heard a bolt slide back, a chain removed and a latch lifted. The door opened.

A tall black woman in her late twenties was standing there, her expression guarded, and her feet planted firmly on the ground. She wore a red sports hoodie, black yoga tights and training shoes, and in her right hand was holding a rubber-coated dumb-bell.

The partner, Thelma Dundas, Caton guessed, although he wasn't prepared to risk her ire by assuming so. Nuan Lau saved him the trouble. She appeared at the woman's side.

'It's okay, Tee,' she said, 'it's Detective Chief Inspector Caton.'

'You can't be too careful,' her partner said, stepping aside to let Caton in. She pulled the door to behind him. 'Anyone can wave a false photo ID.'

'Very wise, Ms Dundas,' Caton said.

'Thelma,' she retorted. 'I don't do titles,' echoing what Poppy Rea had said to him the previous afternoon. Simple discourse had become a minefield. Difficult enough for him, but he had no idea how anyone in the force over forty was going to avoid giving offence, let alone the misogynist dinosaurs.

Lau led him into the lounge. It was a lovely apartment, identical to the one that he and Kate had shared until Emily had come along eight years ago. Eight years? He wondered where all those years had gone and wished there was a way

The End Game

he could put a brake on the passage of time.

Lau sat on the sofa while her partner, arms crossed, remained standing.

'Tee,' Lau said, 'why don't you go and get Mr Caton a drink? What would you like, Mr Caton: tea, coffee, water?'

It was an obvious ploy to leave the two of them alone, one that Caton was happy to go along with.

'Hot water would be fine, thank you,' he said.

'Don't take any nonsense, Nu,' Dundas retorted. 'This has to be sorted.'

She stalked into the kitchen, half hidden behind a hand-painted room divider depicting a smiling Buddha and two temples.

'Please sit down, Detective Chief Inspector,' said Nuan Lau, 'and don't mind Thelma – she's only anxious for me, though I've told her there's no need to be. I don't have a car because I can't drive. I do have an electric scooter that I keep here in the apartment. I don't think anyone would be so foolish as to break in to blow that up, not with all the CCTV in these apartments.'

Caton could see that she was serious. Jokes were not part of her mindset.

'I'm sure that's true,' he said, 'but your partner is wise to counsel caution. We have no way of knowing what else this person, or persons, may have in mind.'

'Which is why I've tried to convince Jake that we should comply and remove the threat entirely. I believe it would be the most pragmatic and ethical thing to do.'

'You'll understand that I can't be seen to be colluding with a criminal enterprise,' Caton responded, 'but I would be interested to know why Mr Gorlay disagrees so vehemently?'

'I think it's because he feels the need to prove himself,' she said. 'He always has to be a winner. To never show weakness. I think it's something to do with the way his father treats him.'

'And yet his father, like yours, invested in the company, and Jake was happy to accept his money?'

'As a loan, yes. His father saw the money as an investment; he attached strings that meant it would be paid back with interest.'

The End Game

'You said "the way his father treats him". What did you mean by that?'

'On the few times I've seen them together, there's always been an atmosphere. I believe Jake's father takes pleasure in humiliating his son in public.'

Caton could see how that might go a long way to accounting for Gorlay's pig-headedness and short temper. But he wanted to find out a little more about Thelma Dundas before she brought the drinks through.

'Tell me about your partner,' he said. 'You met at university?'

Nuan launched, as he had hoped, into a cross between a Wikipedia entry and a dating app. She began by correcting him.

'The University Library Service, where she's a senior administrator. I was searching for a scholarly article on fifth-generation advanced game design. Tee helped me find the article and showed me where I could refill my water bottle with filtered water. We share a passion for reading and cooking Asian food, and we're both vegan. Thelma has a ten-year-old son, Langston. He's amazing. Profoundly deaf and dumb from birth due to an acquired congenital recessive gene from his absent father, he has never allowed that to define him.'

Thelma Dundas appeared, carrying a plain white mug, which she handed to Caton.

'Which is why,' Thelma said, 'Langston doesn't deserve to be placed in danger as a result of this vendetta against Nu and the other directors.'

'It may be,' Caton responded, 'that the perpetrator hasn't made the connection between the two of you, and in any case, there's no evidence that he intends to target anyone other than Nuan, Jake Gorlay and Louie Ellish.'

'"May be" does not reassure me,' Dundas retorted, 'and in the words of Carl Sagan, "Absence of evidence is not evidence of absence."'

Caton was tempted to disprove that assertion, just as Sherlock Holmes had done when referring to the curious incident of the dog in the night-time, in Conan Doyle's mystery *The Adventure of Silver Blaze*. One look at Thelma

Dundas was enough for him to decide otherwise, drink up, and make a quick exit. He stood up.

'Between ourselves and the security firm Mr Gorlay has hired,' he said, 'there will now be a significant and highly visible increase in security around Nuan and the other directors but, just to be on the safe side, it might be best if you and your son were to move out until the threat has gone away.'

'I'm going nowhere,' she said. 'Nu needs me.'

'No, Tee!' Lau said. 'I'm not going to allow you to put yourself and Langston in danger. Go back to the barge and change your mooring. I'll be fine.'

Caton was stunned by the effect this had on Thelma Dundas. She stared at her partner for a moment before lowering her head and turning away. Despite her bluster and commanding presence, it was obvious now which of the two was the stronger. Caton seized the opportunity to make his exit.

'I have to go and check on Mr Gorlay and Mr Ellish,' he said. 'Try not to worry. I'll make sure that more protection is put in place. I'll see myself out.'

Chapter 49

Nexus House, 5 p.m.

As Caton stood up, the room came to order. The events earlier that morning had resulted in a quantum shift in the seriousness accorded by every member of the syndicate to Operational Sentinel, and a day of frantic activity. But then again, it could have had something to do with the strangers sitting on his left: a man and a woman, arms folded, eyes alert, faces expressionless.

'Thank you,' Caton said. 'We'll start with our senior SOCO who's just received the report of the Royal Logistics Corps, Explosive Ordnance Disposal Unit.'

He sat down and Jack Benson walked over to the interactive whiteboard. As Benson spoke, salient points appeared on the screen, together with images taken at the scene, and others supplied by the bomb squad.

'All three devices were identical,' he said, 'and, unlike the device used at the offices of MancVG, these were not incendiary devices. They were all designed to cause controlled explosions and placed in such a way as to damage the engine, gearbox and transmission of the target vehicle such that it would be written off. While all such devices are by definition reckless, these weren't completely irresponsible. The placement and timing of the explosions strongly suggest a desire to avoid significant collateral damage to the owner, surrounding vehicles, nearby properties and passers-by.'

Benson paused to check his notes, then continued.

'Fragments recovered from the scene, together with explosive residue, indicate expertly assembled RCIEDs –

The End Game

that is radio-controlled improvised explosive devices – incorporating a modified mobile phone connected to an electrical firing circuit. Transmission of a paging signal from another mobile phone would have been sufficient to initiate the circuit and detonate the device.'

'Not an amateur job then?' DI Carter said.

'In theory,' Benson replied, 'someone could have followed any one of the online instruction manuals most commonly found on the Dark Web. The report states that these devices had the hallmarks of a trained bomb-maker, but that does not rule out an amateur who has gained significant expertise over time.'

'Like a terrorist bomb-maker?' DC Powell suggested.

'Possibly,' Benson said, 'except that terrorists and insurgents don't hold the monopoly on anti-personnel and anti-vehicle explosive devices. There are many professionals who will have been trained to detect, avoid and defuse IEDs, but also to construct, deploy and initiate them.'

'Such as?' Carter asked.

Benson answered by bringing up on the screen a list taken directly from the report. It read:

- *explosive ordnance disposal officers and technicians*
- *private demolition contractors*
- *explosives and blasting operatives in mining and quarrying industries*
- *members of elite units in the military*
- *Special Forces in the military*

'That's thousands then,' someone muttered.

Benson returned to his seat. Caton stood up again.

'You may have noticed that we have visitors,' he said. 'Colleagues from Counter Terrorism Police North West. I'm going to ask them to introduce themselves and explain why they've joined us today.'

The man alongside Caton stood up. He was tall, in his early fifties, and built like a second row forward in a rugby team.

The End Game

'I'm Len Iredale,' he said, 'one of seven Senior Responsible Officers in Counter Terrorism Policing North West. Each of us is responsible for a thematic strand. I'm responsible for Investigations. My colleague, Nel Moody, is responsible for Intelligence.' He paused and scanned the room. 'Our time is precious, as I'm sure is yours, so I'll be brief. The threat to the UK from terrorism is classified at this moment in time as substantial. We're a small unit and we're currently run off our feet. Based on the information you've sent us, what we've heard today, and our own comprehensive intelligence analysis, Operation Sentinel does not fall under our remit.'

'Thank God for that,' DC Franklin muttered.

Iredale chose to ignore it. 'It seems clear to us ,' he said, 'that what you have here is a rogue individual, or individuals, carrying out a personal vendetta against a small and defined group of people. The attacks that have taken place to date have demonstrated an intent to disrupt business and intimidate known individuals. Your own investigation has still to discover if this is commercially or personally motivated. Whichever, it does not yet, in our view, constitute a threat to the wider public. I say, *yet*, because it isn't clear if this is part of a wider plan to terrorise an entire industry, or could escalate into a more dangerous form of violence. Unless such a pattern does emerge, we won't be seeking to become operationally involved, but we'll keep a watching brief.'

As he sat down, his colleague stood up.

'Moody,' she said.

Franklin clocked Caton staring at him and decided to keep his mouth shut.

'As the Reporting Officer for Intelligence,' she said, 'I'll be receiving regular updates on Operation Sentinel and we'll run any relevant details through our national database. Should we discover anything that may be of assistance to you, I will immediately notify your DCI Caton. Should anything arise that presses alarm bells for us, we'll immediately consider setting up a joint or parallel investigation with you.'

She and her colleague received simultaneous SMS alerts. She checked her phone and turned to look at her partner. Iredale nodded and rose to his feet.

'I'm sorry,' Moody said, 'we have to leave.'

Caton waited until the door had closed behind them.

'Right,' he said, 'we'll take a break. Grab yourselves a drink and bring it back here. Detective Constable Franklin, my office, now!'

Chapter 50

'Here you go, Boss.'

Carter handed Caton a mug of boiled water. The two of them watched a chastened DC Franklin returning to his desk.

Carter sipped his coffee. 'How did he take it?' he asked quietly.

'Like a lamb,' Caton replied. 'I told him he'd be getting a written warning. His constant grandstanding and sarcastic remarks were already wearing thin, but being rude to visitors like that reflects badly on the syndicate and, ultimately, on me. I know he's not quite crossed the line, but am I the only one who detects sexist and racist undertones?'

'You're not,' Carter said, 'and it certainly hasn't gone unnoticed by Nair and Patel. They avoid him like the plague. Although he's been careful not to wind Henry Powell up. Probably frightened of how he'd react.'

'He's in danger of becoming a bad influence on the younger members of the team,' Caton mused.

'I'll have a word with him,' Carter responded, 'make sure he's got the message.'

'He'd better have,' Caton said. 'I'm not having a far-right clique develop right under my nose. Tell him one more strike and he's on his way.'

He put his mug down and called the room to order.

'Any thoughts?' he asked.

Henry Powell raised a hand. 'We should have had their cars checked after the firebomb on their offices.'

'Water under the bridge,' Caton replied, 'and besides, we'd have had to check them on a continuous basis or have

The End Game

them under surveillance twenty-four seven. We don't have the resources. When Gorlay and Ellish find replacement vehicles, maybe that firm of private detectives can add that to their list of jobs?'

This was met by laughter that eased some of the tension.

'We do now have the location of those two vehicles over the past forty-eight hours,' Caton told them. 'That covers the period since the perpetrator's Level Three warning was issued. I've already instructed DC Franklin to obtain and check all of the passive media covering those locations for suspect persons and vehicles. DC Gadd, I'd like you to give him a hand. Mr Wallace, where are we up to with the list of names the charity promised?'

'It arrived an hour ago,' Wallace replied. 'There are fifty names to work through, seven of whom are volunteers. We've also been trawling social media and search engines for mention of suicides attributed to video gaming. That has produced hundreds of instances, and counting. We've prioritised those in the UK first. I'm planning to cross-reference them with any mention of games marketed by MancVG. It's not going to be easy though. Hardly any of them give details of the particular game the deceased was into.'

'Well done,' Caton said. 'Just do your best.' He looked at the progress board. 'Where are we up to with Castlefield Digital Creations?'

'We've drawn a blank on that one,' Carter said. 'The directors all have alibis for both sets of attacks, and we've just heard that they've withdrawn their offer to buy out MancVG.'

'Makes you wonder why they were so defensive when we interviewed them?' Caton said.

Henry Powell raised his hand. 'I think I know why that is, Boss.'

'Go on.'

'You recall that when I did that background check on the father, Harry Draper, I thought his accounts looked less than transparent?'

'I do.'

'Well, I dug a bit deeper. It turns out that CID had suspicions that he was behind a gang of illegal loan sharks and was laundering their ill-gotten gains through his cash and carry business. They think he still is, only they've been unable to do anything about it because they're so understaffed.'

'Aren't we all?' said Carter.

'Anyway,' Powell continued, 'now they've just recruited one hundred and forty-three new detectives, they're going to see if they can get him bang to rights.'

'If the son is anything like the father, that would explain it,' Caton reflected. 'DS Hulme, let CID know about our interest in the Drapers, and ask them to give us a heads-up if they come across anything that might be relevant to Sentinel.'

He checked the board again. 'Do we have anything on any other companies that could be sniffing around MancVG?'

'No obvious suspects,' Wallace responded, 'which doesn't rule out someone preparing the ground for a takeover bid. But if they produce games with in-game purchases or betting, why would they insist on donations to that charity? And the resultant publicity would be bad, not just for them but the whole industry?'

'I understand,' Caton said, 'but we have to explore every avenue, especially now that we've not been able to connect Derek Terry to Operation Sentinel. Regardless, he remains a person of interest. We have to consider that he may have used an accomplice, someone he met in the Army Reserve, for example. Which reminds me, what we heard earlier from the bomb squad reinforces what we already surmised about the perpetrator. We're looking at someone who plans meticulously, can evade surveillance, has expert bomb-making skills, and acts with military precision. But it also now seems clear that this person actively seeks to minimise the risk of death or injury.'

'The dog being an exception?' DC Gadd pointed out.

'The dog's injuries all came from being struck by a car, or cars,' Carter reminded him. 'Unless the person who stole the dog threw it in front of a car, I think we can take it that it was an accident.'

'So, this is someone with a conscience,' Caton said, 'and possibly conflicted. Over to you, DI Carter.'

Carter stood up.

'Conflicted he may be, but *convicted* is what we're aiming for,' he said. 'Preferably before he blows up half of Manchester. Back to work, everybody, and pull your fingers out.'

Chapter 51

Millgate Lane, Didsbury, 7.15 p.m.

Caton flicked between the channels, searching for something that would take his mind off Sentinel. Emily was on the mend but tucked up in bed for an early night. Kate was in the kitchen preparing dinner. He heard his phone ring and realised he'd left it on the kitchen table. As he rose from his chair, Kate appeared with it in her hand.

'It's DS Hulme,' she said. 'Dinner will be on the table in five minutes.'

Caton took the phone. 'Jimmy?'

'Boss, Duggie Wallace has found a strong possible!'

'From the charities list?'

'From the internet. Hang on, I'll put him on.'

'Boss?'

'What have you got?' Caton asked.

'It's from a newspaper report back in 2020. None of the dailies picked it up because it was during the first period of lockdown, but it was in the *Bristol Post*. Son of a soldier serving in Somalia found hanging in their garage. His mother found him. It says the police remained non-committal, possible misadventure, and they weren't looking for anyone else with regard to the incident. The rest of the report consisted of quotes from neighbours and the headteacher of his school about what a lovely boy he was, and how it was completely out of character.'

'What did this have to do with video games?'

'When I saw the military connection, I decided to dig a bit deeper. I searched through the archives until I found a report of the inquest. It made page three of the *Hereford Times*. The verdict was that he took his own life while the

The End Game

balance of his mind was disturbed.'

'Those exact words?'

'Yes, Boss. And the coroner went further. She said that from evidence recovered from his computer, and the note he left for his parents, it was clear that the trigger for taking his own life was the debt he'd built up on one of his mother's credit cards while playing video games. He couldn't bear the guilt, the shame, and the sense of failure.'

'Sounds promising,' Caton said.

'There's more, Boss. The father was unable to attend the funeral because he was engaged in sensitive operations in Somalia. He made it to the inquest though. Sounds like he wasn't only distraught, but positively incandescent. He had to be physically removed from the courtroom.'

Caton felt the adrenaline begin to flow. 'When was this?'

'July 2020.'

'Right,' Caton said, 'I'm coming in.'

'No, Tom! Your dinner's on the table.' Kate stood in the doorway, arms folded.

'I'm sorry, love,' he said. 'Pop it in the fridge. I'll grab a takeaway on the way in.'

She placed a hand on each of the door jambs, barring his exit, her face set in stone. 'Let Carter handle it, Tom. That's what deputies are for.'

'Boss, are you there?' Wallace said.

'On second thoughts,' Caton responded, 'before you go home, see if you can get me this man . . .?'

'Masters, Maxwell Masters.'

'Maxwell Masters's address and phone number. First thing in the morning, I want a comprehensive search – HOLMES, the internet, social media. We need to know about his friends, family, his activities and behaviour since that inquest. And above all, his present whereabouts.'

'I've already drawn a blank on an address or phone number for him,' Wallace said, 'but I managed to get a phone number for his ex-wife, and a photo of the son from the newspaper.'

'Text them both to me,' Caton said, 'then get off home. I'll see you bright and early in the morning. And, Duggie, well done.'

Chapter 52
Day Five
Tuesday 6th September

Nexus House, 8.15 a.m.

'Mrs Masters?' Caton said. 'Mrs Sandra Masters?'

'Yes,' she replied. 'Who is this?'

'Mrs Masters, I am Detective Chief Inspector Tom Caton, Greater Manchester Police. I'm trying to trace your ex-husband, Maxwell. I was hoping you could help me find him?'

There was a pause at her end of the line. When she replied, there was a catch in her voice.

'What has he done?'

'We don't know that he's done anything, Mrs Masters, but we do need to speak with him as a matter of urgency.'

'I'm not sure I can help you,' she said. 'I haven't seen or heard from Max in over three years, except for a short note I received over a year ago telling me to get on with my life. I did.' Her voice dropped to a whisper. 'For all I know, he may be dead.'

Caton had the impression that she thought this a definite possibility. Now was not the time to explore it.

'Can you tell me briefly why you filed for divorce?' he said.

He heard a long sigh, as though this was a story she had long since tired of telling and had no desire to revisit.

'Do you know what happened to our son, Mr Caton?' she said.

Caton looked down at the newspaper image Wallace had placed on his desk. 'Yes, I do,' he said, 'and I'm sorry for your loss, Mrs Masters.'

The End Game

'It was a long time ago,' she said, 'although the pain never goes away. At least I've found ways of living with it, unlike Max. Maxwell was unable to come to terms with our son's death and was obsessed with the fact that no one was going to be held accountable. He was inconsolable. His mood alternated between bouts of rage in which he blamed me, the faceless companies that owned the games our son was addicted to, and the government for not regulating them, as well as himself for not being there to prevent it all happening. To be honest, Mr Caton, there were times when I feared for myself, and for him. After that he completely turned in on himself for long periods – would scarcely even talk to me.'

She paused.

Caton remained silent. He knew that simply talking about that tragic period of her life would bring back some of the emotions and hurt that came with it. He regretted that he had to take her there, but it came with the territory. The earlier that you interviewed a victim of serious crime, and the more detailed their account, the greater the chance of solving the crime and securing a conviction. But while he never forgot those stories, there was no way to achieve damage limitation, for them or for him.

'It was obvious to me,' she continued, 'that Max was deeply depressed. Eventually I told him that either he would have to move out or I would. He went to stay with one of his colleagues in Hereford. He tried to bury his grief by returning to the army. I was surprised they let him go back, Mr Caton. He didn't last long. I was told that he'd been given a medical discharge about five months after his return. I'd heard nothing from him since he left home, I was still grieving myself and, to be honest, I was terrified of what he might do. I filed for divorce on the grounds of unreasonable behaviour.'

She paused again. Caton waited.

'Max had become distant and unpredictable long before our son died, Mr Caton, but I'd never felt frightened of him. Danny dying like that tipped him over the edge. He needed help. I wasn't able to give him that.'

'You mustn't blame yourself, Mrs Masters,' Caton said.

The End Game

'You were grieving yourself. And by the sound of it, your husband was not only grieving but suffering from post-traumatic stress disorder. That would have required specialist support way beyond anything you could have provided.'

There was silence at the other end of the line.

'You were telling me,' Caton prompted, 'that you filed for divorce?'

'I did my best to track Maxwell down so I could obtain written consent. I tried the army, his friends, and those of his comrades if I knew their whereabouts. My solicitors even asked the regional divorce centre to try to trace him through governmental departments. Then out of the blue, December 2020 it was, I received a brief letter from him saying he was sorry that he'd let me down. That I could keep the house and should move on with my life, and that I wouldn't see or hear from him again. That was enough for me to be able to go ahead with the divorce. I've never heard from him since, and because hadn't put an address or a phone number in that letter, there was no way I could contact him.' She paused. 'I don't even know if he's aware that I've just received the decree absolute.'

'What regiment was Maxwell in, Mrs Masters?' Caton asked.

There was a long silence. Caton sensed her brain whirring, and tried some prompts as Mrs Masters continued to hesitate.

'There was more than one? Who was he with when he was discharged?'

'That was from the Second Battalion, The Rifles.'

'And before that?'

She hesitated. 'He was with the Special Reconnaissance Regiment.'

'I don't think I've ever heard of them,' Caton said.

'Not many people have, Mr Caton. It's a Special Forces unit that specialises in on-the-ground reconnaissance, mainly behind enemy lines.'

Caton's heart skipped a beat. 'Where are they based, Mrs Maxwell?'

'I'm not really supposed to share that information.'

The End Game

'I'm sure I can find out from the MOD.' Then a thought occurred to him. 'Did you always live on or near the base during the years that your husband was in the army?'

'When we got married, we lived close by his first regiment, The Royal Green Jackets. It merged with other regiments to form The Rifles.'

'Which was where?'

'Bulford, in Wiltshire.'

'Did you have to move when he transferred to the SRR?'

Yet another hiatus. He waited.

'No.'

'Am I missing something?' he said.

'I didn't have to.'

'But you did?'

'Yes.'

She had told him that her husband had insisted that she keep the house. Could she still be living there? The house where her son took his own life?

'Mrs Maxwell,' he said. 'You've been really helpful. And I'm truly sorry to have to ask this, but I would like one of my officers to come and see you tomorrow.'

'I'm not sure there's anything else I can add to what I've already told you,' she said.

'Even so, I would appreciate it.'

'Very well,' she replied. 'I'm not working tomorrow. I'll be in all day.'

'I'll need your address,' he said.

He wrote it down as she read it out. She was still living there. Credenhill, Herefordshire, home to Sterling Lines, headquarters of the Special Air Service, and presumably of the SRR. It was such common knowledge, Caton wondered why she'd been reluctant to tell him.

'Thank you,' he said, 'you've already been a great help.'

'Mr Caton,' she said, 'if you find him, will you tell me?'

If, not when, he noticed.

'I promise to let you know that he's alive,' he said, 'but I'll need his permission to tell you where he is.'

'Thank you,' she said.

Chapter 53

Caton went straight to his computer and searched for the Special Reconnaissance Regiment. He had a hit first time of asking. Part of the United Kingdom's Special Forces, it was established in the wake of the seven-eleven attacks in New York in 2001 that sent a shock wave across the West.

Based alongside the SAS, at Stirling Lines barracks in Credenhill, and initially recruited from members of the 14th Intelligence Company who had been performing a similar role in Northern Ireland, it drew its personnel, referred to as operators, from existing special forces units and from across every branch of the British Armed Services. Both men and women were accepted onto the rigorous assessment process.

Consisting of somewhere between two and seven hundred personnel – such was the secrecy surrounding it, nobody could be sure – its primary role was to carry out covert surveillance and reconnaissance across a wide range of operations at home and abroad, involving highly classified methods and activities. Some but not all of these included close target surveillance on behalf of, and sometimes together with, MI5 and the Secret Intelligence Service, otherwise known as MI6. Part of the role of the SRR entailed counterterrorism activities. It also filled a role that was formerly covered by the SAS and the Special Boat Service, namely the infiltration of military and intelligence personnel behind enemy lines, and their exfiltration – also known as extraction – from sticky situations.

Caton scooted his chair away from his desk. If this was their perpetrator, it would explain how he had managed to evade detection while carrying out such highly visible attacks. From what Sandra Masters had told him, there was

The End Game

a strong motive and a potentially obsessive driving force. Masters was the full package: opportunity, motive and means, the very definition of a prime suspect.

Caton called the number for Gordon Holmes's syndicate. Much to his surprise, it was Gordon who answered.

'Tom, unto what do I owe the pleasure?'

'I've a massive favour to ask, Gordon.'

'You can but try.'

'I urgently need someone to pay Stirling Lines a visit, and...'

'I'm way ahead of you. You were just wondering, given she's familiar with the place, if DI Stuart happened to have a spare day or two?'

'One at most.'

'Because this syndicate has bugger all to do, and my team just sit here twiddling their thumbs?'

'I wasn't...'

'Only kidding,' Gordon said. 'As it happens, Jo was due in court today and tomorrow, but the scrote in question jumped bail last night. We've got an all-ports out on him and the case has had to be adjourned.'

'Gordon, you're a star!' Caton told him.

'Don't thank me, thank the criminal justice system – they should never have given him bail in the first place. Give me a second.'

Caton heard Gordon asking someone where DI Stuart was, then he was back on.

'Jo's on the phone at the moment,' he said. 'I'll send her over shortly.'

'I owe you one,' Caton told him.

Gordon laughed. 'And the rest.'

Caton went in search of DS Hulme. He found him in the conference room. 'What are you doing?' he asked.

'My computer's had a wobbly, one of the techies is fixing it, so I came in here for some peace and quiet while I updated the casebook.'

'Well, I'm sorry,' Caton told him, 'but given that Ged is off with that bug, I need you to track down a number for the Special Reconnaissance Regiment at Stirling Lines in Herefordshire and tell them that I'm sending two detectives down there tomorrow morning.'

The End Game

'They're going to want to know why, Boss.'

'Tell them it's regarding a rapidly evolving major investigation, potentially involving a former member of the regiment. That should grab their interest.'

'Do I give them his name?'

'You might as well. It'll give them a chance to dig out his details and save time in the morning.'

While Jimmy Hulme rang the MOD, Caton called Sandra Masters. She assured him that she would be in all morning and was willing to speak with the detectives. He had just come off the phone and had DC Whittle join him when Joanne Stuart knocked on his door. He waved her in and stood up.

'Jo!' he said. 'I'm delighted Gordon could spare you.'

She grinned. 'Truthfully? He can't manage without me, but I was intrigued.'

She turned to Carly. 'Hi, Carlz, hope this means we're working together again?'

'I have no idea,' Carly replied, 'but I hope so.'

DS Hulme appeared in the doorway. 'It's sorted, Boss,' he said. 'They must be rattled because they've found a window to meet with a Lieutenant Colonel Ian Valentine, officer commanding the regiment, at 11 a.m. tomorrow at Sterling Lines.'

'Thanks, Jimmy,' Caton said. 'Jo, Carly, take a seat, but don't get too comfortable.'

'Sterling Lines,' Jo Stuart said. 'Now I know why you asked for me. But you do know I've only been there twice, even then only to use the Killing House? It's hardly going to cut the mustard, least of all with the commanding officer of the SAS.'

'SRR,' he told her. 'We have a DC who's ex-forces, but I need someone with the kind of experience you and I gained in Northern Ireland dealing with people like this. No offence, Carly.'

'None taken, Boss.'

'Good,' he said. 'I've been told I have to give a report to the Command team in half an hour, so I'm going to leave you to bring DS Stuart up to speed. You need to find out everything you can about Masters, without giving too much

211

away. Especially anything that may help us track him down. The same with his ex-wife, Sandra. I've spoken to her, but I think she has more to tell. I'm particularly interested to find out why she's kept her married name.'

'I can think of lots of reasons,' Jo said.

'I get that,' he said, 'but what are hers? And does she really not know his whereabouts? But go easy – between her husband and her son she's been dealt a rubbish hand.'

Chapter 54
Day Six
Wednesday 7th September

Credenhill, 09.15 a.m.

Jo turned right at The Bell Inn and took the shortcut past Credenhill Wood. From the moment they had left the A49 it had been a long and picturesque journey through the sparsely populated county of Herefordshire.

'This is lovely,' Carly Whittle said. 'I'd always pictured Herefordshire as flat.'

Jo smiled to herself. She had felt exactly the same the first time she visited Stirling Lines. It had struck her then as incongruous that the headquarters of Britain's most elite Special Forces nestled below wooded hills, surrounded by apple orchards, amidst villages consisting of quaint black and white cottages.

'It depends how you come at it,' she replied. 'The good news is, we're almost there.'

They had left Manchester at 6 a.m. and made good time until they hit rush hour north of Whitchurch. Then it had been stop-go, until they turned off at Moreton-on-Lugg. They were now on a narrow road leading past farm buildings and into the heart of the village. Dwellings over a century and a half old made way for uniform, mid- and late twentieth-century homes.

'Are these army houses, do you think?' Carly asked.

Jo slowed down so she could read the numbers by the doors.

The End Game

'Not as such. Last time I came, I passed some older houses that looked like they were probably MOD service family accommodation, but a lot of the families live off the patch now, mixed in with the locals.'

She pulled up outside a large semi with a low hedge and neat front garden.

'This is it,' she said. 'Why don't you take the lead on this one? I'm still trying to get my head round Operation Sentinel.'

A woman stood in the partly open doorway. She was tucking the tails of a white blouse into a pair of tailored jeans. She looked to be in her late forties, early fifties even, her face careworn.

'Mrs Masters?' Carly said. 'It *is* Mrs Masters?'

The woman smiled faintly. 'Yes, but please call me Sandra.'

'I'm Detective Sergeant Whittle, and this is my colleague, Detective Inspector Stuart.'

Sandra Masters stepped back into the hall. 'Please, come in,' she said.

The hallway was lined with photographs. A wedding photo of herself and her husband. Her holding a baby, and her husband proudly looking on. One of her husband in his Green Jackets Regimental Number Ones. Jo noted that none of them showed him in his Special Forces uniform.

They were led into the living room. A three-seat sofa, one armchair, a coffee table, and a modest flat-screen television. On the mantelpiece in the living room there were pictures taken of her son taken at his primary school, and right through his teens. Portraits in which his smile was tentative, informal photos of him smiling broadly in his sports kit, holiday snaps of him diving into a pool and emerging from the sea, and sitting proudly on a mountain bike. None gave the slightest hint of the tragedy that had followed.

'Can I offer you a drink?' Sandra Masters said.

'I'd love a coffee if you have one?' Carly replied.

'Me too,' said Jo.

'Would you like a toasted teacake with that?'

They didn't need asking twice. It had been over three

The End Game

hours since they'd snatched a quick breakfast. They waited until they could hear her busying herself in the kitchen, then spoke in hushed tones.

'That's interesting,' Jo said, nodding towards the display on the mantlepiece. 'None of him with his father?'

'She's not ghosted him though,' Carly observed, 'he's prominent in the hallway. Interesting that she's kept her married name?'

'And that she still lives in the house they all shared together.'

'Do either of you take sugar?' Sandra Masters called from the kitchen.

'No thanks!' they chorused.

'Doesn't look as though she's really moved on since the divorce,' Carly whispered.

'Or come to terms with her son's death,' Jo said.

Sandra Masters appeared with a mug each and handed them to the two detectives.

'Here you go. Teacakes are on their way.'

They thanked her, and sat in silence sipping their coffee, until she returned with the teacakes and a mug for herself.

'I hope you wanted butter,' she said, setting two plates on the coffee table. 'I should have asked.'

She placed her mug on a side table, sat down in the armchair and folded her hands in her lap.

'Thank you for agreeing to see us, Mrs Maxwell,' Carly said.

'Well, you were lucky I don't work Wednesdays,' she replied. 'And it's Sandra.'

Carly smiled. 'What is it you do, Sandra, workwise?'

'I'm a senior pharmacy technician.'

'That must be hard, coping with the Covid fallout?'

'It is. You wouldn't believe the number of people with complications. And now that we're offering vaccinations too...' Her voice tailed off.

What had seemed like a good way to help put her at her ease had misfired. Carly decided to cut to the chase.

'Perhaps you could begin by telling us about your husband,' she said.

The End Game

'Where do you want me to start?'

'At the beginning? How you met?'

Mrs Masters took a deep breath and let it out like a sigh. 'He was a private fitness instructor at my gym. We clicked straight away. We'd only been together six months when I fell pregnant. We got married shortly before Danny was born.'

She smiled.

'He was twenty-two, I was twenty-one. Max was a fitness fanatic and adrenaline junkie. He loved hiking in the Peak District, the Lakes, tackling the Munros. He even started rock-climbing. One of the guys he met there was a marine. That was when he got the bug to join the army. He should have joined the Paras or the Royal Marines, but he joined The Green Jackets because it had been his father's regiment. His father served with distinction in Burma after the Second World War. Max always wanted to outdo him. I think that's why he went on to apply for Special Forces selection.'

'How did your husband get on with his son?' Carly prompted.

'He doted on Danny, partly, I think, because he was our only child. I had a difficult pregnancy, and after Danny was born, they told me I'd not be able to have another.'

Her face softened.

'When Danny was little, Max took turns in reading to him. And he loved playing football with him in the yard. As soon as Danny was old enough, he'd take him up on the moors. They went camping and fishing together in the Lakes. But several years into his time at Stirling Lines, all that began to change.'

Her face clouded over and when she spoke, she sounded sad and regretful.

'At first it was gradual. Each time he returned from active deployment, he was that little more distant. There were times when he seemed ... I don't know ... vacant? As though he was still back there ... wherever he had been. He was either up early out running, or up on the fells ... or else he'd sleep in. He was no longer interested in spending time with Danny or going out with me of an evening. He

The End Game

preferred to stay in watching television and drinking. It was obvious he couldn't wait to go back.'

'How did that affect your son?'

She looked up. 'Danny never understood why his dad had changed. I think he began to blame himself. He became increasingly turned in on himself and moody. During lockdown he spent most of his time in his room. He'd only come downstairs to get food which he took back to his room. He was obsessed with his video games. At first, he fitted them in around his online lessons.'

She paused, and then shook her head.

'It was only after Danny had . . . gone, that his school told me he'd missed loads of sessions and stopped doing his online assignments.'

She took a tissue from the pocket of her jeans and dabbed her eyes. Then she pushed herself out of her chair.

'I'm sorry,' she said. 'You'll have to excuse me.'

She picked up her mug and left the room.

Chapter 55

Five minutes later, Sandra Masters returned, clutching a glass of water. She apologised and sat down.

'There's no need, Sandra,' Carly told her. 'I'm sure that anyone in your position would feel exactly the same. I know I would.'

Mrs Masters took a sip of water.

'Thank you,' she said, 'but you'll have to forgive me, I won't be able to talk about the day Danny died... the day I...'

'It's fine,' Carly responded. ' You don't have to do that. But if you could tell us how it affected your husband, that would be really helpful.'

Sandra Masters looked relieved. She put her glass down.

'When Max came back from the last tour,' she said, 'immediately after Danny had died, it was awful. He was consumed by grief and guilt. It was made worse because the Covid lockdown restrictions meant that the coroner had granted an interim death certificate and listed Danny's death for an inquest later in the year. I had no idea how long it would be before Max could return home. The funeral went ahead.'

She shook her head. 'I should have waited. But the mortuaries and funeral directors' chapels were all full. Both my parents had Covid. I wasn't thinking straight.'

Her eyes began to fill with tears. She bowed her head. Nobody spoke. Eventually she looked up at the two detectives, as though seeking absolution or, at the very least, understanding.

'I can't imagine how difficult that must have been,' Carly said.

The End Game

Sandra Masters appeared to draw strength from this. She dried her eyes and breathed in deeply.

'There were only three of us there. Me, my best friend Hazel, and the regimental chaplain. Five days later, Max arrived home. He was grief-stricken, but also furious with me for letting the funeral go ahead. He insisted on watching it alone on the recorded video the funeral director sent us. When it was over, he took a bottle of whisky from the drinks cabinet, went to Danny's room, and locked himself in. He didn't come out for two days. Then he went straight back to the regiment, but they sent him back home. They told him he needed time to deal with his grief, that in any case he was due R&R after his last tour.'

'How did he respond to that?' Carly wondered.

'Badly. He had the same routine every day, come rain or shine. He slept in the study bedroom at night, got up early, took his bergen or a rucksack, and drove off. When he got back, he'd go straight upstairs, have a bath or a shower, and go straight to bed. He'd help himself to breakfast and that's it.'

She picked up her glass of water, realised it was empty, and put it back down.

'Two weeks this went on, then he went back to work. He started speaking again, but it was all perfunctory. No real conversation, and certainly nothing about Danny. But then... in May it would have been... we watched the inquest via a video conference. I watched down here on my laptop; he insisted on watching it upstairs in his bedroom.'

Her face crumpled. She gripped the arms of her chair.

'It was awful. The paramedic who pronounced Danny dead, the police who responded, and the officer who investigated, they all gave their evidence. Then I had to answer questions about Danny's state of mind. And about the debts he'd racked up on my credit cards playing those games. Max kept interrupting. Then when the coroner started summing up, Max demanded to know why the companies who sold the video games Danny was playing, the ones where he was buying in-game purchases, hadn't been required to give evidence.'

She dabbed her eyes again.

The End Game

'It really was awful. The coroner kept threatening to exclude Max from the inquest. When he gave his verdict, I heard Max howling as though in pain. Then he was shouting and swearing and there were crashing sounds from upstairs. I ran up but he started cursing me, and he wouldn't let me in. I was scared, for him and for me. I went round to Hazel's – she lives next door – and her husband was in Max's troop. She called Tony. He arrived in minutes. When he got no response, he broke the door down, took one look at Max, and told me he had no option but to call Stirling Lines. Max's regimental sergeant major arrived with a doctor and the chaplain.

'They were in there in less than twenty minutes and waited until the arrival of an army ambulance. The doctor explained that Max had experienced a psychotic episode. Like a mental breakdown, he said, but where he'd lost all sense of reality. He said he was confident that Max would recover, and they were taking him to a specialist Forces hospital in Portsmouth. Then he and the RSM left. Tony and the chaplain stayed with me until Hazel arrived to take over.'

She shook her head.

'It took the two of us to clear his room up. The bed was upside down, doors had been ripped off the cupboards, the desk chair was a twisted mess, the computer, keyboard and monitor all smashed to smithereens.'

She picked up her glass again, stared at it, and put it back down.

Carly stood up. 'Let me get you some more water?' she said.

Sandra Masters nodded. 'Please.'

Carly took the glass and returned with it full. After drinking deeply, Sandra Masters continued her account.

'He was away for six weeks. When he returned, the RSM was with him. It was weird. Max wouldn't speak to me. He went straight upstairs to pack a case and his bergen. The RSM told me he was much improved but that he wouldn't be able to continue at Stirling Lines, and was being returned to his home regiment, The Rifles, where he would be on light duties, and receive support to help his continued recovery.'

The End Game

She looked at each of them in turn.

'But it didn't work out like that, did it? After that, whenever he came home for a couple of days, he looked physically fine, but we barely spoke, though Lord knows I tried. I could see he was a broken man. Not only had he lost his son, but having to leave the regiment, and in that manner, he'd lost his identity too. It was like a double grief. He wasn't the man I'd married. I was having enough trouble dealing with my own pain; I couldn't deal with his as well.'

She fell silent and hung her head.

Jo nudged Carly on the arm, nodded to her untouched teacake, and took over the questioning.

'What did you do, Sandra?' she asked.

Mrs Masters looked up. 'I told him I was going to stay with my parents. That I needed a break.'

'How did he react?' Carly said.

'He just shrugged and said, "Fine. Whatever."'

Her tone and expression changed. She searched their faces, desperate for them to understand. 'You see, I'd already lost my son. I didn't want to be here when something else bad happened.'

She took another sip of water. 'Then I heard that Max had been discharged, but according to Hazel, he didn't show up here. When I contacted The Rifles, they had no idea where he was either. Work had kept my job open, and we'd bought the house a few years back, so I came home. I've been here ever since.'

'You told my colleague that your husband sent you a note?'

'That's right.'

'Do you still have it?'

'I do.'

'Could I possibly see it?'

'Of course.' Mrs Masters stood up.

'I'm sorry to have to ask you this, Sandra,' Jo said, 'but do you have any photos taken within a year or two of your husband's disappearance?'

Mrs Masters frowned. 'I'll have to see. It wasn't a time when we took many pictures. Max was away much of the time, and when he was here, there weren't many occasions

The End Game

for photographs.' She left the room.

Jo leaned closer to Carly and whispered, 'I'd like a quick look upstairs. Can you keep her talking?'

Sandra Masters returned and handed Jo a photo. 'I found this,' she said. 'We were invited to a New Year's Eve party in 2018 with a few of his colleagues and their wives. Max didn't want to go, but I made him.'

Max Masters was smiling at the camera, holding a champagne glass and wearing a black tuxedo with an open-neck shirt. His dress tie was tucked into his breast pocket. He had short brown, slightly receding hair, with a hint of grey at the temples. He had a square face with a slightly prominent jaw, but what held the attention were the eyes. Although piercing in their intensity, they appeared completely devoid of emotion. It put Jo in mind of a book with an arresting cover that gave no hint of what lay inside.

She handed the photo to Carly. 'Before we go, Sandra, could I possibly use your toilet?' she said. 'We were on the road for nearly three hours.'

'Of course,' Mrs Masters replied. 'It's at the top of the stairs, on the right.' She turned to Carly. 'There's one in the kitchen too, DS Whittle.'

'I'm fine,' Carly said. 'Thank you.'

Jo headed upstairs and paused on the landing, heard them talking, and proceeded to open each of the doors in turn. The first was a bedroom with a double bed. From the tubs of make-up and brushes on the dressing table, she assumed it to be Sandra's room. Behind the next door was a box room kitted out as a study. The third room was a revelation. This had to have been Danny's room, much as he had left it.

One wall was fitted with bookshelves that held stacks of DVDs and games, as well as books and knick-knacks. Along the opposite wall, a fitted desk held a television, a computer and monitor, and twin speakers. Above them, a poster proclaimed the signature *Star Wars* catchphrase 'In A Galaxy Far, Far Away'. A pair of headphones were draped over the back of the desk chair. On one side of the desk, two guitars – one acoustic, the other a red electric guitar – hung from wall mounts. A small double bed covered with a plain

The End Game

grey duvet faced the window. Behind the bed, a large print of a popular poster was displayed. It showed a chimpanzee seated on a box and holding a can of spray paint, beside a paint-splattered canvas bearing the slogan in red paint to *Follow Your Dreams*. The irony was not lost on Jo.

On the far side of the bed, she spotted a framed photo on the bedside cabinet. She quickly crossed the room and examined the image. It was Max Masters, wearing the uniform of his home regiment, The Rifles, but with a navy-blue belt and an emerald-grey beret. The beret bore a badge displaying a Corinthian helmet pierced by an upward-pointing dagger, and a scroll bearing the label 'RECONNAISSANCE'. Jo took a shot with her phone and hastened to the doorway, where she took another of the room. In the bathroom at the end of the landing she flushed the toilet, ran the tap for a few seconds, and then hurried downstairs.

As Jo entered the living room, Carly stood up.

'I'm afraid we'll have to leave, Sandra,' she said. 'We have an appointment with your husband's commanding officer. But thank you so much for your hospitality, and for answering our questions. We know how difficult it must have been for you.'

'Yes, thank you,' said Jo, turning and heading for the front door.

'You will let me know,' Mrs Masters called after them as they walked down the path, 'if you find him?'

***

'Put your foot down!' Carly exclaimed as she fastened her seatbelt. 'I'm bursting!'

Jo started the engine. 'Why didn't you go when I came down?'

'Because I didn't want to arouse her suspicion. Did you find anything?'

'Suffice it to say, she definitely hasn't moved on from her son's death like she said she had. His room looks untouched, apart from being tidy and spotlessly clean. It's like a shrine. I'll show you when we get there. '

'That'll be why she hasn't moved away,' Carly said. 'She can't bear to leave him behind. Maybe that's why she hasn't reverted to her maiden name? Because it was their son's name too. And it's beginning to look like, despite the divorce, she's still not over his father?'

Jo turned right onto the A480.

'Could be,' she said, 'but unless she knows where he is and isn't saying, that doesn't help us.' She slowed down and indicated right. 'Here we are,' she said. 'You'd better pray they're expecting us, and they've got a loo handy.'

Chapter 56

Stirling Lines, Credenhill, 10 a.m.

'Unfortunately,' the adjutant said, 'Lieutenant Colonel Valentine has been called away at short notice. He's arranged for Major Hodgkiss to take his place.'

He double-tapped on the door to the meeting room, stood back to let them pass and closed the door behind them.

Two men seated at the table stood up; a third man sitting in the corner of the room did not. The shorter of the men standing inclined his head in greeting.

'Welcome to Stirling Lines,' he said. He pointed to the the chairs immediately opposite. 'Please, take a seat. My name is Major Hodgkiss,' he continued, 'and this is Captain Subedi, my second in command. Lieutenant Colonel Valentine has asked me to offer you his apologies, but I assure you that both Captain Subedi and I are well placed to assist you.'

'I am Detective Inspector Stuart,' Jo said.

'And I am Detective Sergeant Whittle,' Carly told them.

Jo turned in her chair so she could take a look at the third man, the placement of whose chair who was off to the left and slightly behind the two detectives. In his early fifties, he wore a navy suit and matching silk tie with silver twin bar stripes she recognised as belonging to one of the elite public schools – Eton, she thought, or Harrow?

'Excuse me,' she said, 'and you are?'

He smiled thinly. 'From the Ministry,' he said, 'as an observer.'

Ministry of Defence, she guessed, or more likely MI5 or MI6 Liaison. She held his gaze for a moment then turned back.

The End Game

'You've been here before, Inspector?' Major Hodgkiss asked.

'That's correct,' she replied, 'for advanced firearms skills training.'

He nodded. 'The Killing House. Have you ever had cause to use what you learned here, Inspector?'

'Yes.'

'And did it help?'

'Yes.'

'Good.' He sat back in his chair and folded his arms. 'So, how can we help this time?'

'I'm hoping,' she began, 'that you can provide us with some background information about a Maxwell Masters, a person whom we understand to have served with the Special Reconnaissance Regiment for over nine years.'

The major nodded and tapped the file on the table in front of him. His colleague had a similar file she noticed.

'Former Staff Sergeant Masters,' Hodgkiss said. 'Why exactly do you need this information?'

'Mr Masters is a person of interest in relation to an ongoing investigation.'

'I'm aware of that much. What is the nature of the investigation?'

'Extortion, among other things.'

'Blackmail?'

'No, extortion.'

'The difference being?'

'The difference being that extortion involves the threat or application of violence.'

The major's eyes widened a fraction. 'Do you have any concrete evidence that connects Sergeant Masters to your investigation?'

'No.'

'Then I don't understand how you think we can help you.'

'The methods being used by the perpetrator suggest someone with a military background such as we understand Sergeant Masters to have had, together with a credible motive in this case.'

The major's face remained impassive as processed the information. 'And what are these *methods* exactly?'

226

The End Game

'With respect,' Jo said, 'there is only so much that I'm able to disclose in relation to our investigation and, as I'm sure you'll appreciate, my colleague and I are here to ask questions rather than to answer them.'

The captain leaned forward and was about to object, but the major placed a restraining hand on his arm.

'It's alright, Captain,' he said. 'So, Inspector, what is it you wish to know?'

'Thank you, Major,' she said. She clicked on her tablet. 'As I said, background information. Anything that may help to confirm or refute our suspicions, and especially anything that might help us find him, so we can speak with him.'

The two officers exchanged a glance.

'Very well,' said the major. 'What exactly do you mean by *background information*?'

'His operational deployments. The particular skills and knowledge he acquired. His mental health at the point at which he left the army.'

Hodgkiss leaned back in his chair and folded his arms. 'With all due respect, Inspector, I'm sure that you'll appreciate that we're bound by Queen's Regulations? There is only so much that we can share with you, given that any period of service he may have had with Special Services is covered by the Official Secrets Act.'

Touché, thought Jo.

'Naturally,' she said, 'but I can assure you that as far as we're aware, there's unlikely to be any direct connection between our investigation, and anything he may have been involved with in the army, other than the skills he used and his mental health.'

Another look passed between the two men. Jo sensed that they had expected this and prepared their script meticulously. The major opened his file, removed the first two pages, and laid them side by side in front of him.

'Masters,' he began, 'joined the First Battalion Royal Green Jackets in 1999. He served twice with them in Iraq on Operation Telic from 2003 until 2007, during which time he was promoted to corporal. In February 2007, his regiment ceased to exist and became the Second Battalion The Rifles, with whom he continued on Operation Telic until December

The End Game

2007. He was then involved in operations in Afghanistan, where he served with distinction, until 2009. During this time, he was promoted to sergeant. He had already applied for Special Forces selection in late 2008. He passed the selection process in mid-2009, was identified as a good fit for the Special Reconnaissance Regiment, and was deployed to Northern Ireland.'

He paused, put the first sheet down, and took up the second. 'From 2009 until 2011, he served in Northern Ireland. From 2011 until 2016, he was engaged in operations in Libya.'

He looked up for a moment, then back at the sheet.

'In 2013, he was given permanent cadre status and retained his substantive sergeant's rank. From 2016 until 2018, he served in Yemen and Somalia. At the end of the tour, he was invited to join our selection team and became a member of the directing staff with the rank of staff sergeant.'

There was a long pause, during which he and the captain caught each other's eye.

'In June 2019,' the major continued, 'there was a tragic accident. A thirty-year-old Para died during his final endurance TAB.' He looked up. 'Nobody's fault. Masters seemed to have come to terms with that, but in January 2020, he requested a return to his squadron and was deployed with them on operations in Somalia.'

He returned to his notes.

'On 20th April 2020, his son committed suicide. It was thirteen days before Masters could be extracted and returned here to Credenhill. There was no way he was fit for duty, so we sent him home to process his grief, and recover from what had been a particularly hairy operation. Two weeks later, he was back with us, initially on light duties. He seemed okay, if not back to his best, and did take part in a training exercise. Then there was the incident concerning the inquest into his son's death.'

'Mrs Masters told us about that,' said Jo.

Major Hodgkiss looked relieved not to have to go through it again. 'So you'll know about his breakdown?' he said.

'Yes.'

'And also that he was returned to The Rifles, in administrative terms at least?'

'Administrative terms?'

'Back on their books. Their responsibility. No further immediate expectation of active duties.'

'I see.'

The major looked at the sheet. 'In September 2020, he was given a medical discharge, and returned home. A duty of care check in December 2020 stated that he had gone off radar. We were informed.'

'Duty of care check?'

'Standard procedure for anyone with a medical discharge. Strictly speaking, it became the responsibility of his parent regiment, in this case, The Rifles. This involved periodic welfare checks to make sure he was safe and accessing appropriate ongoing support. With former Special Forces personnel, additional checks are carried out by us and by the intelligence services.'

'Additional checks?'

'Checking that he was not a danger to himself... or others.'

'And that he was not a security risk in terms of breaches of the Official Secrets Act?'

'Indeed.'

'But you weren't able to do that because he'd taken himself off?'

'He had left home. No forwarding address. Nobody knew where he was living. He had withdrawn the whole of his lump sum. His army pension was sitting in his bank account. Other than the lump sum, he had made no withdrawals, and no use of his credit cards. His mobile phone was dead and untraceable. Nothing on social media – he'd closed it all down when he joined Special Forces. Standard procedure.'

'Can you tell us how much his lump sum was?'

'Is that relevant?'

'It could be. It would tell us what resources he had available to him.'

He checked the file. 'Thirty-four thousand, two-hundred and forty pounds.'

The End Game

'That's quite a lot?'

'It could have been more if he'd stuck around, and asked Veterans UK to assess his entitlement to additional benefits from the Army Compensation Scheme. As it was, the fact that he was no longer fit for military employment was deemed not to have been directly caused by his military employment, only aggravated by it. That could have been challenged, as could his degree of fitness for alternative employment.'

'Can you tell us more about his behaviour following his son's death?'

Captain Subedi responded. 'When Masters returned from compassionate leave, he insisted he was fine, but we had him assessed by our medical team as a matter of course. They found him fit for duty. But as time went on, we noticed that he was not his usual self.'

'In what way?'

'Normally he was positive, focussed, self-contained but okay with the banter, but now he was uncharacteristically quiet. Seemed to prefer his own company. When asked if he was okay, he'd shrug and make no effort to join in. That gave us cause for concern. We operate in small teams. There has to be a special bond between everyone in the team. They need to know they can rely on each other in the most extreme circumstances. The tipping point came after he'd viewed his son's inquest by video link. He went berserk and smashed up his room. His wife was frightened of what he might do to her, or himself. We sent a medical team round, he was sedated and taken by ambulance to an army hospital in Portsmouth. He was diagnosed with grief disorder and associated PTSD. Once he was discharged from the hospital's care, we had no option but to return him to his regiment.'

'How did he take it?'

He must have known it was coming. He appeared to be resigned to the fact. But you'd have to ask them.'

Jo checked her notes.

'You were going to tell me,' she said, 'about the particular skills that he acquired through his military service.'

She sensed movement behind her, and a chair being pushed back.

The End Game

The major stood up and nodded for his second in command to do the same.

'We need to take a break,' he said. 'We shouldn't be too long.'

Chapter 57

In less than five minutes, the three men returned.

'Thank you,' Major Hodgkiss said. 'Now, where were we? Oh yes, skills and training.' He steepled his fingers. 'Well, there's quite a list. Captain Subedi will enlighten you. Anil?'

'There are the basic infantry skills,' Subedi said, 'such as battle fitness, weapons training, patrol support, field skills, self-defence – those are a prerequisite for selection. Maxwell will already have been well versed in those. Then, of course, there followed Special Services initial training.'

He leaned forward, warming to his narrative.

'We have a catch-all term for our core skills,' he said. 'SERE, which stands for Survive, Evade, Resist, Extract. This includes survival skills, surveillance and reconnaissance training, and signals, high, low, and free-fall parachuting and counterterrorism. When he'd finished all that, there came the squadron-specific training. In his case, this meant covert surveillance, identification of key hostile targets, planting bugs and tracking devices, hidden cameras, covert entry to buildings and vehicles, advanced driving, close-quarter battle, advanced signals training, and intensive language training.'

'In which languages is Mr Masters proficient?' Carly asked.

'Arabic, Pashto, and, to a much lesser extent, Dari Persian and Somali.'

'That's very impressive,' Jo said.

Subedi smiled. 'All of our operatives are sent on intensive language courses, and most are multilingual.

The End Game

Now, where was I? Oh yes, he also had infil and exfil training...'

He saw the look on Carly's face.

'... the process of avoiding discovery while infiltrating a hostile target area or site, and the reverse, extracting persons – friendly or hostile – from a hostile area.'

He sat back, signalling that he had finished.

'In relation to Sergeant Masters's training,' Jo said, 'you haven't mentioned anything about the preparation of explosive devices. Is that something with which he may be familiar?'

'Ah...' said the major. 'Well... as we've already explained, the role of the Special Reconnaissance Regiment is to carry out *covert* operations. Engagement with the enemy, indeed, anything at all that might draw attention to their presence, would critically undermine that mission and threaten the entire operation.'

He paused, his fingers tapping the file in front of him.

'However...?' Jo said.

The major's eyes looked past her, towards the man from the unnamed ministry, and back again.

'Once in a blue moon, a squadron may find it necessary to employ an explosive device.'

'For what purpose?'

'For example, to create a diversion in the face of an imminent threat of detection. To evade capture. Or, in extremis, to protect friendly forces.'

'All of our personnel are able to identify IEDs, and how to avoid them,' the captain added. 'As for defusing them, devices are so varied and unpredictable, that's best left to experts in Ordnance Disposal.'

'So, to be clear,' Jo said, 'Sergeant Masters would have known how to prepare and deploy an explosive device, improvised or otherwise?'

'Yes.'

The two detectives look at each other. Carly nodded. Jo closed her file.

'I think that just about covers it,' she said, 'except for asking again if you have even an inkling of where he might be, or how we might locate him?'

The End Game

The two soldiers looked at each other, and then shook their heads in unison.

'That's a no, I'm afraid,' Major Hodgkiss said.

'In that case,' said Jo, 'thank you for your time and your cooperation.'

'We always seek to cooperate with the relevant authorities,' he said, 'wherever possible.'

As Jo and Carly gathered up their bags and tablets, the captain and the major rose to their feet.

'If I may ask a question?' said the man in the corner.

The two detectives turned to face him.

'Go ahead,' said Jo.

'You stated at the outset that if Sergeant Masters does turn out to be implicated in the case that you're investigating, you think it unlikely that it has anything to do with his military service per se?'

'That's correct,' she replied, 'unless there's something significant about his service that you've not yet shared with us?'

'Major?' the man said, his face expressionless.

'No,' Hodgkiss responded, 'but would I be right in thinking that the possible motive to which you referred may be connected with his son having taken his own life?'

'I'm afraid we're unable either to confirm or deny that while the investigation is ongoing,' Jo said.

Carly had her hand on the door when the man from the ministry spoke again.

'One last thing, Detective Inspector,' he said. 'When it was discovered that Sergeant Masters had gone off radar, we made two subsequent attempts to locate him, without success. He clearly does not wish to be found. Frankly, if *we* were unable to find him, I think it highly unlikely that you will.' He smiled thinly. 'But if you do, please let us know.'

Jo returned his smile.

'Likewise,' she said.

Chapter 58

Nexus House, 7 p.m.

'That about covers it,' Jo said, wrapping up her report to the syndicate briefing. 'Although both DS Whittle and I had the feeling that so far as the military were concerned, at best, they were treading on eggshells, and at worst, deliberately hiding something.'

'The presence of that anonymous man from the ministry wasn't helping,' Carly added, 'and they were bound to be worried about the potential embarrassment and attention that a trial might bring. Especially when we weren't disclosing much about our investigation.'

'If our hunch was right, and the man *was* from one of the secret services,' Jo said, 'he'd almost certainly have known about the IED attacks, because Counter Terrorism will have flagged them.'

Caton stood and joined them beside the whiteboard.

'Thank you,' Caton said. 'Great job. Now grab a drink and have a sit-down. You must both be knackered.'

'We've been sitting down all bloody day,' Jo quipped, drawing sympathetic laughter as the two of them walked over to the coffee machine.

Caton brought up an image of Maxwell Masters on the whiteboard. It was one of the photos Carly and Jo had brought back with them.

'Right,' he said, 'this is our prime suspect. Maxwell Masters. As you've just heard he has an impelling motive, driven by grief over his son's suicide, together with an overwhelming sense of guilt that he wasn't there to prevent it, nor to attend his funeral.'

The End Game

'Aggravated by him and his missus splitting up?' Carter suggested.

'And devastated that it led to him being kicked out of the army,' said Jimmy Hulme.

'Medically discharged,' Jo Stuart corrected.

'Same difference,' Jack Franklin responded.

There were groans.

'Sorry,' he said.

It was Jimmy Hulme all over again, Caton reflected, before his miraculous conversion following his promotion. Except that promotion was the last thing DC Franklin was looking at.

'Given his Special Services background,' Caton continued, 'he has an almost unique ability to reconnoitre his targets and carry out the attacks covertly, remain undetected and evade arrest.' He paused. 'So how do you propose that we track him down? Any ideas?'

Josh Nair raised a hand. 'He must have a vehicle of some kind.'

'Not necessarily,' said DC Gadd.

'What are you suggesting?' Nair responded. 'That he's travelling back and forth on the Metrolink and the number 8 bus with a bag full of explosive devices?'

'He wouldn't be the first. And he'd know we'd be looking out for a motor or a bike of some kind?'

Jimmy Hulme twisted in his seat. 'He'd also know that every bus and every Metrolink tram has CCTV cameras, and that we'd be checking those as a matter of course!'

'Which we have been doing,' said DC Franklin, 'around the clock. And we've not identified anyone who looks remotely like him, or even anyone who leaves or boards a vehicle in the vicinity of more than one of the crime scenes in a whole two-hour window either side of the known or estimated time of each incident.'

'What about the rest of the passive media?' Caton asked.

'We've checked and double-checked all the images from CCTV around the crime scenes, and the static and mobile traffic and general surveillance cameras.'

'And?'

The End Game

'Nothing. Same with the ANPR cameras, all of which are some distance from the crime scenes. They record so many vehicles it's like looking through a haystack unless you know what vehicle you're looking for.'

'Keep trying,' said Caton.

He stared at the image. Maxwell stared back at him. A blank stare, giving nothing away. Here was a man used to yomping miles at a time, carrying seventy kilos or more, practised at blending in, staying invisible. They would have to try another tack.

'We need to get inside his head,' he said, 'to think like him. Manchester is a hostile environment. How does he remain undetected?'

'Change his appearance and identity and hide in plain sight?' said Carter.

'We should have pressed Sterling Lines to let us have a list of any false identities and legends he may have been given while he was with Special Services,' Jo said ruefully.

'Probably as well you didn't,' Caton said. 'That might have made them even more cagey. But we can still do it. DS Hulme, I'll leave that with you.'

'He'll have to have a base of some kind,' Carter pointed out. 'It's unlikely to be a hotel or a short let – he'll know we'll be checking those.'

'What about an Airbnb?' someone called out. 'He could easily move from one to another.'

'That's possible,' Carter said, 'but he'll know he's leaving a credit card trail even if it is with a false identity.'

'Wouldn't he be more likely to pose as a homeless person?' Amit Patel suggested. 'He'd be as good as invisible during the day, move around freely at night without arousing suspicion, and kip down in a different doorway or railway arch every night?'

'Or alternatively,' Henry Powell said, 'he could have a one-man tent and bivouac anywhere on brownfield sites or out on the hills.'

'In which case, how would he get from the hills to Jake's house, say, or into the city?' Caton asked.

'He could have a mountain bike, or a motor of some kind parked up nearby. Besides, he's used to yomping for miles on foot.'

The End Game

'Anyone else?' Caton asked.

This was met with silence.

'Very well,' he said. 'Let's move to actions. Ged – good to see you back! – can you note these for us, please?'

He waited for the office manager to sit with her laptop, and then began.

'One, contact the city council homeless outreach team, Street Support, as well as hostels and soup kitchens, and set up a force-wide alert. Two, get the Digital Imaging and Reconstruction Team to produce a four-pack of the photo the wife gave us, along with three new images showing how he might look now without a disguise, or with a beard, glasses, and a change of hairstyle.'

'Do you intend to release these images to the press and media?' Jimmy Hulme asked.

'Yes, but only the undisguised one to be going on with. Let's start with the GMP Twitter and Facebook feeds, and then the *Manchester Evening News* in the form of an appeal stating that we believe this person may have some vital information; that we would like him to come forward to assist us; and if any members of the public see him, please to let us know . . . et cetera, et cetera.'

'That's going to alert him to the fact that we're on to him,' Carter pointed out.

'I have no doubt that he'll already have assumed that,' Caton said. 'Besides, our first priority is to protect the victims from further harm. And even if it does force his hand, it may cause him to rush his next move and make a mistake.'

He paused and turned to where Jo and Carly were perched with their mugs of coffee.

'Remind me,' he said, 'did we get a line on any friends or former colleagues?'

'According to his wife,' Jo said, 'he didn't really have a lot of friends. He was always a loner, but more so since he joined Special Forces. There was one former colleague though who she thought was the closest thing he had to a friend. They'd sometimes meet up for a drink. And she'd heard them talking on the phone a couple of times.'

The End Game

'That's right,' Carly said. 'Tony Bates. Nickname "Tiny". Lived next door to Masters. His wife, Hazel, was Sandra Masters's best friend. Like Masters, he's also divorced. Now lives up here in Liverpool, the wife thinks.'

'And you know all this because?' Caton said.

All eyes were on Carly.

'I decided to do some digging while Jo was driving us back. I called Mrs Masters, got her friend's number, then I called her.'

'That's called being a detective, ' Caton said to those at the back of the room. 'Good work, DS Whittle.'

Carly kept her head down and focussed on her coffee. There was going to be banter later. Nothing she couldn't handle.

'Right,' said Caton. 'Duggie, I need his address, tonight. DS Whittle, you go and see him in the morning and take DC Powell with you. DS Hulme, get onto The Rifles and find out if they carried out a psychological assessment before his medical discharge and, if so, what it tells us about his mental state.'

'That's confidential information, Boss,' Hulme reminded him. 'They don't have to tell us.'

'Make a Section Two application,' Caton told him, 'prevention or detection of a crime, then use your legendary charm to persuade them.'

He looked at the board on which Ged had just finished typing the final action.

'That should do it,' he said. 'The rest of you carry on with the tasks you've been assigned. We're getting closer.'

He went over to Jo and Carly.

'Thank you for today,' he said. ' It was a pleasure to have you on the team again, Jo, if only briefly. I hope we can do it again.'

'Let's hope so,' she said, 'but next time, can we keep it local? Somewhere north of the Watford Gap would be good.'

Chapter 59
Day Seven
Thursday 8th September

'How much further?' Carly asked.

Henry checked the satnav. 'Two miles,' he said. 'Remind me. Why did we have to meet him here?'

They were on the Wirral Peninsula, six miles southwest of Liverpool, a stone's throw from the M53, surrounded by fields and hedges.

'Because he's working. Something he couldn't get out of. And the only window he had all day was between nine thirty and ten fifteen this morning.'

Henry pointed to the screen. 'We're already five minutes late.'

Carly grimaced. But for that pile-up on the M62 they'd have been fine, despite the rush hour. 'Hang on,' she said, putting her foot to the floor.

'Slow down,' he told her. 'You're going to miss it.'

'Don't worry about me,' she told him, 'just keep looking for a sign.'

'I think we just passed it.'

She cursed. 'Why didn't you say?'

'Because it was only a tiny sign, and you were going too fast.'

It took another two minutes to find a passing place she could reverse into.

'I told you,' Henry said, pointing to a small brown board with gold letters, set back on the grass verge.

He had a point, Carly conceded, as she steered between

The End Game

the metal gates and up the long winding tree-lined drive bordered by daffodils.

'Did you Google this place?' she asked.

'Yep. It's a five-star luxury boutique hotel with coach house. Limited number of bedrooms. Big on weddings and exclusive events. I wonder what brings an ex-SAS trooper here.'

'Ex-SRR trooper,' she reminded him. 'That may be an important distinction for him, and we don't want to piss him off before we're even started.'

He grinned. 'Right-ho, Boss.'

She glanced at him. 'And you don't want to piss *me* off either!'

The gravel drive ended in a wide-open space in front of an Edwardian mansion.

'Looks like we have a reception committee,' she said.

There were three large black vehicles, with privacy glass windows. Beside each one stood identical black-suited males: stocky, hair close-cropped, alert, a single coil of wire extending from behind their collars to a silicone earpiece. On the steps behind them stood a woman identically equipped.

'Now we know what he does,' Henry observed. 'Close protection. I'm betting that Beamer is an X5 VR6 Protection model, and the other two are Range Rover Sentinels. Bullet-proof, bomb-proof, blast-proof, they may not look like it but they're mobile fortresses!'

Carly had to hand it to him – he certainly knew his cars.

'Well over a million and a half all told, I'd say,' he added.

'Pretty special VIPs then,' she said, slowing to a halt. 'I'm guessing this is not Protection Command?'

'You'd guess right,' he replied. 'I often came across that lot while I was in the Met. This is definitely a private outfit. We're talking high-net-worth individuals – crooked or straight – former and exiled heads of state, visiting foreign royal families, former prime ministers and presidents, foreign dignitaries not covered by the Vienna Convention, and celebrities believed to be vulnerable to stalking, theft or kidnap for ransom. Plus, anyone receiving death threats who can afford this kind of protection.'

The End Game

The woman descended the steps, strode over to where the car had stopped and indicated for Carly to lower her window.

'You are?' she said.

They held up their ID cards.

'Greater Manchester Police, for Mr Bates,' Carly said. 'We have an appointment.'

The woman nodded, stood up, and turned her head as she spoke into her lapel mike. She turned back and pointed to the opposite side of the drive.

'Park your car in one of those bays, please,' she said, 'and then join me.'

They were halfway up the steps when a man appeared at the top. Around six foot three, and fourteen stone, his muscular build was evident in a navy double-breasted suit and charcoal-grey trousers. He exuded an air of quiet confidence.

'Tony Bates,' he said. 'Welcome.'

'I'm sorry we're late,' Henry said. 'The traffic was horrendous.'

'Unfortunately, that now means I can only spare you twenty minutes,' Bates replied as he led them into the building. 'You can't be here when the client arrives.'

'I take it you provide security services?' Carly said.

'My employer does, together with VIP executive protection.'

He led them through the large hall into an even larger room on the left, with views out across manicured lawns. He indicated two sofas either side of a coffee table.

'Take a seat.'

He waited until they were comfortable and then sat down opposite them.

'I gather you wanted to talk about Peanuts?' he said.

'Peanuts?' Carly responded.

'Maxwell Masters, M&Ms . . . Originals obviously. We all had a moniker in regiment – mine was "Tiny".'

'Obviously.'

'Mine was "Sooty",' said Henry.

'Who were you with?' Bates asked.

'First, The Queen's Dragoon Guards.'

'Respect!' Bates said. 'Were you in Helmand?'

'The winter of 2011, out of Camp Bastion. I drove a Jackal 2.'

'We were redeployed around then,' Bates said. 'I guess our paths never crossed.'

Henry laughed. 'I think I'd have remembered you if they had.'

'Can we get this interview started?' Carly said. 'Time's slipping away.'

Bates raised his eyebrows. 'Interview?'

'Only in as much as we'll be making notes.'

'In that case, there'll be a limit as to what I can tell you.'

'DC Powell and I have signed the Official Secrets Act,' she said.

Bates smiled thinly. 'It's more complicated than that,' he said. 'Why don't you crack on and we'll see where it leads?'

The door opened. A man dressed like the rest of Bates's team stood there.

'You'll have to excuse me,' Bates said. 'I won't be long.'

Chapter 60

Bates sat down.

'Sorry about that,' he said. 'Please, carry on.'

'I gather you and Masters were close?' Carly said.

'Close as you're likely to be when your lives depend on having each other's backs. Besides, we were neighbours.'

'On the estate in Credenhill?'

'Correct.'

'So you saw a lot of each other off duty?'

'I didn't say that. We might have seen each other over the garden fence. Had the occasional barbecue. But as far as I was concerned, R & R was family time. Anything to do with work was off limits. Besides, it was important for our personal security that we all kept a low profile. Didn't advertise what we did, or who we did it with.'

'But your neighbours must have known?'

'Only that we worked on the base. But they had no idea who was admin and who was Special Forces. And that's the way we kept it.'

'Is that how Masters saw it?'

'Peanuts didn't need to be told. He was a natural introvert. He took fitness to a whole new level. He'd rather run up and down a mountain or cycle 50 K than go down the pub. His idea of a rest was to camp out in the wild. He took Danny with him a few times – to toughen him up, I guess. But it wasn't the boy's thing. They had a falling out.'

'Not according to his wife,' Carly said. 'She said it was her husband who lost interest in taking his son with him?'

Bates frowned. 'I didn't know that. But it makes sense.'

'How come?'

'Of all of us, Peanuts found it hardest to come down after a tour. Sure, we all had reactions: the occasional nightmares and night sweats, irritability, short tempers, bouts of solitary drinking. It was hell for wives and partners. That's why so few of the marriages lasted, mine included. Most of us found a way of coping well enough to be able to function. A couple of us had allotments. One guy took up watercolour painting. Another joined the local folk club. All of us kept up our fitness regime.' He shook his head. 'But Peanuts got more and more detached. Turned in on himself. Especially after Danny died.'

'Were you there when he found out?'

'Yes.'

'And?'

There was a long pause.

'Some of what I'm about to tell you has no direct relevance to your investigation. It's just context. Understand?'

'Yes.'

She put her tablet aside. Henry followed her lead.

'We'd been deployed to Somalia,' Bates began. 'Our mission was to locate and identify targets for elimination. Intel had got wind of a meeting between some corrupt officials in Eritrea who were diverting funds to support al-Shabaab, the Islamist militant group. We were holed up two hundred miles west of Mogadishu, in the hills overlooking Bardhere. Upwards of forty degrees heat, tropical downpours. It was the kind of place we'd stick out like a sore thumb, but we had a local asset with eyes on the place where the meeting was to take place: a small compound containing half a dozen single-storey concrete houses on the edge of the city. But there was a problem. We were told the meeting had been delayed by a week. And then our asset got sick. Fever, coughing, breathlessness.'

'Covid?' Hunt ventured.

Bates shrugged. 'Who knows? It meant he couldn't monitor the conversations captured by the parabolic microphone we'd installed on our asset's roof.'

'Didn't you have a KingFish?' Henry asked.

Carly stared at him.

'Mobile traffic intercept and location-tracking device,' he explained.

'We did,' Bates said, 'but we were too far away from the target to divert the signals from local cell towers. Besides, the asset wasn't trained to use Kingfish. The upshot was we were sitting on the side of a mountain with only visual data to go on. We had no option but to send someone in under cover of darkness. Peanuts spoke Amharic and Arabic better than the rest of us put together. We didn't have to ask – he volunteered.'

His face clouded over.

'That was April twentieth. The night his son died. Only we didn't find that out until we were back in the UK.'

'Why not?' Carly asked. 'Surely they were able to communicate with you?'

'We had short-burst sat-com between them and us, and Bowman tactical radios between us and Peanuts. But we were at a critical point in the op, and Command were between a rock and a hard place. Do they tell him, and risk the operation, or wait till we're out of there and risk his ire?'

'They had a duty of care,' Carly said.

Bates nodded. 'They did. But you could argue that not telling him was the lesser of two evils. There was no second-guessing how the news might affect him. If knowing that his son had just killed himself compromised his ability to focus on the job in hand that was likely to jeopardise the mission, his safety, and ours too.'

'Couldn't they have flown in a replacement, and got him out of there?' Henry asked.

Bates turned to him. 'You should know better,' he said. 'Bardhere was bristling with competing militia groups. Neither the Somali intelligence and security service nor the Somali police force were aware of our presence; we had to keep it that way. To make it worse, on the morning of the twenty-first there was a major build-up of al-Shabaab fighters in and around the target compound. They threw a ring of fighters – most of them trigger-happy teenagers – around the district, including our asset's house. There was no way Maxwell could have been ex-filed and a replacement flown in, without compromising the mission.' He paused.

The End Game

'You've heard of Black Hawk Down?'

'I saw the film,' Carly responded.

'Me too,' Henry said.

'Then you'll understand. We're talking potential bloodbath.'

'What did you do?' Henry asked.

'We had no option but to sit it out. Ten days passed, then we received the heads-up that the meeting was on. Late afternoon on day eleven we watched the convoy arrive. Four SUVs and two pick-ups full of heavily armed militia. The objective was to send confirmation and get the hell out of there. But there was a problem.'

'How to get Maxwell out too?' Carly ventured.

'Exactly. Then we had a stroke of luck. That ring of fighters I told you about was redeployed to form a shield around the compound. As soon as darkness fell, Maxwell made his way back to us. We sent confirmation, and then headed for an RV forty miles away in the mountains. Twenty-four hours later, we were back at Sterling Lines.'

'But too late for his son's funeral?'

'Don't forget, it was early days in the pandemic. The bodies were piling up and the hospital morgues and funeral directors were overwhelmed. Only members of the immediate household could attend, but because Max's mother was dead, his father out of it, and Sandra's parents had Covid, she was allowed a family friend. Hazel, my wife, accompanied her to Danny's funeral. It was a bleak affair by all accounts. The hearses were backed up at the crem, and it was all over in under ten minutes.'

He shook his head and scuffed the toe of his shoe on the back of his trouser leg.

'So much for closure.'

'You said Masters's father was out of it. What did that mean?'

'After his wife died, he took to the bottle. For the last ten years of his life, he was an alcoholic.'

'Was?'

'Sandra told Hazel he'd died of Covid sometime in the autumn of 2020, around six months after Peanuts lost Danny.'

The End Game

Carly looked at her notes. Henry filled the silence.

'How did Sergeant Masters deal with his grief after his son died?' he asked.

'I don't believe he did. To me he was in denial. Insisted he was fine. He even fooled the compulsory psych evaluation into believing he was fit for duty. You have to remember that he'd been trained to hide his feelings. To fool interrogators. To get on with the job whatever happens. But we could all tell he wasn't right. The only surprise was that he lasted as long as he did before he cracked. The trigger was him watching the inquest by video link. He locked himself in his room, smashed it up, and refused to come out. Sandra was beside herself. She didn't want to call the police, so she told Hazel, who called me. We tried talking him down, but he didn't respond. There was just silence.'

'What did you do?'

'I broke the door down. The room looked like a hurricane had swept through it. Even the fitted wardrobes had been torn off the wall. The bed was upside down. We found him under the mattress, curled up in a foetal position. I had no option but to call it in.'

'What happened?'

'The RSM, our regimental medic and the chaplain arrived. He was sedated by the medic and transferred to the specialist Defence Medical Service facility in Portsmouth. He was there for over six weeks. He came home to get his gear, but not to Stirling Lines. We were told he'd been returned to his regiment.'

'Did you have any contact with him after he came home?'

'I tried, but he never returned my calls. Sandra couldn't take it any more and went back to live with her parents. Then I heard he'd been given a medical discharge. That would be late summer 2020?'

'September,' Carly told him.

'Yeah, well I was away on my last tour then. When I got back, early November, the second national lockdown had kicked in. Peanuts was long gone, and no one knew where.'

The door opened. The female from the steps stood there with a hand to her right ear.

The End Game

'Incoming,' she said. 'Five minutes.'

'Thank you,' Bates responded.

His colleague left, leaving the door ajar. Bates stood up.

'That's it, I'm afraid,' he said. 'You can't be here when the client arrives.'

Without waiting for them, he turned and strode towards the door. Carly caught up in the hallway and fell in step with him.

'You didn't ask us why we wanted to talk to you about Masters,' she said.

'I didn't need to,' he replied.

'You already knew?'

He nodded.

'Who told you? SRR? MI5?'

'Does it matter?'

'Not really.'

He smiled. 'Good,' he said.

She set off down the steps, and then turned. Henry was on the step above. She had to put a hand up to prevent him from colliding with her.

'Steady, Boss!' Henry said.

Carly waved him to the side so she could make eye contact with Bates.

'One last question,' she said. 'There was mention of a tragic accident involving a member of the parachute regiment. How was Masters involved?'

Bates's face clouded over as he stared down at her.

'June 2019, the Brecon Beacons. A Para on his final endurance TAB was overcome by heat exhaustion. He got disorientated and fell down a slope into a small ravine, in the course of which his GPS tracker was damaged. He must have known he was in trouble because he decided to slip his kit off and sit in the shade of a bush. That's where they eventually found him. Masters was manning the last checkpoint the Para passed through. He thought he should have recognised signs of heat exhaustion. Both the inquest and the MOD enquiry exonerated him. He appeared to accept that, but I had a lingering feeling that he still blamed himself.'

He glanced skywards. They could hear the sound of a chopper approaching.

The End Game

'Right, I need you to leave sharpish. Anything else you want to know, leave me a voicemail.'

***

'Sooty!' Carly said as they climbed into the car. 'How did they get away with calling you that?'

'It wasn't exactly racist,' Powell said. 'Our corporal was a Henry too, and they'd already christened him "Sweep", because he went round shouting "Izzy Wizzy, let's get busy!"' He grinned. 'Got my own back though – I bought a high-power water pistol and soaked the lot of them five minutes before a barracks inspection.'

Carly shook her head, started the engine and set off.

'Big boys' games,' she muttered.

Chapter 61

Naval Street, Ancoats, 3 p.m.

'Come away from that window,' said Louie. 'You're making us nervous.'

Jake failed to respond.

'Speak for yourself,' Nuan said.

'Okay, you're making *me* nervous. What are you doing anyway?'

Jake turned and walked towards them. 'Checking they're still there,' he said. He sat down on the sofa next to Nuan.

'Are they?' she asked.

''Course they are. They daren't move after the bollocking I gave them when our cars got torched.'

'That wasn't their fault,' Louie pointed out. 'I still think we'd be safer working from home – after all, they're guarding our homes as well as this place.'

'I'm not at home, remember?' Jake growled. 'I'm in a hotel. And that's under surveillance too.'

'You know where I stand,' Louie said. 'Let's just do what he wants and get it over with.'

Jake stared at him. 'Aside from the money and the adverse publicity, how do we know that would be the last of it?'

'We don't, but it's better than living like this. We have no idea how many levels this game has. He's going to keep going till we pay up or the police find him, and there's bugger all sign of that happening. And what about our nearest and dearest? What if he starts targeting them? We can't have them all watched.'

Nuan stood up.
'Where are you going?' Jake asked.
'Home,' she said. 'I need to talk to Thelma.'

***

New Islington Marina Apartments

Nuan had only just arrived back at her apartment in New Islington when the doorbell rang. It was Thelma. Looking flustered and tense, she brushed past Nuan and threw her bag on the island in the middle of the kitchen.

'What's so urgent I had to leave work early? And why couldn't you tell me over the phone?'

'Because I have no idea whether or not The Boss has hacked our phones?'

'Stop calling him The Boss,' Thelma said. 'You're just giving him power over you, which is exactly what he wants.'

'No, I'm not,' Nuan protested, 'that's just what he calls himself.'

Thelma threw her arms up in despair. 'Exactly my point! Why don't you call him shit-face instead?'

Nuan frowned. 'Because we've never seen his . . .'

'Aargh!' Thelma responded. 'Why do you have to take everything literally?'

She saw Nuan's expression and immediately regretted having reneged on her promise to herself never again to raise the subject. The amazing talents that accompanied Nuan's spectrum diagnosis far outweighed the small, if irritating, characteristics.

'I'm sorry, Nu,' she said. 'Why don't we just call him *he*,' she grinned, 'with a small aitch, to match the size of his penis?'

Nuan's expression didn't change. 'I'm worried,' she said, 'that *he* will target the apartment next. Or that he may come after you or Langston.'

Thelma walked around the island, sat down next to Nuan, and placed an arm around her. 'Relax, Nu,' she said, 'Langston is still with Trev at the moment, and the marina has CCTV and regular security checks around the clock.'

Nuan frowned. 'I thought Trev was going back to Dubai tomorrow?'

'He is. He's going to drop Langston off here this evening.'

Nuan sat up. 'No! That's a very bad idea. Langston hasn't been here for the past three weeks. This person probably has no idea who he is.'

'You can't know that for certain.'

Nuan shook her head. 'Why take the risk? Move the *Harlem* today. There's that marina closer to Langston's school. Go there. You can come back when the police have arrested the guy.'

She folded her arms, her face blank, eyes staring at an imaginary point on the wall. Thelma knew this look. It spoke of unshakeable resolve. There was no arguing with Nuan when she was like this. Any attempt to do so would see her retreat into herself and her work. Then it would take days to coax her back to the comfortable and mutually affirming relationship it had taken them months to create.

Thelma picked up her bag. 'Very well, I'll do it for you, Nu, but I'll worry about you all the time. So there's one condition: I'll text and FaceTime you morning, noon and night to check you're okay – and you will *always* pick up. Agreed?'

Nuan nodded. 'Agreed.'

Thelma walked over to her, gave her a hug, and kissed her gently on the cheek.

'We're good?' she said.

'We're good,' Nuan repeated, though her mind was plainly elsewhere.

Chapter 62

New Islington Marina

Thelma left the building and turned towards the marina. There were times when she wondered if this relationship was worth it. True, Nu had helped to claw her back from a dark place when the decree absolute came through.

Cold hard logic had more than made up for her emotional deficit. Thelma had a surfeit of friends offering gin and sympathy. There were even a few who had been there themselves and were genuinely empathetic. But Nu alone listened without judgement, refused to take sides, and never offered advice. Her questions – clinical and thought-provoking – had enabled Thelma to chart her own way out of depression, to own the process, and to come out stronger and more resilient.

Furthermore, Nuan had been great for Langston. Within a week of their having met, she had applied herself to learning British Sign Language with the same intensity that she applied to her work. Within a fortnight she had become fluent, and she and Langston had become as thick as thieves. They had recognised in each other the loneliness that often came with being different. The shared experience of attempting to communicate with others – those who quickly tired of the effort required to communicate with him, and those who misinterpreted Nuan's lack of emotion and her candour as rude and contemptuous. Since they had found each other, Langston had blossomed, at home and at school.

Thelma paused alongside the narrowboat. Everything looked secure. She stepped over the side and down onto the stern well-deck. The cylinder lock on the cabin door was just as she had left it. She opened the app on her iPhone. The image from the hidden camera showed an empty cabin, and the alarm was shown as active. She pocketed her phone, lifted the hatch over the engine, and knelt so that she could reach down and remove the cork bung she had inserted in the air inlet. Replacing the hatch, she then stood up, brushed off the knees of her jeans and climbed back onto the bank. She inspected the heavy-duty nylon ties around the mooring ropes, and then walked towards the stern so she could check the chains securing the three bikes to the roof. All was well.

Turning slowly through three hundred and sixty degrees, Thelma scanned the marina, its paths and green areas, and the blocks of apartments on either side, for anything suspicious or out of place.

Across the water a swan emerged from the reeds, and slid gracefully into the water. Students sat at the scattered tables pretending to study. A young couple lounged on one of the benches in the park, arms around each other as though for mutual warmth or consolation. Here and there, people rested on park benches: a young man in a leather jacket and jeans reading a newspaper, and a woman in her sixties reading a paperback; two girls in school uniform, side by side, ear pods in, staring at their mobile phones.

A man of indeterminate age, clad in a thick woollen overcoat, and sporting long lank hair and a tangled beard, sat eyes closed, head thrown back, warming his face in the welcome autumn sunshine. One of his hands rested on a large bundle tied with string. There was no sign of the person supposedly assigned to watch the entrance to their apartment. Thelma mentally corrected herself – to *Nuan's* apartment – but nor should there have been. Not unless they were putting deterrence before detection.

She turned her attention back to the narrowboat. Picked out in gold against the sleek black hull, the name glinted in the sunlight. *Harlem Renaissance*. She smiled. Turning this boat into a home for herself and Langston had changed her life. Had been *her* renaissance. It had brought Nuan into their lives. She was not going to let some deranged stranger take that away.

The End Game

She climbed back on board, took the ignition key from her bag, and started the engine. Then she returned to the towpath, released the bow and stern mooring ropes, lifted the fenders, and pushed the boat gently away from the bank before stepping back onto the well deck. Having checked that way ahead was clear of traffic, she slipped the gear out of neutral and after a brief burst of speed settled the engine into a steady idle as her floating home eased out into the channel, heading east, away from the city. She checked her watch. Five hours to the Portland Basin, though she could do it in just over half an hour by bike.

The bearded man watched through hooded eyelids until the narrowboat disappeared from view. Then he placed his right hand on the top of the bench for support, rose with the practised caution of a chronic rheumatic, bent to retrieve his bundle, and limped towards the metal bridge.

Chapter 63

Ashton Canal, close to the Portland Basin,
Ashton-under-Lyne, 8.30 p.m.

Thelma placed her hand on Langston's arm. When he turned, she signed that he should slow down. The mooring ropes were difficult to spot now that the sun had set: an accident waiting to happen.

Langston remained on the bank while she stepped into the well deck and unlocked the door. Then he handed her his rucksack and school bag before climbing on board and joining her in the cabin.

He stowed his bags and sat on the dinette sofa watching his mum put the shopping away. He could see from her expression and the way she slammed the fridge door that she was mad about something.

'What's the matter, Mum?' he signed.

'I've forgotten to get the milk and cereals for breakfast in the morning,' she signed back. 'I'm going to have go out again.'

'Mum, you haven't told me why we're here?'

She shook her head. 'It's complicated. But you're much nearer school, so that's good, isn't it?' She picked up the shopping bag. 'I'll take my bike. I'll only be ten minutes or so. You'll be okay, won't you? You can play one of your games on your iPad. And don't forget to lock yourself in.'

Thelma closed the cabin door and removed the lock securing a folding bike to the side of the well deck. She lifted it onto the towpath, unfolded it and locked everything into place, before cycling off towards the marina. As she disappeared from view, the watcher stepped out from the bushes beside the bridge and approached the narrowboat.

The End Game

He had followed the progress of the *Harlem Renaissance* on a bike he had stolen from the roof rack of another boat. Seeing her mooring up, he had assumed that the vessel would remain here overnight and decided to cycle to the farm and back to check that everything was still secure, and to collect some tools. It was fortuitous that he had arrived back just in time to see her leaving.

He paused to check that he was alone, then stepped onto the deck, checked that the cabin door was locked, and knelt down in the well deck. He used a screwdriver to lift the engine hatch, then unscrewed the weed hatch, raised it up and turned his attention to the starter motor. He used the screwdriver to short-circuit the contacts. The engine jolted into action. Within seconds, water began to flood from the weed hatch into the engine compartment. Masters returned to the towpath, untied the forward mooring rope, freed the one at the rear, then placed a foot against the hull and pushed. He watched as the stern, already low in the water, swung slowly away from the bank, leading the boat towards the middle of the canal.

Chapter 64

8.45 p.m.

The instant that she rounded the corner, Thelma knew something was wrong. She pedalled as fast as she could, yelling his name as she went.

'Langston! Langston!'

It was instinctive, as much a cry of fear as of alarm. She braked hard, leapt from the bike, and ran towards the edge of the canal. Her foot caught in a coil of rope and she fell hard onto the towpath, twisting her ankle and bruising her ribs. Oblivious to the pain, she rolled over, untangled her foot and got to her feet.

The *Harlem Renaissance* lay in the middle of the channel. Only the roof, and some twenty inches of the top of the cabin were visible. A plastic plate, two plastic mugs, a fire blanket, and a solitary life jacket drifted on the surface of the canal.

Wild-eyed, Thelma looked up and down the empty towpath. She searched the opposite bank of the canal, where a ten-foot-high stone wall came sheer to the edge of the water. No path, no handholds. She remembered her mobile phone and called her son. The phone was Langston's constant companion, his lifeline. It vibrated strongly to alert him whenever he had a live relay text. An impassive voice informed her that this phone was not available. She screamed twice for help, then dialled 999, her hands shaking.

Thelma's cries of distress carried on the still evening air. As she spoke to the emergency services operator, she saw a man, a woman and a boy in his teens running down

The End Game

the towpath towards her from the direction of the marina. Another man emerged from a narrowboat moored up forty metres away. He looked to see where the screams had come from. She activated the torch on her screen, pointed it towards the sunken boat, and yelled,

'My son is inside there! Please, help me!'

The man unhooked something from the roof of his boat and hurried towards her. As he approached, she could see he was carrying a two-and-a-half-metre-long aluminium and plywood gangplank. Her heart sank. She knew it would never reach. She was trying to talk to him at the same time as to the police on the phone when the trio from the marina arrived.

'What's going on?' the woman asked.

'Her son's in there,' the man with the gangplank told them. 'He's deaf and dumb.'

'I'm going in,' the youth declared.

'Don't you dare, Danny!' the woman said. She turned to Thelma. 'Have you called 999?'

'They're on the phone now,' Thelma said. 'The police and the fire service are on the way.'

'Listen to your mother,' said the other male. 'Leave it to the emergency services.'

'They're not supposed to go in themselves,' the youth said, kicking off his trainers, 'not till their specialist teams arrive.'

He pulled his sweatshirt over his head and, before anyone could stop him, jumped into the canal. The water came up to his chest. He part waded and part swam out to the sunken vessel.

'Should have kept his shoes on,' the plank man observed. 'There's all sorts dumped in there.'

'Be careful, Danny!' the mother shouted.

The youth reached the boat. He tried to pull himself onto the roof but kept slipping back.

'Take a look through the windows,' shouted the plank man.

The youth ducked under the water and disappeared. His mother screamed. He reappeared, spluttered, edged his way along the boat, took a breath, and disappeared again.

The End Game

When he surfaced this time, he clung to the side of the boat, exhausted. Then he flopped back into the water and began to scull with his arms towards the towpath, where the two men grabbed him by the arms and heaved him out.

'What did you see?' his father said.

The boy shook his head. 'Not a lot. It was murky. The water was about a foot from the inside of the roof. But there was no sign of movement.'

They heard the sound of sirens drawing closer. Blue lights strobed the street through the industrial estate on the opposite side of the bridge over the canal. The sirens stopped and a succession of fire officers hurried across the bridge with two police officers hard on their heels.

Three of the firemen carried a short extension ladder, which they proceeded to manoeuvre into place, one end on the towpath, the other on the roof of the barge towards the stern of the boat.

A fourth officer, in a flotation vest, yellow helmet and with breathing apparatus, inched across the ladder and lowered himself onto the well deck. His head and shoulders remained well above the waterline until he ducked through the open door and into the cabin, where the beam of light from his torch swept from side to side towards the front of the boat. Here he seemed to pause to take stock, before slowly returning. After what felt like an age to Thelma, he emerged from the interior, and they heard over the radio, the message, 'All clear!'

The senior fire officer turned to Thelma who was waiting between two male police officers.

'That leaves two possibilities,' he said. 'That your son climbed off the boat before it even left the side of the canal, or he escaped from it before or after it settled on the canal floor. How tall is your son?'

'Four foot eight,' she sobbed.

'In that case, he only had to stand, or climb onto a bunk or a bench to keep his head above water. Can he swim?'

'Yes. And he knows all about how to stay safe on the boat and in the water.'

'Then it's unlikely any harm has come to him.'

'Then where is he?'

The End Game

'Well,' said one of the police officers, 'if he left the boat to go to the shops or come and meet you, then he probably doesn't know the boat has sunk.'

'No,' she said, 'he wouldn't do that, and even if he did, he wouldn't leave the cabin door open. You have to find him.'

The senior fire officer, who had been deep in conversation with his colleague, turned and approached her. The look on his face filled her with dread.

'There are a few things we don't understand, Ms Dundas,' he said. 'The mooring ropes have clearly been untied, and both the engine hatch and the weed hatch are open. This doesn't look like an accident.'

Thelma's hand flew to her mouth. 'Oh my God!' she exclaimed. 'It must be them! They've taken him! They've got my son! They've taken Langston!'

Chapter 65

Jet Amber Fields, Hyde, 1.5 miles from the Portland Basin, 9 p.m.

Maxwell cursed himself for his carelessness as he pushed the boy up the drive towards the deserted farm.

He should have checked there was no one else aboard, but she had definitely been alone when she'd left New Islington. It was only when he'd heard a bolt being pulled back, seen the cabin door thrust open by the onward rush of water, and the pale startled face peering around the door frame, that he knew he'd been mistaken.

He checked his watch. It was thirty minutes since they'd left the Ashton Canal. Even if the boy's mother had been close behind them, it would have taken her time to raise the alarm, for emergency services to respond, and for them to discover that the boy was missing. She was bound eventually to put two and two together. That would mean putting a search force together. Calling in the police helicopter, dogs. On the plus side, they'd have no idea where to start. There was no point in panicking. He made a decision. He would lock the boy in the barn. Give himself time to get away. Get rid of his beard, change his clothes. Then, if the boy hadn't been found by morning, he'd send them another message. Let them know where to find the lad. Pretend it was all part of the plan.

He unlocked the padlock on the barn door and pushed the boy inside, closing and bolting the door behind him. Then he dragged a chair in front of one of the thick wooden posts supporting the roof braces, beckoned the boy over, and signed for him to sit down and not to move.

The End Game

Keeping one eye on the boy, he crossed to a pile of wooden crates in the corner, where he had spotted a ball of twine he could use to bind his captive's arms and legs to the pillar. As he stood up, twine in hand, the radio scanner he was using to monitor police transmissions squawked into life. He picked it up from the battered table.

Instead of the usual cryptic radio traffic, he heard a series of exchanges around some recent statement about all officers having to be prepared for significant changes to rosters, including probable overtime and the cancelling of all leave, in response to Operation London Bridge. It was a phrase he'd heard before. One he knew was important. In his current state, it heightened his anxiety, but he was damned if he could remember why.

He put the scanner down, switched on the small portable radio and tuned into Radio Manchester in the hope of catching the latest news bulletin. Unusually sombre music was playing. He was about to change station when the music was interrupted.

> *'This is a BBC public service announcement. We have suspended normal programming following this announcement, earlier this evening, from Buckingham Palace:*
>
> *'"The Queen died peacefully at Balmoral this afternoon. The King and the Queen Consort will remain at Balmoral this evening and will return to London tomorrow."'*

Maxwell froze. Time stood still. He forced himself to confront the enormity of what he had heard. Then he remembered the phrase that he and his comrades had long prepared for.

'London Bridge is down!'

He experienced an overwhelming sense of grief, of impotence, and regret. All over the UK, 21 SAS and 23 SAS would be mobilising. Rapid-response Sabre Squadrons at Sterling Lines and in London would be on highest alert. His own regiment, the Special Reconnaissance Regiment, would

The End Game

already be liaising with GCHQ and Anti-Terrorism Command. And here was he. In a godforsaken ruin that perfectly mirrored the life he now led, with a child he had kidnapped and very nearly killed. Maxwell turned to check on the boy.

His heart skipped a beat. The room was empty, the door was open, the boy had gone. He rushed outside and stopped to listen. Hearing the slap of trainers on the towpath, he raced down the drive and onto the path where it wound through the woods. He could tell the boy was heading north, back the way they had come, and set off again. He was level with the bridge crossing the canal by the industrial estate when he heard the squeal of brakes, a thud, and the blaring of a horn. He could no longer hear the sound of running feet. His heart was tight in his chest as he hurried over the bridge and sprinted through the tunnel of trees lining Dunkirk Lane. Where the trees ended and the tarmac began, he stopped.

Thirty metres ahead, a white van stood broadside in the middle of the street. On the pavement, beyond the van, a man was standing facing away from Masters, a phone to his ear. Someone in a yellow high-vis jacket was kneeling on the pavement, with his back to him. A woman and a man came running over from a large industrial unit to Masters's left. As they reached the scene, the person in the high-vis jacket sat back on his heels and turned his head to speak with them. The woman removed her anorak and handed it to him. He laid it carefully over someone on the ground in front of him, whose white trainers were now visible alongside the bushes edging the pavement. Masters turned and jogged back the way he had come.

Chapter 66

Manchester Children's Hospital, 10.30 p.m.

Nuan stood alone in the corridor. DCI Caton and DS Whittle were speaking with a doctor outside the door to Langston's room. The fire doors swung open and Jake and Louie appeared.

'How is he, Nu?' Louie asked.

'He's suffered severe bruising, shock and mild concussion,' she said. 'They're keeping him in overnight for observation as a precaution. Thelma is with him now.'

'What the hell happened?' Jake demanded.

She shook her head. 'I don't know all the details, but it seems that Langston came out of nowhere, running down the middle of the road. A van swerved to avoid him, but he was caught a glancing blow, and thrown onto the pavement.'

'Where was this?' Jake asked.

'Dunkirk Lane, the police said, on the Hyde and Dukinfield border. It's about a mile and a half from where their narrowboat sank.'

'I thought Thelma's barge was moored up in town,' Louie said, 'opposite your apartments?'

Nuan began to sob. 'It was my fault.'

'*Your* fault?' said Jake. 'How can it have been your fault?'

'I told Thelma to move her boat, and that she and Langston should stay away from me until whoever's behind all this is apprehended. But the marina she decided to move to was full, so she had to leave it on an isolated stretch. They must somehow have found it and sunk it. Thelma thought Langston was inside. And now this!'

The End Game

She stared at each of them in turn. 'We have to do what this maniac says before one of us is killed.'

Caton and Carly approached. Jake turned on them.

'How did you let this happen?!' he demanded. 'You do realise it's the same person, don't you?'

'Until we've spoken with Langston, we don't know that for sure,' Caton told him, 'but we are indeed working on that assumption.'

'*Working?* What the hell does that mean?'

'We have officers searching the area around the marina, interviewing potential witnesses, and gathering evidence. As soon as we know anything concrete, I'll let you know.'

The doctor called from the doorway of the side room.

'You can go in now, Detective Chief Inspector,' she said, 'and Ms Dundas would like Ms Lau to join her.'

'Come on, Louie,' Jake said. 'We'll go and grab a coffee, but we'll be back.'

***

Langston Dundas, his head bandaged, sat propped up on a couple of pillows. His face was pale, but eyes were alert as he watched them enter the room.

His mother was sitting next to him. Nuan joined her and the two hugged as though their lives depended on it. Caton and Carly stood awkwardly at the foot of the bed, waiting for the right moment.

Nuan detached herself from Thelma's embrace and began to sign to Langston. The meaning was obvious to the two detectives.

'How are you?'

'Fine.'

'Fine?' she repeated.

He shrugged. 'Okay.'

'I'm sorry,' she said.

He shook his head and his finger. 'Not your fault.'

'I'm sorry to interrupt,' Caton said, 'but if we're going to catch the person who's responsible, we're going to need some answers. Could one of you interpret for us?'

The End Game

Thelma Dundas stood up. 'I will.'

'Thank you,' Caton said. 'Can you please explain to your son that we're police officers?'

'He already knows. I told him. And he knows why you're here. He's anxious to help. Langston is able to lip-read, but I'll also sign what you say.'

'Thank you,' Caton said. 'In which case I shall speak directly to Langston and pause for you to correct any misunderstanding.'

'That would be best,' she said.

Nuan sat down on the seat Thelma had vacated, and Caton began.

'Langston,' he said, 'my name is Tom. My colleague's name is Carly. We're very sorry that this has happened to you. We'll do everything we can to catch those responsible.'

The boy was nodding well before his mother had finished signing.

'Rather than us asking you questions,' Caton said, 'please tell us what happened exactly as you remember it. Is that okay?'

The boy nodded.

'Good,' Caton said. 'When you're ready.'

Chapter 67

The boy turned towards his mother, winced, placed a hand on his chest for a moment, and then began to sign. His mother started to interpret, sticking as closely as possible to his own words.

'When Mum left, I bolted the door like she said, then sat on the sofa with my tablet and began to play *Heleram The Guardian 2*.'

'That's one of his accessible video games,' his mother explained. She signed for him to continue.

'I'd only been playing for a short while when I felt the boat sway a bit, like another boat was going past. I carried on playing. Then I felt the vibrations that come when the engine is running, so I got up and went to check. I'd got as far as the bottom step when the boat jerked. I fell against the wardrobe. I managed to get up and I slid the bolt back. As soon as I opened the cabin door, water began to rush in. I held onto the edge of the door and pulled myself up. The well deck was full of water, and the boat was drifting away from the towpath. The stern was almost completely under the surface.'

The boy turned to face the two detectives. 'There was a man...'

His mother touched him on the shoulder and signed for him to wait. 'This'll work best if I come around to your side of the bed, Detective Chief Inspector,' she said. 'Langston won't have to keep turning his head, and you'll be able to see his expressions.' She went and stood beside Carly Whittle.

'That's better,' she said. 'Please say that again, Langston.'

The End Game

'There was a man with a beard standing on the towpath. He looked surprised to see me. He grabbed the mooring rope and pulled the boat back to the bank. I'd got one hand on the roof and both feet on the side. He waved at me to jump.'

Langston frowned and looked sad. 'I thought he was helping me, but he grabbed my arm and held it tight while he kicked the *Harlem* back away from the bank. Then he dragged me down the towpath, over the bridge, and left along another canal that led away from ours.'

The boy paused and again put his hand to his chest.

'What's the matter?' his mother said, signing at the same time. 'Are you alright?'

Langston nodded and signed something.

'He says it's just a bit sore,' she told Caton and Carly. 'He thinks it might help if he sits up.'

'I can lift him,' Caton said.

'I'll go round the other side,' said Carly. 'It'll be better if we lift him together.'

The two detectives hooked an arm each under the boy's armpits and gently lifted while his mother plumped up the pillows behind him.

'How's that?' Caton asked.

The boy smiled and gave a double thumbs up. He signed again.

'Langston says thanks, that's much better,' his mother continued.

Caton gave him a thumbs up in return. 'Good,' he said. 'You were saying, he took you onto a branch canal?'

Reading Caton's lips, the boy replied instantly and his mother began to interpret again.

'When we were away from the bridge, the man stopped, pulled a bike out from the bushes at the side of the path and then turned and spoke to me. I think that's when he realised that I couldn't hear him or speak to him. He looked surprised. Then he stood close to me and let go. I couldn't see his lips clearly because it was quite dark, but he knew some basic signs. He told me he didn't mean to hurt me, that he was going to let me go. He pointed to his watch. Moved his finger round the clock face twice.

The End Game

I thought he meant in a little while. Maybe two hours?'

His mother turned to Caton. 'I get that he didn't know that Langston was on the boat,' she said, 'and that he didn't want him giving the alarm, but if he didn't mean to harm him, how did he end up in here, like this?'

'Why don't you let Langston answer that,' Caton said. 'He's doing really well.'

She turned back to the bed. 'I'm sorry, Langston, carry on.'

'The man led me through a gate in the hedge and up a track to some old ruined farm buildings. He took me into a barn and made me sit down on an old chair with my back to a wooden post. I thought he was going to tie me up, but he was fiddling with something and got distracted. I crept to the door, slid back the bolt and escaped. I ran down to the towpath, crossed the first bridge I came to, and then ran down a dark lane and out onto the street . . .'

He hesitated and his face went pale. His mother sat on the bed, and took his hand. He looked into her eyes.

'I didn't see it coming,' he said. 'There was just this bright light...'

She leaned forward and gently cradled him in her arms.

Carly whispered in Caton's ear and then left the room. Caton waited until mother and son had composed themselves and then he opened a file on his tablet and showed it to Langston.

'This man who took you to the barn,' he said, 'could this be him?'

The boy stared at the shot that Sandra Masters had given Jo Stuart – the one taken at a New Year's Eve party. He frowned in concentration.

'Take your time,' Caton said.

Langston signed, 'I'm not sure.'

Caton swiped the screen to reveal the photo Jo had captured on her phone in Danny Masters's bedroom.

Langston's eyes widened. He turned to his mother. 'He's a soldier.'

'Yes,' Caton responded, 'but is it him?'

'I can't be sure,' the boy replied. 'His hair was long and he had a beard ... but—'

'But?' Caton said.

The boy looked at Caton, and then back at the photo. *'But I think it's him.'*

Caton breathed out slowly. 'How certain are you,' he said, 'out of ten?'

'Nine?'

Caton smiled and switched off the tablet. 'I have just one more question for Langston if that's alright?' he said.

'As long as it's only one,' Thelma replied. 'You can see it's taken a lot out of him. He's very tired.'

The boy signed, 'It's alright, Mum.'

'Thank you,' Caton said. 'It's just you were on that towpath for quite a while. I was wondering if you saw anybody else? They could be witnesses?'

The boy nodded.

'Langston says there was a man on a bike, and also a woman with a dog,' Thelma said.

'In his own words, please,' Caton prompted.

She turned back to the bed. 'Sorry, Langston,' she said, 'carry on.'

'The man was riding a bike; he was wobbling a bit because the woman had the dog on a lead, and she was going slow. The soldier man was holding my hand so I couldn't say anything, and they wouldn't have been able to see my face properly.'

'Can you describe them at all?'

Langston shook his head apologetically. 'Not really. It was getting dark. But he was quite tall, and youngish, and she was short with short hair. But I think the dog was a German Shepherd.' He looked as though he had let them all down.

'I'm sorry,' he said.

'You have nothing to be sorry about,' Caton told him. 'You've been really helpful, and very brave. You should be proud of yourself. Just concentrate now on getting better.'

Nuan stood up, and Thelma put her arm around her. Caton thanked Thelma, promised them both that he would keep them updated, and turned to go. He knew what the two of them were thinking. That it was he who should be apologising, and that he had absolutely nothing to be proud of. He didn't disagree.

Carly was in the corridor, looking excited. She held up the screen of her mobile phone.

'I think I've found it,' she said. 'He was right. It's an old farm. Right where he said it was.'

Chapter 68
Day Eight
Friday 9th September

Jet Amber Fields, Hyde, 12.05 a.m.

Five of their vehicles were parked beyond the woods less than two hundred metres away. A patrol van blocked the entrance to Dunkirk Lane. A black bomb-squad Land Rover Discovery and an armed response vehicle waited fifty metres away by the bridge. The officers on foot were hunkered down behind a hedge by the track that led to the derelict farmhouse.

'What are the odds he's still there though?' Carter whispered.

'Less than evens,' Henry Powell said, 'though he could be lying low until he reckons everyone's left the scene of the accident.'

'The traffic officers left over an hour ago,' DC Nair pointed out, as he adjusted his stab vest.

'Enough,' Caton told them. 'I'm trying to concentrate on our eye in the sky.'

He crouched beside the drone operator who was staring at the screen of his laptop.

'No car, no obvious heat sources,' the operator said. 'Nobody hiding in the woods.'

Caton turned to the dog handler.

'I'd like you to send him in first,' he said. 'Don't get too close and try to stay out of sight. We'll be following both of you on the livestream from the drone.'

The End Game

'I'll have to be close enough to issue verbal warnings if he confronts someone,' she said, 'as well give him instructions. Standard operating procedure.'

'Then use your initiative,' he told her. 'You'll have two of the firearms unit with you.'

'Sir!' she said. 'Sabre... come!'

She set off with the dog on a lead with the two firearms officers either side of her. From two hundred feet above, the drone began to track their progress: three white shapes and one smaller one, moving ghostlike towards the farm. Caton and the operational firearms commander watched on the screen as she knelt to release the dog. Sabre set off at pace, pausing every ten metres or so to check for scents. He headed straight for the barn to the left of the farmhouse, circled by the door, and tracked back to the farmhouse door. He paused to look back down the track to where his handler was crouching in the dark.

Caton spoke into his radio.

'This is Silver Command. All clear so far. K9 appears to be awaiting instructions. Over.'

'Copy that,' the handler replied. 'I propose to join K9. Over.'

'Roger that,' Caton responded. 'Maximum caution. Do *not*... I repeat... *do not* approach, or attempt to enter, any buildings.'

'Roger that,' she replied.

'I propose we send in the remaining AFOs,' the firearms commander said. 'With all these buildings, those three don't have anywhere near enough cover.'

'Do it,' Caton said.

The three firearms officers appeared on the screen and jogged up the track, where they fanned out to create a semicircle of bright white figures moving slowly towards the buildings. The dog, responding to verbal commands, circled the farmhouse, and then the barn, before exploring the exterior of the remaining outbuildings. Caton and the firearms commander watched as he returned to his handler and sat at her side.

'Sit rep, Silver Command,' she said. 'We have Zero contacts. That's *Zero* contacts.'

'Copy that,' said Caton. 'All officers to withdraw a safe distance, remain vigilant, and await instructions. I'm sending in the Explosive Ordnance Unit.'

'Roger that,' the handler and the rifle officers replied in unison.

Caton looked down at the screen. 'I take it you've not spotted something I've missed?' he said.

'No,' the drone operator replied. 'No sign of any heat sources, and there's been no movement all the time we've been here, other than what looked like a fox, or maybe a badger.'

'That's it then,' Caton said. 'Gold Command, this is Silver Command.'

'Go ahead, Silver Command,' said ACC Gates from the relative calm and absolute safety of GMP Headquarters.

'I propose to send in the bomb squad,' he said. 'As soon as we have the all-clear, I'll send in the SOCO and the tactical aid search team. Over.'

'Copy that, Silver Command,' Gates replied. Caton imagined her raising an eyebrow and flicking imaginary fluff from the collar of her immaculate uniform. 'It's your call, Detective Chief Inspector.'

***

It took twenty minutes to complete the operation. Caton stood in the doorway of the barn watching the scene of crime officers gathering evidence under the glare of Nomad LED floodlights. Every now and then, one or other of them called for the lights to be dimmed or switched off altogether so they could use their specialist handheld lights to check for potential footprints, finger marks or trace evidence. Caton waved Jack Benson over to join him.

'What have you got?' he said.

'A portable radio, a scanner that's tuned to our frequency the remains of some papers that have been burned in a brazier, a tin mug with some decent prints. That's it, but it's early days.'

Caton had already spotted the wooden chair and length of rope that confirmed the boy's story.

The End Game

'Nothing that tells where he may have gone, or what he's planning to do next?'

'Not yet,' Benson said. 'Sorry, Boss.'

'I'm going back to Nexus House,' Caton told him. 'DI Carter will hang on here. Make sure he's told the minute you find something significant.'

'Will do, Boss.'

Caton used his tactical torch to light his way as he hurried down the farm track. He glanced at his watch. Half past midnight. Just over three hours since the accident had been reported. That meant the perpetrator could be well away by now, unless he'd chosen to find another place to hide, draw breath, and decide on his next move. One thing was certain, the boy had not been part of his plans. Dealing with that and the aftermath would have knocked him off kilter. Made him unpredictable, and even more dangerous.

Chapter 69

Nexus House, 1.17 a.m.

The incident room was a hive of activity, the atmosphere electric.

Jimmy Hulme rose from his desk and waved Caton over.

'We tracked down the crew of the ambulance that responded to the 999 call,' he said. 'The paramedic recalled seeing a Land Rover Discovery pass them going in the opposite direction on Dunkirk Lane. He can't swear to it, but he reckons it was a Series 2.'

'Opposite direction?' Caton said. 'Away from the lane that leads to the canal path?'

Hulme had a map up on his screen. He pointed to the spot. 'Either from the Jet Amber car park, this other car park to the east, or his hideaway at the farm?'

'How long did it take the ambulance to respond?'

'Nine minutes.'

'Just time for him to belt back to the farmhouse, pack everything and leave.' Caton straightened up. 'We need the camera footage from the ambulance.'

'That's in hand,' Hulme said. 'We should have it shortly.'

'Shortly isn't soon enough,' Caton replied. 'We need it now. And we need all the footage from any cameras on Dunkirk Lane.'

'Uniform located a number on the industrial units,' the DS said. 'I've got officers tracking down keyholders and night security staff, but it's going to take time.'

'Time we can't afford,' Caton said.

Hulme was busy moving the cursor around his screen with the mouse. He clicked on an email and then on an attachment.

'We've got the images from the ambulance,' he said, opening the file. Caton leaned in.

The time on the webcam was nine twenty-nine in the evening. The strobing lights of the ambulance, and a diffused glow from the walls of industrial units set back from the tarmacked lane, fashioned an other-worldly scene. A dimly lit huddle of figures, backs to camera, hid the focus of their attention. The ambulance began to slow down, and then moved to the right to avoid a vehicle coming towards it. A vehicle without lights, hugging the nearside shadows. The licence plate was partially obscured.

'Pause that!' Caton said.

Hulme ran the footage back and hit the pause button. He zoomed the screen in. Caton was able to make out the last two letters, an H and an R.

Hulme pressed play. They watched as the ambulance came to a halt, then he pressed pause.

'The paramedic was right,' he said. 'That shape is unmistakeable. It's definitely a Disco' Series 2. Late Nineties to 2004.'

'Franklin!' Caton shouted.

The DC came to join them.

'This vehicle,' Caton said pointing to the screen, 'is a Land Rover Discovery Series 2, partial plate ending in HR. Last seen on Dunkirk Lane, Hyde, at nine twenty-nine last night. I need every capture you can find within our famous ring of steel.'

'Yes, Boss.'

It took Franklin less than four minutes.

'Put it on the screen,' Caton told him.

The core team stopped what they were doing and joined Caton in front of the whiteboard.

'This is the first sighting, at nine thirty-one, on the A627 Dukinfield Road, heading south from Dunkirk Lane,' Franklin told them. 'Here it is again three minutes later on Manchester Road. The next capture was here on the A626 Marple Road, and again on the A523, London Road, and

The End Game

finally here on the Manchester Airport Eastern Link Road, at nine fifty-seven.'

'He's staying within the speed limits then,' Henry Powell observed drily.

'Thank God for the GMP ring of steel,' Carly Whittle observed. 'We just need to see that on the rest of the system.'

'Get on to the national ANPR service, Jack,' Caton said. 'We need to find out where he goes and where he ends up.'

Jack, not *Franklin*, the DC thought. *That's a turn-up for the cards.*

'Yes, Boss,' he said. 'Two of those captures caught a clear image of the entire front licence plate. I've already put it through the PNC.'

'And?'

'It belongs to an identical vehicle owned by a farmer in Norfolk. And, since the vehicle isn't flagged as stolen, we can assume the plate has been cloned.'

'Excellent work,' Caton told him. 'Call me the minute you have the national service data running.'

'Yes, Boss!' said Franklin. He had a wide grin on his face as he scurried back to his carousel.

***

Forty minutes later, they reconvened. The screen was filled by a map that covered the entire road network from South Manchester all the way down to Cardiff in the southwest. As soon as Franklin ran the program, yellow dots began to appear on the map showing any camera capturing the vehicle as it passed. They watched transfixed as DC Franklin provided a commentary.

'From the Link Road, he heads for Wilmslow,' he began, 'then Holmes Chapel, Nantwich, and Whitchurch. As you can see, he's avoiding the motorways and most of the A-roads. But here, at Prees Heath, he joins the A49 towards Shrewsbury, then heads south on the A488. Here he is leaving Minsterley. Then there's nothing, until he trips this camera at Knighton, where he's heading east on the A4113.'

The End Game

He turned to face them. 'The system's got a bit of a glitch here,' he said. 'It freezes. We just have to give it a moment.'

'Where the hell is he going?' Henry Powell wondered.

'Home,' said Caton. 'Credenhill, even though he doesn't live there any more.'

'I think I know where he's headed,' Carly said. She pointed on the map. 'The Brecons. Where this all started.'

'You win the prize, Sarge,' Franklin said.

As Carly stepped back, the yellow dots began to appear again.

'Here he is on the A438 at Bronlys, heading west,' Franklin told them, 'then on the B4602 entering Brecon, and then briefly on the A40 south of Brecon heading west, before this final capture at 1 a.m., at the roundabout where the A40 meets the A470.'

Caton checked the wall clock. It was one twenty in the morning.

'Wherever he was going,' he said, 'the odds are he's already there.'

He looked at the map.

'We need him found, and I need to be there when he is.'

'It took him three hours fifty minutes to get there,' Henry Powell said. 'He's got some head start, Boss.'

Caton turned to his officer in the case.

'Jimmy,' he said, 'get on to NPAS and find out if there's a fixed-wing plane available out of Doncaster Airport – they're still based there for the moment. And get someone else to contact the local force out where he is. I'm going to speak to Central Park and see if I can get approval. Carly, since you seem to know what's going on, you're coming with me. You can explain it all on the way.'

Chapter 70

Barton Aerodrome, Eccles, 2.55 a.m.

The Vulcan 68R lifted off.

It had taken thirty minutes for the plane to reach Barton Aerodrome and less than five for Caton and Carly Whittle to board. They were now seated behind the pilot and the tactical flight officer.

'How did you swing it, Boss?' Carly asked. 'I thought to get a lift in one of these, we had to demonstrate a significant level of threat, risk or harm posed to an individual, to communities or to property, and that it's essential we're able to support police officers on the ground?'

'Hark at you,' Caton said. 'Have you just looked that up or are you working on another promotion?'

'No, seriously, Boss,' she replied, 'how did you wangle it? I'm interested.'

'I said that not only did we suspect this person of being responsible for attempted extortion, an arson attack, two car bombings, and the sinking of a houseboat, but he's also put a child's life in danger. And that although he appears to have fled the scene, he's now highly unpredictable, and a clear and present threat to those he's been targeting.' He grinned. 'What I failed to say is that he's an expert in avoiding surveillance, a slippery bastard, and this may be our only chance of catching him.'

'When you put it like that,' she said, 'although . . .'

He turned to face her. 'Go on.'

'You missed out the fact that he may well pose an even greater danger to himself.'

The End Game

'Because he's unstable?'

'It's more the cause of his instability,' she said. 'Obviously he's still grieving the loss of his son, angry about what led to his suicide, and that he wasn't there to stop it, or even attend the funeral . . .'

'As well as the fact that gaming companies continue to enable a gambling habit among minors,' he said.

'That too. But even before that, there was the Para who died during the final stage of the SAS selection process, for whose death Masters blames himself. Throw PTSD into the mix, and anything's possible.'

'He was exonerated by both the army and the inquest though?' Caton said.

'That's right,' she said, 'although the army came in for a deal of criticism from the coroner with regard to what she described as a cavalier attitude with regards to their duty of care for those seeking selection.'

'How exactly?'

'Unreliable GPS trackers, insufficient water at some checkpoints, a mindset that deaths were inevitable if they were testing the participants' ability to survive in the kind of extreme weather conditions they might encounter on special ops. Nevertheless, the verdict was still accidental death.'

'But avoidable?'

'There wasn't enough evidence to support that. The army successfully argued that in this case it was one man's burning desire to complete the final selection task that led him to push himself beyond his limits, and to make several fatal decisions.'

'Such as?'

'Not to tell the truth when Maxwell asked him the standard health check questions at the final checkpoint; choosing to take an even more challenging shortcut that he was in no state to tackle; not to voluntarily withdraw before he was too disoriented and too far gone to do so; hunkering down in a spot that made it difficult for the DS – Directing Staff – to find him when they came looking.'

'This Para,' Caton said, 'Maxwell Masters blamed himself?'

The End Game

'I only have the word of Tony Bates, his former troop colleague, for that. And he said it was just a feeling he had. Masters's commanding officers thought he'd moved on, and his wife didn't mention it at all.'

'He'll have spent a hell of a lot more time with his troop than with either the command team or his wife,' Caton reflected. 'And when you live cheek by jowl with others in situations where your lives are in each other's hands, I'd trust a colleague's intuition every time.'

'A bit like us?' Carly said.

'Us?'

She shrugged. 'FMIT. Our syndicate. I bet we all know things about each other that our partners don't.'

'Like?'

She shifted in her seat to face him. 'How we cope at murder scenes, at autopsies. How we celebrate a win and how we let off steam when it's all gone bottoms up. Who's playing away from home, and with whom . . .'

Caton held up a hand. 'I get the drift,' he said, 'but I'd rather know what Masters is doing right now.'

'Maybe he's got another hideaway somewhere. After all, he has an intimate knowledge of the area. Or like I said, perhaps he's looking for closure.'

They were flying through thick cloud. It was a metaphor for how Caton's head was feeling.

'Why now?' he said. 'When he still hasn't achieved his goal? It can't just be because Langston escaped, and can describe him?'

'That is one possibility,' Carly said. 'What if he believes that Langston is dead? It was dark, his headlights were off, and the presence of the ambulance would have told him it was bad. He didn't stay around to find out exactly how serious. Instead, he fled. That must tell us something?'

Caton sat up and turned towards her. She had just lifted his brain fog.

'You're right,' he said. 'Let's think it through. His motive is pretty much a given, but his MO is unique. He's using a gaming methodology to force MancVG to do what he wants.'

'A deadly game.'

The End Game

'But it hasn't been deadly, has it? He's not motivated by greed. This is partly about revenge, but he's also trying to prevent others from going through what happened to his son. Think about it. He's gone out of his way to ensure that nobody is harmed, at least not physically. The arson and the explosive devices were built and timed in such a way that only property was damaged. The report on Gorlay's dog's death proved it was an accident. And he had no idea Langston was on board that boat when he set out to sink it.'

He let this hang in the air.

'And now,' Carly said, 'while attempting to avenge his son's death, he's become responsible for Langston being knocked down, injured, and for all he knows, killed. Another innocent death on his conscience. The state he's in, that's going to blow his mind.'

'Exactly,' Caton said.

He turned to stare out of the window. The clouds had cleared. On the ground below, a patchwork of orange and white lights stood out as pinpricks against a blue-grey background. Roads snaked across the landscape like rivers. It was calm and peaceful up here. He felt completely disassociated from the earth below. He glanced across at Carly. She was staring out of the window on the other side. The only noise was the sound of the engines, and the voices of the aircrew as they communicated with air traffic control. They lapsed into silence, alone with their thoughts.

***

Twenty minutes later, the flight officer turned in his seat.

'We'll be flying directly over the mountains in three minutes,' he said. 'Do you want us to carry out a search pattern or just a low pass?'

'How long before we reach St Athan?' Caton said.

'It's a clear night, no traffic reported, we should have you there in fifteen minutes,' the pilot responded. 'There's a Eurocopter, ready to go, sat there waiting for you. They can get you here, on the ground, in much the same time.'

'In that case,' Caton said, 'just a low slow pass, please.

The End Game

If he's here, I don't want to spook him.'

'Roger that!' said the pilot.

The Vulcan was already descending. The sky was full of stars, their brightness fading closer to the horizon where the twilight presaged dawn. The mountains appeared as an irregular dark grey mass, intersected by ribbons of black where trees and bushes populated the valleys.

'Activity on the port side!' the flight officer announced.

Caton unbuckled his belt and went to sit on the arm of Carly's seat.

The two of them strained to see through the gloom. The pilot banked to give them a clearer view.

'There,' he said, 'at the southern end of the reservoir.'

'Got it,' Caton said.

There were a cluster of vehicles at the bottom end of a large expanse of water that lay like a vast mirror reflecting the sky. The shape of the vehicles was unmistakeable, and they could see identity markings on the roofs of police cars.

'Patrol cars, vans and several Land Rovers,' said Carly. 'Looks like the locals have pulled out all the stops.'

'Indeed,' said Caton.

They had even responded to his request for no blues and twos, so as not to alert Maxwell to their presence. Caton returned to his place. The plane was gaining height now and a sudden acceleration pushed him back into his seat. He fastened his seatbelt and composed his thoughts.

Not long now.

Chapter 71

Pen y Fan, The Brecon Beacons.

Masters paused to restore the balance of his bergen, tightened the waist belt, and set off towards the summit, pushing hard.

Even when clouds obscured the moon, and plunged the stone-strewn path into darkness, Masters never missed a stride. He had an intimate connection with these mountains, forged through blood, sweat and tears. Cribyn, at the foot of whose south-eastern slope he now was, had been a loyal comrade, a familiar adversary, and had helped forge the man he had become. The man he needed to rediscover. He checked his watch and pressed on.

An hour later he stood at the summit of Pen y Fan, staring up at a sea of diamonds that stretched to infinity. Stars like those he had gazed on from an observation post on Camlough Mountain in South Armagh, in the frozen mountains of Somalia, on a high desert plateau in Libya, and the searing Afghan plains. There had been moments such as this when he had contemplated the infinite expanse of the universe, the mystery of creation, the existence or otherwise of a god.

He remembered a memorial service at Camp Bastion. The padre informing the assembled troops that over 100 billion persons had died since the beginning of the world. That every single atom that made up their bodies remained here on Earth, or out there beyond the stars, travelling the furthest reaches of an infinite universe, while their souls returned to the God who had created them.

He recalled a hurried funeral. The pitiful remains of a twelve-year-old boy, caught by Pashtun militants carrying

The End Game

messages between informants and the British. He had watched, drenched in perspiration in a stone and mud-brick *qal'ah*, as silent prayers were said over the tiny white shroud. He had heard the village mullah implore the Angel of Death to instruct the soul to 'depart to the mercy of God'. Maxwell had no doubt that Danny's soul resided with God, if such there be. As for his own soul, he was past caring.

Half a mile south of the summit of Corn Du, a pile of stones marking the Craig y Fan Ddu cairn emerged from the predawn mist. Twenty-five minutes later, avoiding the ridge path, Masters followed a narrow sheep track down the treacherous eastern flank, littered with grass-covered sandstone ledges from which the unwary might plunge down the rock-strewn mountainside. On reaching the twisted remains of the wartime Spitfire that had been his final marker, he left the path and began the sheer descent to the valley below.

Chapter 72

The Storey Arms Outdoor Education Centre,
Brecon Beacons, 5.50 a.m.

The helicopter landed on the road just north of the Beacons Reservoir by the Storey Arms Outdoor Centre. More than four hours had elapsed since the suspect's vehicle had disappeared off the grid seven miles northeast of here. It wouldn't get light for nearly an hour still, but already the darkness was less opaque and there was the sound of birds laying claim to their territory.

Caton and Carly were met in the car park of the outdoor education centre by the officer in command of the local search team, a uniformed superintendent. Towering over Caton, he had the build of a second-row forward. He held out a meaty hand.

'Alwyn Hughes, Dyfed-Powys Police,' he said, 'welcome to Bannau Brycheiniog. And this is Captain Anil Subedi, from Sterling Lines.'

The Special Forces captain stepped forward. Though short and wiry, he had an air of quiet confidence and a grip of steel.

'Detective Sergeant Whittle and I were together less than forty-eight hours ago,' he said. 'I wasn't expecting us to meet again so soon.'

'Nor I,' Carly replied,' but I'm relieved to see you here.'

'We're always keen to help the police,' he said, 'more so when a former colleague may be involved. I've brought with me a team of five, including three Special Forces selection, directing officers. None of them have worked with Sergeant Masters, but they've been briefed about his

The End Game

background before he left. And, for the record, none of us are armed.'

'I have an armed response team,' Hughes said quickly, pointing to two BMW SUVs parked ten metres away, one plain black, one with its flanks marked with bold chevrons. Four firearms officers stood beside them, three bearing Heckler & Koch assault rifles. He waved a hand towards the other vehicles in the car park. 'I also have a tactical aid team comprising eight officers, a police dog handler, and a drone. And the helicopter that brought you here is at our disposal, although it could be diverted if an immediate emergency should arise.'

Caton and Carly exchanged a look. With all of that resource why had they wasted so much precious time? Surely they could have found him by now – always assuming he was somewhere out there. The Welshman read their faces.

'We thought it best to wait for you,' he said, 'not least, because we would have been unable to arrive at a robust risk assessment without you.'

Hughes could see they were unimpressed.

Caton noted that Captain Subedi had distanced himself by turning away and pretending to study a map, lit by an LED lamp, spread out on the bonnet of an army Land Rover. The superintendent continued to plead his case.

'There was no point in putting anyone at risk if there wasn't an immediate threat to life, and besides, with a search area of nigh on nine hundred square kilometres and such a small resource at our disposal, we needed a lot more to go on before setting off. Plus, we've been waiting for the fire rescue drone, which was diverted from this operation to assist with a large blaze at a car warehouse in Swansea...' He tailed off. 'It's only just got here.'

Captain Subedi came to his rescue.

'Detective Chief Inspector,' he said, 'why don't you start by telling us why you're looking for this person, and why you suspect that he may be Maxwell Masters?'

'The second question first,' Caton said. 'We have a witness who's seen our suspect at close quarters. He can't be one hundred per cent sure because this person had long

The End Game

hair and a beard, we believe in an attempt to disguise himself, but from photographs we showed the witness, he's ID'd him with ninety per cent certainty. As for why we need to find him, we suspect that he's been targeting a small computer games company as part of a campaign to stop in-game purchases of the kind that led to his son committing suicide. In the process, he's carried out an arson attack on their offices, stolen a pet dog that subsequently got run over, written off two of their cars with controlled explosions, and just six hours ago, sunk a narrowboat where the partner of one of his targets was living, and kidnapped her mute son who was on board at the time. The boy, who subsequently ID'd him, managed to escape but was then hit by a car.'

'Maxwell's car?' Hughes asked.

'No, but we think he saw it happen. That's when he set off to drive down here.'

'How's the boy?'

'Bruising, shock, concussion, but the doctors say he'll be okay.'

'Does Maxwell know that?'

'We don't think so. I told the hospital not to give out any information, and also to let us know if anyone contacted them asking about the boy. So far, nobody has.'

'What do you believe to be the state of his mental health?' Hughes asked.

'He was suffering from severe depression and PTSD, which led to his being medically discharged from the army,' Caton told them. 'Since then, his wife's divorced him, he's changed his identity, gone to ground, and started this campaign. Now he believes this may all have been responsible for that lad's death. Draw your own conclusions.'

'Is he armed?'

'We don't know for sure, but his former wife says he definitely kept a handgun hidden in their garden shed. A trophy, he told her, from Afghanistan. After he'd gone, she went looking for it, but it had disappeared.'

'Then we have to work on the assumption that he *is* armed,' Hughes said. 'Do you believe he may be intending to kill himself?'

The End Game

'Honestly? I have no idea,' Caton said. 'We're still waiting for the MOD to respond to a request we made for information on his mental state prior to his discharge. Specifically, if there was any suicidal ideation or potential for violence to others. In the absence of further intel, we can't rule out either possibility.'

'Including suicide-by-cop then?' asked the firearms inspector.

One of the Directing Staff NCOs stepped forward. 'I'd be surprised if he goes that route,' he said.

'What make you say that?' Hughes asked him.

'Because it's a coward's way out. Given his training and his active service, he's anything but a coward. Besides, from what you've told us, I reckon what happened with that lad will have been a wake-up call. I lay odds that right here, right now, he's more rational than he's ever been.'

Caton checked his watch.

'I think it's time we got going,' he said.

Chapter 73

They gathered around the bonnet of the car on which, alongside the OS map, stood a laptop displaying satellite imagery of the area.

'Over to you, Captain Subedi,' Hughes said.

'Staff?' said Subedi.

The senior member of the directing staff took the reins. 'He's got a good head start on us,' he said. 'We have no idea whether he's carrying a bergen or travelling light. Even though it's night-time, he knows these hills like the back of his hand. So, we've worked on the assumption that he's on foot, and he's moving at between five and seven klicks an hour, depending on the route he's taken. Unless he had another mode of transport waiting for him, that would put him somewhere inside this circle.'

As he spoke, his index finger moved clockwise around the map, centred on the point where the car was last captured by an ANPR camera.

'Going south, he could easily have reached the outskirts of Merthyr Tydfil by now. Southwest would put him around Aber-Llia or Ystradfellte. West places him on the A4059 then he can head south towards Penderyn or, at a pinch, further west onto the A4067. A bit further north, he hits Sarn Helen – the old Roman road. If he's headed northeast, he could already be on the A40, similarly, if he struck east, although I doubt he'd have got further than the B4558 north of Talybont.'

'If he took the path through Sirhowy Valley,' one of his colleagues said, 'he'd probably be close to Trefil by now. That puts him within spitting distance of the A465. I suggest

The End Game

we put the 'copter up and ask them to start with a circuit of this perimeter of the circle, and then spiral in towards the centre.'

Alwyn Hughes's radio squawked. He held up a hand requesting silence.

'Say that again?' he said.

'Talybont? Where exactly? Stay there. I need eyes-on in case he comes back. If he does, I want to be the first to know.'

He turned to the others.

'The target Land Rover has been found in the car park on the far side of Talybont Reservoir.'

He pointed to the spot on the map.

'How far away is that?' Caton asked.

'Seven and a half miles as the bird flies,' the directing staff responded, 'but because of this mountainous terrain in between, it's nearer twenty by road.'

'What's he doing there?' Hughes wondered. 'There's nothing but the reservoir and the youth hostel. Unless . . . he's in the reservoir?'

'It's where you park if you're going to do the Four Peaks Circular,' one of the directing staff said. His finger traced the route. 'Fan y Big, Cribyn, Pen y Fan and Corn Du.'

'Only it won't be there and back,' Carly said. 'There's somewhere in particular he wants to be.'

They turned to stare at her. She looked to Caton for support.

'That Para,' she said. 'We both know that's why he's here.'

'DS Whittle,' Caton explained, 'has a theory that Masters is returning to the scene of a tragic accidental death during a Special Forces selection exercise. One for which he blamed himself. I think she may well be right.'

'June 2019,' said another of the directing staff. 'We did wonder.'

One of his colleagues pointed to a spot southeast of where they stood.

'Wasn't he found right here, in VW Valley?'

'That's Nant Crew,' said Hughes. 'I've never heard it called VW Valley.'

The End Game

'It stands for Voluntary Withdrawal,' one of the directing staff told him. 'Just when candidates on their final selection task think it's almost over, they find themselves faced with this near vertical descent followed by an equally treacherous climb, with bugger all to cling to apart from thistles. It's where the majority of candidates decide they've had enough, and voluntarily withdraw.'

'Except for some of them, it isn't a choice,' added another of his team. 'They're that confused with heat exhaustion, dehydration or hypothermia, they just collapse. Some even die unless we find them in time.'

He was almost drowned out by the sound of the helicopter engine starting up on the road. Hughes had one hand to his ear and the other on his radio.

'Damn!' he shouted. 'There's been a fatal hit and run north of Abergavenny. They have a car in pursuit, but the fugitive is driving like a madman. They need the helicopter to try to avoid more fatalities.'

'You've still got the drone,' Caton said. 'I suggest we start the search in that area.'

'*Us*, not you,' said Captain Subedi, 'not dressed like that. We've got some gear in the Land Rover. I suggest that you and your colleague boot up.'

He turned to Hughes. 'It'll be daylight in twenty-five minutes. Let's RV at the lay-by at the foot of the valley by this reservoir, and head out from there up VW valley. When DCI Caton and DS Whittle are ready, one of your guys can run them down there.'

'I suggest your guys stay here,' he said, turning now to the senior AFO. 'It's not ideal terrain for carrying a weapon. Besides, he was one of us. We're best placed to talk him out. We can always radio Superintendent Hughes if we need you.'

The super and the senior AFO had a brief conversation, then Hughes turned back and addressed Subedi.

'Very well,' he said, 'but you remain in continuous contact and take no risks. Is that understood?'

'Roger that,' said the captain. 'Give us ten minutes, and then you can put the drone up. And please, make sure it's high enough that he won't spot it. We don't want to spook him.'

Chapter 74

Nant Crew, 6.29 a.m.

Maxwell Masters sat on his haunches gazing at the drought-bleached escarpment, beyond which lay the ridge of Craig y Fan Ddu. Silhouetted against the dawn sky, a pair of buzzards circled languidly over the Beacons.

A raven landed on a bush on the opposite bank of the stream. It cocked its head, regarded him with a beady eye, and with a flap of its wings flew off towards the head of the valley.

Unhurried, the sun began to emerge from below the horizon, painting the sky with layers of russet and gold, until it became a blinding starburst disc, whose rays crept down the mountain's eastern flank towards him.

***

Caton and Carly shaded their eyes against the blinding sun as they struggled to follow the sandy silt bed and strewn stones, over which a trickle of water wound its way past them towards the reservoir.

A gunshot echoed around the mountains, shattering the silence, scattering the birds. The two detectives stopped, stared wordlessly at one another, and then carried on, their pace less urgent now.

***

Captain Subedi, stood with his back to them. Beside him knelt two of the directing staff, while their remaining

The End Game

colleague stood opposite. He spotted the two detectives and spoke to Subedi, who turned to face them. The captain's expression confirmed their fears. He issued a brief command and his two colleagues on the ground stood and stepped aside to let the detectives through.

Maxwell Masters lay face up on the bank, his boots dangling in the margins of the stream. The hair at the back of his head was saturated with blood, which had begun to pool on the stones beneath him. He was dressed in a windproof camouflage jacket, on the left breast of which was pinned a row of medal ribbons. His right arm lay by his side, his hand folded around a pistol. On a tussock of grass, a metre behind the body, a khaki bergen stood upright, like a headstone.

'It's a Makarov,' Subedi said, pointing to the gun, 'Russian, point-three-eight semi-automatic. He likely brought it back from Afghan.'

Masters's left arm was outstretched, as though flung there when the explosion propelled his body backwards. Beside it lay a photograph, face down. Caton took a pair of crime scene gloves from his pocket and put them on. He gave a wide berth to the body until he'd reached the far side, then bent down to pick up the photo, turned it over, and held it up for Carly and the others to see.

A young man stared back at them. In his mid-teens, with the whole of his life ahead of him, he wore a school rugby shirt and a broad grin that radiated confidence and hope. It was the face in the newspaper article that Duggie Wallace had shown Caton. The face that had been in every frame on the mantlepiece in Sandra Masters's home. It was Maxwell Masters's son, Danny.

Overhead they heard a sound resembling an approaching swarm of bees.

Caton looked up. The drone circled above them, spiralling ever closer. Too late to make a difference, he reflected, though he doubted that anything would have deflected Maxwell Masters from his chosen path.

Chapter 75
Day Nine
Saturday 10th September

Naval Street, Ancoats, 9 a.m.

Nuan Lau approached the office. The only evidence that there had been a fire here was the scorch marks on the stone lintel beneath the windows over the cellar. She held her pass against the keypad and leaned her shoulder against the door. As she climbed the stairs, she heard laughter.

The stench of smoke that had permeated the office had been replaced by the scent of jasmine. There was a gentle hum downstairs that told her that the replacement servers were up and running.

Jake and Louie were seated in the lounge area. Between them, on the table, stood a battery-operated oil diffuser, an ice bucket and three champagne flutes. Louie held a glass in readiness as he watched Jake do battle with the bottle.

'Good timing, Nu,' Jake declared. 'Come and join us – it's celebration time!'

He popped the cork and filled Louie's glass, oblivious to the foaming bubbles running down the side of the bottle and spilling out across the table. Nuan placed her bag and phone on the couch between herself and Louie and sat down.

'It's early for fizz,' she said. 'What are we celebrating?'

'What the hell do you think?' said Jake, proceeding to fill the remaining glasses. 'I had a call from Caton to say the threat's been removed. He said he couldn't tell us more until they've issued a press release, probably sometime tomorrow. But he said it's definitely over.' He grinned. 'And we haven't

The End Game

had to part with a single cent, except for that security firm that was worse than useless. The insurance is going to pay out for the damage to our servers and the cars, and we can move on with our next venture.'

He lifted his glass. 'Cheers, everyone!'

He and Louie chinked their glasses and downed their champagne in one. Jake immediately refilled them.

'What did he mean, the threat has been removed?' Nuan said. 'How has it been removed?'

'Well,' Jake said, oozing smugness, 'what Caton doesn't know is that the one thing the security firm we hired is good for, is having an inside track on police operations. Linslade gave me a call half an hour before Caton. He gave me a name. Asked if I recognised it. He said the word was GMP had put out an all-ports warning for this guy, and that the rumour was he'd topped himself sometime yesterday morning.'

'A man has died,' she said, 'and Langston was lucky to avoid serious injury. I can't believe you think this is cause for celebration?'

Jake waved his glass in the air. 'Why the hell not?'

'This man,' she said, 'who was he?'

'Some ex-army guy, Special Forces.'

'Why did he pick us?'

'Something about his son committing suicide,' Louie told her.

'Runs in the family,' Jake said.

'What was his name?' Nuan demanded.

'Masters,' Louie responded. 'Max Masters?' He looked to Jake for confirmation.

'Maxwell!' Jake replied. 'Like the Beatle's song "Maxwell's Silver Hammer".' He began to sing the lyrics. Louie joined in.

Nuan picked up her phone, and Googled: *Masters . . . Son of army veteran . . . Maxwell Masters . . . Suicide*. There were three returns. One was the report of the inquest in the *Hereford Times*. She read it.

'Stop!' she shouted, stunning them both.

This was not like her. Nu was always composed, calm, unemotional.

The End Game

'What the hell?' Jake said.

'This!' She waved her phone at him. 'This is the reason we were targeted.'

Jake took the phone from her and read the account out loud for Louie's benefit. When he'd finished, he tossed it back to her dismissively.

'That wasn't our fault,' he said.

'We don't know that for sure,' Nuan retorted. 'But if not us, then people like us. Doing what we do. With no thought to the consequences.'

'Get real,' said Jake. He placed his glass on the table. 'We're a business. Our job is to bring pleasure to others and make a buck at the same time. Not to take responsibility for every gamer out there with a mental health problem.'

Louie squirmed on the leather sofa, causing it to squeak. 'He's got a point, Nu,' he said. 'It's a free world. No one is forcing anyone to buy skins or gamble on loot boxes.'

'That's not true,' she retorted. 'Our games are addictive. They all are. We design them that way. *I* design them that way. If people become addicted, it dramatically limits their ability to make that choice.'

Jake rounded on her. 'Addicted to games?! What the hell's wrong with that? It's no different from being addicted to reading, or sport, or . . .'

'Rap music?' Louie offered.

'Exactly!'

Nuan stood her ground. 'But it *is* different, isn't it? *Gamble* on loot boxes, you said. And that's what we're doing. Teaching kids as young as twelve to gamble. Getting them to think that gambling is normal, safe, a bit of fun. Only it isn't, is it? Not for everyone.' She caught her breath before continuing. 'I think we should still donate the money to that charity, remove all in-game purchases and loot boxes from our games, and then take an active role in trying to persuade the rest of the industry to do the same.'

Her colleagues stared at her aghast. Jake recovered first. He rounded the table and towered over her.

'Let him win?!' he said. 'After he's firebombed our servers, killed my dog, blown our cars up, sunk your girlfriend's boat, kidnapped her son and chased him under a car?'

'The man is dead,' she said, 'and so is his son. I don't call that a win.'

Jake seemed lost for words. He turned, picked up his glass, took a sip and slumped down opposite her.

'Since when did you have this epiphany?' he asked.

'Epiphany?' said Louie.

'Moment of revelation,' Nuan told him. She turned to face Jake. 'I've been having doubts for a while.' There was this article in the *Global Bulletin of Computer Game Design*. It said researchers had established a clear and unambiguous link between adolescent gaming and adult gambling, and this could be a wake-up call for the industry. That got me thinking...'

'You're being naive,' Jake told her. 'Besides, even if it's true, we can't afford to be the only ones without in-game purchases.'

'Yes, we can – we made plenty of money before we introduced those features. And I told you, if we take an ethical stand, it may even give us an edge in the market.'

'A tiny niche market! None of the others will follow us. And if you think I'm going to throw money away trying to persuade them to join some self-flagellating pursuit of wokeness, you've another think coming.'

'Louie?' said Nuan.

'I'm with Jake,' he said.

Nuan stood up. 'Then I'll go it alone. I've already had this discussion with Thelma, and she's one hundred per cent behind me.'

'After what he did to her son?!'

Nuan placed her tablet inside her bag. 'You don't get it, do you?' she said. 'And it's clear you never will. My lawyers will be in touch. I'll expect one third of the value of the company based on the valuation in our last year's accounts, and will be claiming my share of the royalties from future sales of games to which I hold shared or individual intellectual copyright.'

'You can't do that,' Jake said.

She pocketed her phone and placed her bag over her shoulder.

'I think you'll find I can,' she said.

Chapter 76
Day Ten
Sunday 11th September

Central Park, 9.45 a.m.

Caton was exhausted. His sleep had been disturbed by flashbacks of the scene on the bank of the Nant Crew. And, if that wasn't bad enough, for the first time in a long while he found himself remembering the day on the Greek coast road when the lorry had come at them head-on. His mother's scream. His father's curse as he swung the wheel. And how he, Caton, had been the only survivor.

Helen Gates did a double take. 'You'd better sit down, Tom, you look exhausted,' she said. 'I take it you didn't get any sleep?'

He collapsed onto one of the only two comfortable chairs.

'Not really, Ma'am. We spent the day being debriefed by the local force and waiting for the post-mortem. And then that was postponed until this morning. NPAS had to fly back without us because they're all involved in the security arrangements following the death of the Queen. The local force gave me a lift to Hereford, and I caught the train back to Manchester. I couldn't sleep.'

'What about Detective Sergeant Whittle,' she said, 'did she not come back with you?'

'I asked her to stay down there and attend the post-mortem in the morning.'

'It was definitely suicide though?'

The End Game

'We won't be able to confirm that until we have the scene of crime, forensics and PM reports. But there's no doubt in any of our minds.'

'And are you sure that he was responsible for the campaign against that video gaming outfit?'

'MancVG,' Caton supplied. 'We found a laptop and a burner phone in a rucksack beside his body, together with a notebook that contained hand-drawn maps, coded notes and the victims' addresses. More than enough to draw a line under the investigation.'

'Why didn't he leave it in the Land Rover? Why trail it up and down a mountain?'

'I'm guessing that he didn't want to risk some opportunist thief stealing it. I believe he wanted to make sure that we found it.'

'Unless that's what someone else wanted us to think?'

'It's not impossible, Ma'am,' he said, 'but highly unlikely.' He forced a smile. 'It's not like you to indulge in conspiracy theories?'

'That's the curse of working on the top floor.'

'The search team were on the scene within a couple of minutes of the shots being fired,' he told her. 'If there had been anyone else there, they'd have seen them.'

'Fair enough.'

She tapped her pencil against her lower lip. It was the least disconcerting of a number of mannerisms she seemed to have developed since her promotion.

'I have to tell you this, Tom,' she said, 'the Chief had a call from Dyfed-Powys Police. Apparently, they had to wait almost two hours for you to arrive? Two hours that they claim could have made all the difference. I hope we're not going to get any comeback?'

'Someone is trying to cover their backs, Ma'am,' he told her. 'They didn't have to wait for me – that was their decision. They claimed they needed to speak to me so they could compile a risk assessment.'

'That's understandable in the circumstances?'

'Then why didn't they call me? I was on a plane, not a different planet. Welsh police Professional Standards Branch are carrying out an internal review overseen by the

The End Game

IOPC. I've already given them a statement, and so has Special Forces liaison.'

'So you think you're in the clear?'

'You', he noted, not 'we'.

'Yes, Ma'am. Besides, Maxwell didn't want saving, just the opportunity to go on his own terms.'

Gates eased her chair back from the desk. 'In that case, Tom, please brief Communications Branch so they can release a statement for the press. Dyfed-Powys Police have passed that particular buck to us, and the hounds are baying.'

'If I may, I'd prefer to deliver the statement myself, Ma'am.'

She frowned. 'Not like you to seek the limelight?'

'It's nothing to do with that, Ma'am.'

'So what is it to do with?'

'I think the public need to know that this was not a random series of attacks. That there was a reason why Maxwell was targeting a video games firm.'

'Isn't that for the inquest to address?'

'That could be months away. Even as much as a year, given the Covid backlog. I think we need to allay fears that it wasn't a random event, or part of a wider conspiracy.'

Gates pursed her lips. 'You wouldn't be going political on me, would you, Tom?'

'No, Ma'am.'

'Only I'm guessing that you have some sympathy with his motivation, if not his methods?'

'Certainly not his methods, Ma'am.'

Gates sighed. 'We can't save people from themselves, Tom. Aside from the fact that it isn't possible, that is not our role.'

Caton sensed that she was weakening. 'It wouldn't hurt to alert parents to the dangers,' he said, 'albeit tangentially? Besides, people who become addicted to gambling are on a quick road to penury for themselves and their families, and we all know that poverty breeds crime.'

His boss stood up.

'Draft your statement, and send it to me,' she said. 'I'll be the judge of how *tangential* it is.'

Chapter 77

Millgate Lane, Didsbury, 11.30 a.m.

Kate threw her arms around him.

'Thank God,' she said. She stepped back. 'You look awful.'

'Welcome home,' Caton said, dropping his bag on the floor.

'I'm sorry,' she said, 'but I've been really worried. Your voice message was cryptic to say the least.'

'It's been full on,' he told her. 'I did try to ring you from the train.'

'I was in a meeting. I called you back, but it went to answerphone.'

'I'd switched to silent so I could get my head down for an hour or so.' He peered through the open door of the lounge. 'Where's Emily?'

'Now that she's fully recovered, Jane's mum took them to a pottery decorating class at the café in Didsbury. She'll back for tea. Harry's slept over. Helen's coming for him this afternoon. He's upstairs on his laptop. Have you eaten today?'

'I had a bacon roll and a cup of tea on the platform in Hereford.'

'What about dinner last night?'

His face told her all she needed to know.

She took him by the arm and led him towards the kitchen.

'You can tell me all about it while I fix you some beans on toast to keep you going till dinner time.'

***

The End Game

'It's very sad,' she said, 'but in a way, heroic.'

He stopped, his fork suspended in mid-air, and looked up. Kate was watching the Queen's cortège approach the outskirts of Aberdeen, on the way to her Lying at Rest in St Giles' Cathedral in Edinburgh.

'It was certainly heroic of her, within twenty-four hours of her demise, to see off one prime minister and see in another,' he said.

'I was referring to your dead veteran,' she told him.

'I agree,' Caton replied, 'but I don't think that's how his intended victims see it, or ACC Gates, come to that.'

'That's because they're not looking at the whole picture. They're trapped by historical assumptions about suicide that have their roots in religious condemnation.'

Caton recognised the academic tone and gave in to the inevitable. He put his fork down. 'Which are?'

'That either there's some evil influence at work, or that mental illness or overwhelming emotional trauma is responsible. That the decision to take one's life is always irrational, and ultimately selfish.'

He continued to play along. 'But it isn't always irrational, is it,' he said, 'to choose to end unendurable pain or suffering?'

'That *is* rational,' she agreed, 'but in most cases, it can be argued to be selfish, unless the primary motivation is to ease the suffering of those closest to you . . . especially your carer. However, there were two more examples of rational and self-sacrificial suicide proposed in 1984 by the philosopher Margaret Battin. To kill oneself for a cause, or to express an emotion such as remorse, for actions you have taken . . . or failed to take. It seems to me that your man meets both definitions.'

'I said as much to Helen Gates,' he responded, 'only she doesn't see the whole picture. Don't worry, I've got it all in hand.' He squeezed a blob of ketchup on his beans and carried on eating.

Kate raised her eyebrows. 'That sounds ominous. You're not going to get yourself in trouble, are you? You have my pension to think about.'

He began to choke and reached for his glass of water.

For emphasis, he now stabbed his fork in her direction. 'Your *half* of my pension. And only when I'm dead.'

She smiled. 'That can be arranged.'

Caton cleared his plate and stood up. 'I'm going to nip upstairs and have a chat with Harry.'

'You'll be lucky,' she said. 'He's playing one of his computer games. I'm surprised he didn't bring a *Do Not Disturb* sign with him.'

Caton knocked on the door, called Harry's name, and when there was no reply, entered the study bedroom. Harry was seated at his desk, wearing headphones, transfixed by something on the screen. It didn't look like a game to Caton's untrained eyes.

Caton sat on the bed. 'Harry,' he said.

His son's eyes remain glued to the screen.

'Harry,' Caton repeated, 'look at me.'

Harry turned his head a fraction. '*Please* can I just finish this, Dad?' he said. 'I'm bidding for Ronaldo and there's only two minutes left before the auction closes.'

'Ronaldo? Cristiano Ronaldo?'

Caton remembered seeing something about an unnamed Saudi Arabian club offering in excess of two hundred million pounds to prise the footballer away from Man U. 'I hope you're not using your mother's credit card?' he joked.

Harry's eyes remained glued to the screen. 'Don't be silly, Dad, it's not real money.'

'And it had better not be any of those bitcoins either,' Caton said.

Harry responded with the shake of the head that children use when their parents embarrass themselves.

Caton stood up. 'When you've finished,' he said, 'come on downstairs. We need to talk.'

***

Kate was seated on the sofa following the cortège, the diminutive coffin draped in the Royal Standard of Scotland and topped with a simple wreath of the Queen's favourite

The End Game

white flowers gathered from the estate. White heather, pine fir, and sweet peas.

Caton saw the tears trickling down her cheeks, sat down beside her, and took her hand in his. His thoughts began to wander. He didn't believe in coincidence. Truth to tell, there wasn't a lot he did believe in any more. His was a job ruled by the mantra enshrined in *Blackstone's Police Operational Handbook*: 'Assume nothing, Believe nothing, and Check everything.' Eventually, he reflected, it became second nature, leaching from your professional work to invade your private life.

There was no way of knowing what Maxwell had been thinking when he fled, or what his intentions were. Nor was it certain that he'd been aware that the Queen was dead as he set out to climb Pen y Fan for the final time. Caton believed that he had. He hoped that Maxwell Masters's decision to end his life had been an act of remorse and escape. But he had a hunch that it was more than that. What if this was a last desperate attempt to shine a light on the corporate greed that had led his son to take his own life? If so, that would require someone to tell his story.

Gates was never going to agree to allow GMP to become involved. The army would find a way of distancing themselves. He could see their press release: 'A tragic loss of a brave soldier unable to live with the death of his son', with no mention of the reasons why the boy had taken his own life. With the passing of the Queen, and all that entailed, Maxwell Masters would be consigned to a footnote in the newspapers or, at best, a couple of tweets from old comrades that would drown in the maelstrom of patriotic memes.

'We'll see about that,' Caton said out loud.

'What's that, Tom?' Kate asked, her eyes still glued to the screen.

'Nothing,' he said.

Among the contacts on Caton's mobile phone was his bête noir, the investigative reporter, Anthony Ginley. Caton couldn't risk using his own phone, but there were three public call boxes in the village. A few pointers from an anonymous source would set Ginley running. By the time the inquest opened, the reporter would have a front-page story.

On the TV screen, people lining the road were throwing flowers onto the bonnet and roof of the hearse. The commentator broke her silence.

'It is as if,' she said, 'the people are fulfilling those poignant words spoken by Her Late Majesty Queen Elizabeth when addressing the bereaved families of the September 11th attac..."Grief is the price we pay for love."'

The words triggered the flashback that had already disturbed Caton on the train in the early hours of this morning, and that he knew would continue to haunt him in the weeks to come. Maxwell Masters's body on the banks of the Nant Crew stream, his blood seeping into the earth, the photo of his lost son beside him.

'And there's no telling where that grief may take us,' he murmured.

Kate glanced at him and placed her other hand on his. They sat in silence watching the final journey of the only monarch either of them had ever known.

Internet Gaming Disorder

Information and Support

Internet Gaming Disorder
In 2017, the World Health Organisation included video and digital gaming disorder as a behavioural addiction in the International Classification of Diseases.

In the UK, Canada, the USA and Germany, between 0.3% and 1% of the population were identified as fitting the criteria for an internet gaming disorder, or IGD.

South Korea have declared video game addiction a national public health crisis, with an estimated six hundred thousand children affected.

The highest prevalence of IGD in the world is in Iran, at 22.8%, according to the world expert in video game addiction psychiatry, Harvard-trained Dr Alok Kanojia, himself a reformed gaming addict.

An international research review published in March 2022 found a clear association between problem gaming and suicidal ideation.
Problem gaming and suicidality: A systematic literature review:
Eilin K. Erevik, Helene Landrø, Åse L. Mattson, Joakim H. Kristensen, Puneet Kaur, Ståle Pallesen (March 2022)

https://www.thebridgechronicle.com/lifestyle/world-suicide-prevention-day-gaming-and-suicide-emerging-connection-55492

A study by York University in July 2020 found in-game practices - including real-money gaming and token wagering - were significantly linked to problem gambling.
https://www.york.ac.uk/news-and-events/news/2020/research/games-problem-gambling/

2021 Report on Advice to the Gambling Commission by the ABSG [Advisory Board For Safer Gambling]
https://www.gamblingcommission.gov.uk/print/lootboxes-advice-to-the-gambling-commission-from-absg

If you have any concerns about your own relationship with internet gaming, or concerns about others in your family, contact:

NHS National Centre For Gaming Disorders
https://www.cnwl.nhs.uk/national-centre-gaming-disorders

https://americanaddictioncenters.org/video-gaming-addiction

Op COURAGE: the NHS Veterans Mental Health and Wellbeing Service
In March 2021, the NHS launched Op COURAGE, which brings together several services to focus on veterans suffering from PTSD and in crisis, who are at risk of self-harm or suicide, or suffering other problems such as homelessness and addiction.

At the time of writing, since the Covid lockdowns, fourteen Armed Services personnel have taken their own lives, including several members of the Special Services Regiments. We too easily take for granted the contribution made by members of our Armed Services and underestimate the toll that it takes on their mental health.

https://www.nhs.uk/nhs-services/armed-forces-community/mental-health/veterans-reservists/

About the Author

Bill Rogers has written seventeen crime novels to date – including *The End Game* - all of them based in and around the City of Manchester. Twelve feature DCI Tom Caton and his team, set in and around Manchester, while four novels in a spin-off series feature SI Joanne Stuart on secondment to the Behavioural Sciences Unit at the National Crime Agency, located in Salford Quays. Formerly a teacher, schools inspector, and Head of the Manchester Schools Improvement Service, Bill worked for the National College for School Leadership before retiring to begin his writing career. Born in London, Bill has four generations of Metropolitan Police behind him. He is married with two adult children and lives close to the City of Manchester.

For more information, and to contact Bill, visit his Amazon Author pages and website.

amazon.co.uk/-/e/B0034NWVC0

billrogers.co.uk

Acknowledgements

As ever, I must acknowledge the debt that I owe to my wife and fellow director, Joan, for her encouragement, work, support, and the companionship that has made the completion of this book a pleasure.

I owe a massive debt to my editor, Monica Byles, as do you, the reader, for her eagle eye and relentless pursuit for accuracy, which have made *The End Game* a far more trouble-free and pleasurable read than it might otherwise have been.

And Suzie Tatnell at commercialcampaigns.co.uk for this, the sixteenth book she has typeset for me.

And finally, to all those DCI Tom Caton fans who have urged me to continue the narrative of both his life and his career, a heartfelt thank you!

Milton Keynes UK
Ingram Content Group UK Ltd.
UKHW011844071223
433887UK00004B/205

9 781909 856318